Future Memories

WILLIAM TANENBAUM

Copyright © 2020 William Tanenbaum
All rights reserved
First Edition

PAGE PUBLISHING, INC.
Conneaut Lake, PA

First originally published by Page Publishing 2020

ISBN 978-1-6624-1166-3 (pbk)
ISBN 978-1-6624-1167-0 (digital)

Printed in the United States of America

"What happens in your life today is unique, be it good or bad. There are no ifs, for that is the past, and there is only the future. Today will become a future memory."
—William Tanenbaum

Dedicated to My Loving Family:

My wife Ronna, My daughters Ruthie and Betty and their families: Robert, Samuel, Rose, and Max Friedman; and Michael, Nathan, and Dori Baron, My brother Robert, my sister-in-law Patricia, and their family, and In memory of my beloved wife Reina Tanenbaum.

CHAPTER 1

The Train Rides, Spring 1940
In Nazi- and Russian-Occupied Poland

The steam-powered locomotive engine belched clouds of smoke as it chugged through the hills of southern Poland. Passing through tunnels as dark as the night without moonlight, and abruptly emerging into daylight, this early twentieth-century relic of a train swayed from side to side. In two adjoining compartments, twelve teenage students sat quietly on hard wooden benches. The floors, covered with linoleum, showed the distress of the times with its tears, scratch marks, and missing pieces in the compartment and corridors. The students' attire copied that of the eighteenth-century aristocracy in Russia, black hats, black coats, black trousers, and black shoes, making them conspicuous like the proverbial black sheep in a flock of white ones. Besides their dress, their sallow-colored faces were covered with the beginnings of small dark beards. Accompanied by a teacher from the yeshiva, the Jewish school, where they studied, this trip was a journey for survival.* Seeking a safe haven in distant Shanghai, China, mixed emotions evoked sadness at leaving their families and the joy of surviving the war.

Joseph Shalosky gazed out the window, his hazel-colored eyes entranced by the beauty of the changing landscape rushing past. The winter freeze was melting into warm spring sunshine. Tiny green buds appeared on bare branches. On the mountain peaks, wet mud-strewn patches of earth broke through the snow covering. Melting snow cascaded down the mountains forming streams and waterfalls. He was fascinated by this display of spring awakening at the end of winter.

At five foot two inches tall, Joseph was the shortest of his classmates and tried to appear taller by standing straight. He was also one of the oldest at age nineteen. With a good sense of humor, he joked about himself, saying that precious diamonds came in small packages. Friends laughed with him instead of at him. His smile radiated a feeling of kindness and gentleness, enveloping his face. Speaking in his husky voice, he made conversations with friends important. The love and warmth given to him by his parents illuminated from the inside out. Joseph removed his hat, keeping his head covered with a yarmulke, a skull cap, which showed his devotion to God. He pressed his forehead against the glass and watched as the forests appeared and

---

* On September 1, 1939, Poland was invaded by the Nazis, and Poland's armies were crushed in three weeks. Using mechanized power of aircraft, tanks, and artillery, the German's military might conquered the country with minimal resistance. After this startling quick victory, a new word entered the language, the word *blitzkrieg*. Based upon a secret pact signed between the Nazis and the Soviet Union, the country of Poland was divided and occupied by the armed forces of each nation. Soviet troops controlled eastern Poland.

disappeared in a few seconds. He remembered life before this journey from Chemelnick, a life filled with love and family. He saw himself at the dinner table with his parents, grandparents, aunts, uncles, and cousins. The men spent many hours each day studying Torah (the Five Books of Moses) and the Talmud (the oral laws of the Torah). Joseph expected to live the same life after completing his studies. While growing up, he believed that nothing would change the normalcy in life other than relatives getting older and dying and infants being born continuing the family. *How many more hours until the train arrives in Hungary?* he wondered. *It does not matter. When it arrives, it would arrive.* He knew he had no control over it. There was no sense worrying about things he could not control as God controlled the outcome. He prayed quickly that the students would arrive safely. He thought of his life during the last month and just last week, and then of a few hours ago. He wondered what day it was exactly that his parents had his shoes repaired? The old heels and soles were replaced with new ones to last a long time, and his mother paid for them at the shoemaker's shop. In a split second, his mind drifted back to his childhood, and he remembered the shoemaker's wife giving him and the other neighbors' children freshly baked cookies. *Will that ever happen again? Of course not. Some things happen in life and then pass by, and all that remains are the memories. Only we do not know when it is the last time. I do not remember the last time the shoemaker's wife gave me cookies although she did it many times.*

Joseph remembered asking his father, Jacob, how he could afford to spend that much money to repair his shoes. Jacob replied by quoting from the Talmudic sages, "A man should even sell the beams of his house in order to secure shoes for himself." Joseph thought about the telegrams and questioned, *Had they changed his life? No, it was the Germans who changed his life. No, it was God who changed his life. Why wasn't it simple anymore as it had once been?* There were the telegrams from America pleading with his parents to leave Poland. Neighbors asked how this war could happen. They knew. They just did not want to see the truth. The newspapers reported the Nazi invasion of Poland on September 1, 1939, and the start of World War II.

He rested his head against the corner of the high-backed wooden seat and closed his eyes. The train rocked from side to side like a baby carriage and lulled him into a dream like state. He floated back in time to 1933,* the year before his Bar Mitzvah. The pending danger caused anguish to creep into his parents' eyes. With all their courage, they tried to insulate him, to protect him. Hitler had become chancellor of Germany in January. Joseph grimaced at that memory and knew then that war was a possibility. Joseph thought about his parents and remembered the letters from the rabbi of Vilna warning of the pending danger. The rabbi urged them to leave Poland. Students from the yeshiva wrote letters urging an immediate departure. His memories brought him to 1939, the year the telegrams

---

* The Nazis constructed their first concentration camp, Dachau, six miles outside of Munich. Gypsies, homosexuals, intellectuals, Jews, and anti-Nazis, such as newspaper editors and church leaders, were sent there to be murdered. The Europeans stayed silent, reasoning this was an internal German matter. They did not have the will or the strength to stand firm against Germany. In March 1936, German troops marched into the Rhineland, breaking the Treaty of Versailles and the Locarno Pact. In 1938, the British and the French appeased Hitler by allowing Nazi annexation of Czechoslovakia's Sudetenland.

began to arrive at the yeshiva in Natrusk. His parents read the telegrams and wanted to flee, but few countries would accept Jews. His parents considered emigrating to Palestine, but Britain in its *White Paper* in 1939 limited Jewish immigration.* His parents' resolve weakened mainly because of the physical weakness of his mother. Remembering these letters and telegrams, Joseph's father pleaded with him to stay, but Joseph was anxious to leave. His mother asked the local rabbi if Joseph should go, and the rabbi said no.

The bouncing of the train caused his head to bump against the window. He moved it back on the headrest. Leaping through time, bits and pieces of memory flew through his brain. He remembered the telegrams from Brooklyn, New York, and how he had to learn the code that deciphered the telegrams since mail and telegrams were censored by the government. The messages sent by Rabbi Weinberg, on behalf of the Lubavitcher Rebbe, the chief rabbi of this Chasidic movement, warned everyone to flee. The first telegram read, "Grandfather wants you to visit him. Stop. Needs you by his side. Stop. Important that you leave immediately. Stop. Terrible things may happen to you if you do not visit me. Stop. Signed, Cousin Weinberg." The meaning was, "Run away from Poland immediately. Do not wait. Do not hesitate. Terrible dangers await those who stay."

---

* President Franklin Roosevelt, not wanting to annoy Marshal Petain and his Vichy government in France, ordered the United States representative in Marseilles not to grant visas to Jews. Jews in Europe were isolated without hope of escape. England and the United States had previously confirmed their actions at the Evian-les-Bains Conference in France. At the conference, in July 1938, the western nations agreed not to allow Jews into their countries. With Nazi officials permitted to be observers at the conference, it became clear to them that the western nations did not care for the safety of Jews in Europe.

But most people prefer to see what they want to see, hear what they want to hear, and believe what they want to believe. Whatever the reasons, the result remained the same, and they stayed. Without those telegrams, Joseph daydreamed life would be the same as it was before. He would be studying in the yeshiva, where he entered in 1935. Remembering the ordeal of the entrance requirement still made him shudder. He had to memorize two hundred pages of Torah, Bible, and commentary. No, he argued with himself, life would not be the same. He fixed his memory on a day in April when the Nazis conquered Denmark after a one day battle. Denmark was one of the few countries in the world that allowed Jews to immigrate from Germany. Within days after Denmark fell, the plan was made for Joseph to leave.

Opening his eyes, he looked out the window and thought how watching the scenery from a moving train was similar to life. Objects that were close seemed to whisk past quickly and were seen briefly, whereas objects in the distance could be seen in greater perspective. Distant memories gave one more perspective on life, while that day's activities seemed to fly by. Until a few days ago, his parents had planned to accompany Joseph to Shanghai, a city where no entry visa was required. Their optimism was misguided, because from the beginning of the war, his mother's health had deteriorated. In her weakened condition, she was unable to travel. At that moment, when Joseph decided he would leave for Shanghai by himself, he had his first disagreement with his parents, a disagreement that bordered on becoming an argument. He remembered that day, and a grimace crossed his face.

His father, a strong, robust man with a protruding belly, entreated Joseph not to leave. "You are our only child. What will become of us without you?" Joseph's face was frozen, his eyes solemn and very wide, like glass eyes on a doll. His lips parted as though he would speak, but he said nothing. He sat on a chair and buried his face in his hands. It was upsetting to disagree with his parents as it had not occurred before. "How can I make you understand?" his father pleaded, his ashen lips trembling as he spoke. "You are all we live for. Every day, you are in my prayers. Without you here, our souls would be like a tree with a hollow trunk that is decaying."

Joseph rose to his feet. He spoke calmly, yet confusion and uncertainty swept through him. Torn between his parents wanting him to stay and his wanting to go, he uttered in a stammer, "You taught me that frankness deserves frankness, and although I want to go, I will stay and take care of you." His eyes locked into his mother's eyes, and in them he recognized fear and anguish. As he said these words, questions flew through his mind. *How can I disobey the rabbi? Must I ignore the messages in the telegrams telling us we must go?* His father's deep-set eyes studied his son's face, and he was gripped by doubt. He looked sadly at his wife, understanding the love and loyalty she bestowed on her family.

Jacob, Joseph's father, quiet by nature, hardworking, and an observant Jew, was crushed by the decision he was about to make. In an awkward but kind voice he said, "Joseph, my son, your mother and I have lived most of our lives already. Naturally, we do not want you to go. Your offer to stay and care for us tells us of your love and devotion to your parents. But this war between the Germans and the European nations will end soon, and everything will return to normal. If you go, then with God's help, you will return from China and continue your life here as I believe God meant it to be." Joseph saw the perplexity in his father's eyes and the displeasure on his mother's face. Joseph's father felt his cheeks burning. The creases on his forehead deepened, a melancholy crept into his eyes, and the dark rings under them became more prominent. He fumbled with his beard trying to smooth it out. The wrinkles on his cheeks extended under his beard. "We need you here," his father continued, "but the choice is yours. If you go, you know we will miss you. Whatever happens to us because of the war, you must have the opportunity to survive. Many things you do not know or understand yet. Your mother and I have done everything to protect you." He stopped speaking and stared upward. "Dear God, what am I to do? Please help us." He lowered his eyes and peered into his wife's eyes.

Sophie said to Joseph, "Go, my son. You have lived your life within the world of Lubavitch, and you know the people and the traditions. From the age of six, you began learning, and now you will enter another world, a world dominated by war, greed, and jealousy. Be cautious, my son. May you go with God's blessing."

His father spoke to Joseph in a tone like he was praying, "If the worst occurs, then you will be the only one from our family to continue the family name. You will be the only one to say Kaddish, the mourner's prayer, for us after we are departed from this earth. I cannot go because a husband's place is with his wife. Since you offered to stay but want to go, may God be with you, and may you have the courage and strength to survive for all of us. Go towards peace, and always remember that we love you more than anything in the world."

Joseph lifted his head and looked into the sad eyes of his father. "Poppa, after the war, we will be reunited. You will see. Our family will be together again." Joseph quickly added, "Although the Japanese attacked China two years ago, and have occupied it ever since, Shanghai is safe. When the war ends, I will come home. This will be a temporary goodbye."

"Joseph, Joseph," his mother sobbed. Her illness made her thin and frail, causing her to hunch over. Her face, withered like shriveled dead leaves in autumn, made her look older than her age. The once-vibrant brown eyes gleamed no more. Placing her hands on each side of her face, she had changed her mind and pleaded, "Please, do not leave us. I love you very much. No matter what was said in the telegrams, leaving me will break my heart. I will never see you again. I just know it. Please, I beg you not to go." Her knees buckled, and Jacob gripped her to prevent her from falling. Jacob was torn between his love for his family, the authority of the rabbi from Brooklyn, and the war. Tears swelled at the corners of his eyes and flowed down his face. Joseph hugged his mother and kissed her on her forehead and kissed his father on the cheek. He had never seen his father cry.

Gazing out the window to the trees on the street, Joseph watched small birds flitting from branch to branch, and his tears flowed.

Departure day arrived. His mother held a handkerchief to her mouth and stifled the cries that tore at her soul. Her cheeks were wet with tears, like the morning dew falling from a leaf. Joseph's father attempted to console her. Like a prophet, Joseph felt a premonition that he would never see his family and the village of Chemelnick again. The life he knew was ended. Without realizing it, he was about to begin another life, a new life, a different life. He concentrated intensely on his parents' faces, imagining his mind was a camera snapping a picture of them. There was silence between them, as fear replaced the comfort and security that once existed. Joseph wanted to remember them always. He thought that how one sees someone for the last time is how that person is embedded in one's memory. His final images would be that of his ailing mother clinging desperately to a life from the past and a father whose world was shattered. The emptiness of missing someone who you love dearly swept over his mother. Her face was ashen white, like she had just returned from a funeral. Her hands were cold and trembling, and his father held them firmly, afraid she would follow Joseph as he boarded the train. In his father's eyes, there was defeat and resignation, like a prisoner awaiting his sentence. Joseph thought how much a person conveys of his essence and attitudes through the eyes. Waving to his parents once, he boarded the train, and as it moved further away from the station, Joseph watched his parents shrink and disappear in the distance. Joseph could not forget that image.

The train rumbled along, and Joseph lost track of how far it had traveled. *Had it passed Radomsko and Czestochowa? Perhaps the train was approaching Cracow. How much lon-*

ger before it stops? Joseph remembered how for years his parents operated a clandestine grocery from their small house in defiance of Polish laws that followed closely to the Nuremberg Laws.* The Polish law declared it illegal for a Jew to own a business. For his grandfather, the law had been different and had allowed him to operate a business selling grain to feed chickens. Many times, Joseph's grandfather traveled to Warsaw to sell his grain. Joseph's parents defied the law and risked being fined and imprisoned. The food, packed in sacks and cans, was concealed in a large wooden chest. The chest was covered with clutter, day-old newspapers, framed photographs, pencils, pads, books, a clock, tea cups with dried tea bags dangling inside, a knitting basket, and a radio. This grocery business provided food to the neighbors and earned enough money for the Shalosky family to survive. With the meager business earnings, Joseph's father gave his customers more food than they paid for and still managed to have enough money to give to charity every week. Every Sabbath, his parents gave a challah, a twisted bread, to a different poor family. Joseph remembered Thursdays, a dreaded day for Jews in Poland. It was the day of the auctions of Jewish personal property. The Polish government passed laws imposing heavy taxation upon Jews. If a Jew could not pay his taxes, then the police removed his possessions from his house and sold them in the public marketplace on Thursdays to collect the taxes owed. Many times, friends and neighbors would buy the possessions and return them to the owner. Once,

---

* The laws allowed the confiscation of Jewish property, forbade Jews access to universities, banned Jews from most professions, and pressured them to leave Germany.

his father bought a prayer shawl at one of government sales and returned it to the owner the same evening. That night for dinner, Joseph's family ate only soup and bread, the rest of the money having been spent to buy the neighbor's prayer shawl.

The call of the conductor brought Joseph back to the present. Wearing a drab green uniform, a cap, and dirty, scuffed shoes, the conductor proceeded down the corridor asking for tickets. Reaching the students, his broad, angular, unshaven face with wild-looking green eyes stared coldly at them. The students trembled in fear at their first encounter away from the security of the yeshiva and their homes. After checking and punching their tickets, the conductor glared at them and, in a threatening tone, barely above a whisper, said, "Your kind won't be around much longer."

Watching the scenery, his mind wandered back to the snippets of conversation he heard as his parents whispered to each other about the horrible events happening in Europe. He remembered the newspaper photo of Prime Minister Chamberlain of England in September 1938 holding up a piece of paper with the caption "Peace in our time." The news in Europe had not frightened Joseph. What frightened Joseph was walking down a street where gangs of Polish teenagers threw stones at him or, even worse, beat him to be left in the street bleeding. Joseph stopped walking on those streets.

The train passed through small stations, stopping only at larger ones. Each stop brought a new sense of terror to the students. They scanned the station platforms for Nazi soldiers, and not seeing soldiers on most platforms restored a sense of confidence. The Germans had not solidified every position in the country, and most stations still operated with Polish guards. In Lublin, it was necessary to bribe the guards at the station to let them board.

Moving away from the window, Joseph put his head back and closed his eyes. Listening to the clacking sound of the wheels on the tracks, he recalled a chapter in his studies about the concept of truth. When God was about to create Adam, the angels divided on whether Adam should be created. Kindness said, "Let him be created." Truth said, "Do not create him." Righteousness said, "Create him." Peace said, "Do not create him." So God took Truth and threw it to the ground and created man. Joseph thought, *Why is it difficult for man to learn to accept truth?*

The train rolled south, occasionally passing through dark, smoky tunnels. Passengers shut the windows lest the engine smoke enter their compartment, making it difficult to breathe. Black smoke stains marred the compartment walls. Emerging from the tunnels, the windows were again opened from the top to allow in air. The train slowed as it crossed trestles over rivers, rivers that crept along as though they were barely flowing.

He concentrated on remembering the Sabbath dinners with his parents, his mother lighting the Sabbath candles, his father reciting the blessings over the wine, and the delicious meal cooked for the occasion. One of his favorite foods was beets, and he remembered how his mother cooked them. Other memories pushed these memories away, and he remembered the morning the police came to the door. It was early, and Joseph and his father were saying morning prayers. His father, Jacob, was dressed in black. Joseph remembered how his father looked when he was learning, his fierce, dark eyes penetrating each word searching for its meaning. Yet speaking to a person, his eyes were gentle and kind, the kindness emanating from the goodness of his soul. This kindness touched the person with whom he was speaking. Joseph wanted his father to speak to him more often, but their time together was usually spent studying or praying.

The unpleasant memory of the police lingered, and Joseph remembered the knocking on the front door, more like a pounding intending to break down the door. His father opened the door and saw three policemen standing there. His mother stopped preparing breakfast and moved behind Joseph, her hands clasped together. The police were unshaven, gruff-looking men wearing wrinkled gray uniforms, with dirty collars opened at the neck, their caps askew, and looked like gorillas dressed for a circus act. Jacob, Joseph's father, recognized Attila, the local police chief. His real name was Ivan, but to the Jewish community, he was known as Attila. His pants, with tears in the material, were splattered with stains, and his shoes were filthy.

"This is the Shalosky house, yes?" Attila inquired in a sarcastic tone.

Joseph's father stood erect, fear emanating from under his heavy eyebrows, and nodded.

"You Jacob Shalosky, yes?" demanded Attila with the smile of a victor. The large nostrils on his broad, flat nose dominated his face. Deep shadows were around his eyes, and his gaze appeared to be that of a pleasure-seeker. "We are here to inspect your house. We heard that you run a business. If that is true, you know the penalty," he added, slowly drawing out the sentence to emphasize his threat. He looked from his father to his mother and then at Joseph, a smirk on his face, his eyes gleaming with joy. "If we find anything, you will go to jail, where you dirty bastard Jews belong anyway." Attila smiled, his teeth uneven and with a few missing, and mockingly said, "Of course, you will not mind if my men come in and look around?"

The tall, skinny policeman with a long neck, like a human giraffe, enjoyed making a mess of the house. Rather than searching for anything, he undid the tidiness that Sophie worked hard to maintain. The third policeman, built like an ox, deliberately searched through everything he could touch. As he searched, he grunted like an animal stalking prey in the forest. Looking under every chair, table, and piece of furniture, he emptied drawers and closets dropping the contents on the floor. Attila stood watching, a grin on his face. After a thorough search of the house and the attic, they found nothing. As the police were leaving, Attila said in a bad temper, "You are lucky this time, yes. Maybe next time you will not be lucky. Anyway, who cares, soon there will be no more Jews in Poland." Spitting on the threshold, Attila slammed the door and left.

Joseph's father watched the policemen walk down the street. Shaking his head in despair, he went to his wife and son and hugged them. Joseph's mother was sobbing. It was one of the rare times that Joseph saw his father frightened, and it was the only time Joseph saw his father put his arm around his mother.

The rumble of the train and his absorption in memories made Joseph drowsy. Folding his hands on the table that separated the compartment into two benches of three seats each, he placed his head on his hands and fell asleep. In a dream, he saw dark clouds forming, and the sky grew bleak. People appeared concerned about the coming rain. The clouds darkened becoming gray and black and swept toward Chemelnick. He saw an image of his parents standing in front of their house watching the daylight turn into darkness. He wanted to cry out and warn them. His mouth opened, but no words came forth. The blackness descended, engulfing the village, house by house, store by store, and street by street. Joseph attempted to warn them, again, but he could not speak. As his parents were swallowed in the abyss of darkness, Joseph cried out, "Run, run, run!"

A hand poked his arm and a voice whispered, "Joseph, wake up, wake up, you are having a bad dream."

Opening his eyes, he forgot where he was. "Where am I?"

"On the train," a teenage boy answered. "Everything is all right. You were talking in your sleep."

Joseph saw Samuel leaning toward him. Samuel was lanky, with curly brown hair and dark stubble on his chin, knowing one day it would become a beard. Joseph met him at the yeshiva, where students learned from early in the morning until nine or ten at night. They were not in the same classes because of the difference in their age.

"What was I saying?" Joseph asked.

"I heard you say 'Run, run, run' over and over again. You seemed to be in distress, as though you were frightened. Are you all right?"

"I think so," Joseph replied, rubbing the sleep from his eyes. "It seemed like a vision more than just a dream.

I mean, it seemed like I was there and it was happening." He stood and stretched to get the stiffness out of his body.

"I do not know what to say," Samuel answered, "because I have not had such dreams. Maybe your dream is a message, like a premonition. Maybe part of your soul was released and went up towards heaven and an angel told what was going to happen in the future." Samuel hesitated. "That can happen, you know."

"I wanted to warn my parents of a blackness that would overwhelm Chemelnick, but I could not speak," Joseph said. "I tried to speak, even shout, but no words came out. I could not warn them. What does the black cloud mean?"

Samuel shrugged his narrow shoulders and flicked his hands palms up and answered, "Only God knows?"

The shout of the conductor interrupted them. "Cracow, Cracow. Arriving at Cracow.[*] Change here for Lvov, Bratislava, and Budapest and hurry up about it. No lingering. Get moving."

The group gathered in the corridor of the train. Rabbi Ariel Stok looked haggard with his heavy eyelids resting over his dull brown eyes, eyes filled with anxiety and stress. A nervous twitch above his mouth and at his cheek distorted his face. Shaped like a bear without a neck, his deep voice sounded like a growl. In a low tone, he warned the students, "No matter what may be said or done to you on the station, do not respond. Do not even look at them, and certainly do not look them in the eye. It is important that we board the next train safely. Now let us go."

---

[*] Cracow possessed buildings and sculptures crafted during the Renaissance and medieval times. The Russians prevented the Nazis from destroying the culture and history of the city.

"You heard the rabbi," commanded a voice. "Let's go." It was Isaac, their leader. He was tall with broad shoulders, heavyset but not fat, and had a large round face with squinty dark-brown eyes covered with brown-rimmed eyeglasses. His brown hair was straight and combed, and his narrow ears set close to the side of his head made him look like a toy doll. Isaac exuded confidence in all he did. His friends relished his optimism. Up to this point in the trip, he had been studying or sleeping, oblivious to the movement of the train or the scenery outside. "Remember what Rabbi Stok said, 'Do not respond to anyone and do not look them in the eye.'"

CHAPTER 2

Cracow to Budapest

Throngs of people rushed about the station searching for their track. On crowded platforms, hundreds waited with their luggage. Since the war began, busy stations became inundated with hordes of people that overwhelmed the station building, like a river overflowing its banks. Following Rabbi Stok, Joseph heard derogatory and anti-Semitic slurs at the sight of their clothing and their *peyes* (sidelocks). His fright at the comments made him wonder how hatred became ingrained in people, hatred that passed from generation to generation. Below the sign at track number 8 were numbers that read Budapest 15:20. Keeping his head down, Joseph peeked at the people glaring at them. The gauntlet of taunts persisted. His parents and his studies taught him that hatred, jealousy, lying, and coveting were sins. Why, he reflected, have not the Polish people learned this? He was proud to be Jewish and desired to be respected by others as a Jew.

A large clock with Roman numerals, supported by two long steel chains, hung above the center of the station. It read two forty. The students waited quietly. Samuel, his light-brown eyes filled with anxiety, his hair fallen over his forehead, nudged Joseph and nodded in the direction of the station entrance. Twelve Polish security guards, one wearing sergeant stripes on his sleeve, approached. The sergeant was a middle-aged Pole wearing a trimmed black mustache, with a short cropped haircut, and dressed in a neat fitting dark-green uniform with a black belt with a large silver buckle. A German officer followed the guards. Draped over his shoulders, the German wore a long dark-gray coat with a black collar over his uniform. His hat covered a large crop of dark-blond hair. His black leather boots were shined spotless.

Recognizing the rabbi as the leader of the group, the sergeant walked to him and in a commanding tone said, "I need to see all of your papers." Sarcastically he added, "I am sure they will be in order." The German officer observed the scene with his hands clasped behind his back.

"Of course, of course," Rabbi Stok, replied as his voice faded as he saw the Nazi standing in the distance. "Everything is in proper order." Fumbling for his papers inside his jacket pocket, he handed them to the sergeant. The students held their papers ready for inspection. The guards checked each set of papers and compared the photograph on it with the face of the student presenting the papers.

The corporal of the guards, whose appearance Joseph thought reminded him of Attila, the police chief in Chemelnick, began laughing, as he quipped to the other guards, "Look at them and look at their photographs. All these dirty Jews look alike." The sergeant stiffened and gave an angrily piercing look at the corporal. Looking at the German officer, the sergeant saw him purse his lips with a glare of anger.

Advancing to the corporal, the sergeant snapped, "Shut up, you idiot, and do your job." The corporal glanced at the German and returned to examining the papers.

"Very good," said the sergeant to the rabbi. "All is in order."

Rabbi Stok exhaled heavily in relief.

"Why are you going to Budapest?" the sergeant inquired. The question caught the rabbi by surprise. His eyes widened, and his cheeks turned red.

"Well, um," he stammered, "It is for a special reason." He struggled for an appropriate response.

"Which is what?" asked the sergeant with a smirk.

"There is going to be a special study session at the yeshiva in Budapest, and we are going to participate."

"I do not see a return train ticket. When might you be returning to Poland?"

The German moved closer to the group. The corporal spurted, "You can see he is lying, the dirty Jew bastard. They all lie. Never trust any of them."

"I told you before to shut up," ordered the sergeant. "I do not think that our friend from Berlin wants to hear your personal prejudices. We must act with obedience on behalf of the Nazi cause, and you are not obeying orders." The Nazi officer smiled. Turning to Rabbi Stok, the sergeant repeated, "The return train ticket, I do not see one for anyone in the group." With polite emphasis in his voice and looking into the dark eyes of the rabbi, he added, "When will you return? And how will you return?"

Regaining his composure, Rabbi Stok replied, "As you see, we have packed our suitcases to stay for several weeks in Budapest. It is a charming city and a good place to learn. Depending on how long the war goes on will depend on whether we travel back by train or travel by wagon. I have heard that the Nazis will win within a few more weeks and everything will return to the way it was before the war. If that is what happens, we will buy train tickets."

A small crowd had gathered, waiting to see what the Poles would do to the Jews. Without warning, the corporal moved forward and quickly grabbed the rabbi's beard and yanked. The rabbi let out a painful scream and, holding his beard, tumbled to the ground.

The crowd laughed and shouts were heard, "More! More!"

Joseph felt Samuel move forward. He tried to grab his arm to stop him, but he was too slow. With the look of a wild animal, Samuel leaped at the corporal. The impact knocked the corporal down, and Samuel fell on top of him. Sitting up, Samuel began punching the corporal in the face. The corporal covered his head with his arms for protection. A rifle butt smacked Samuel across his back. He staggered in pain, losing his balance, and crumpled headfirst to the dirty station floor. Blood ran from his nose as he moaned in pain. Rabbi Stok crawled to Samuel and stuffed his handkerchief into the bleeding nostril. For the moment, Rabbi Stok forgot where he was and concentrated on helping Samuel. The sergeant was bewildered and looked at the Nazi for guidance. The corporal stepped backward, mumbling to the sergeant that it was an accident, a mistake, and it would not happen again.

The Nazi officer tilted his head downward looking at Samuel and the rabbi. For several seconds, he considered the situation. Glancing at the sergeant, he nodded. The sergeant pulled his revolver from its holster. Everyone froze as a hush descended on the crowd, and immediately they began to disperse. Stricken with fear, the students huddled together. Rabbi Stok covered Samuel's body with his own. Disbelief spread over Joseph's face. The sergeant raised the revolver, aiming it at the rabbi. Suddenly he turned toward the corporal. The gunshot reverberated through the railroad station. The rabbi turned toward the sergeant, his cheek twitching. The bullet struck the corporal through the left side of his chest, killing him. In the station, everything stopped except the ticking clock. The sergeant motioned to the guards to move the body. Without hesitation, they obeyed. The Nazi walked to the sergeant and said, "Now you understand what I mean when I say that without discipline to follow orders, you Polish Nazis will never be able to control anyone, let alone the Jews. This will be another job that German troops will have to perform rather than being available to fight at the front. I see no hope that you imbecile Poles can ever be disciplined."

The sergeant apologized and pleaded, "I am sorry for this embarrassing incident. Please do not report this to my superiors. You know how difficult it is to discipline my people. I will demand more of them. Such an incident will not happen again."

The Nazi officer shook his head from side to side, shrugged, and walked back through the station.

The students boarded the train in silence. A student named Mordechai helped Samuel mount the steps and seated him in the compartment. Mordechai was the brightest of the students, the one who knew everything. He had a round face shaped like a balloon. This matched his balloon-shaped, squat body. His slanted eyes were inherited from his ancestors from the east. He had refused to go on this journey, but through the determination and strong will of his parents, he consented the day before departure. In his suitcase, Mordechai carried clothing, prayer books, and photographs of his family. The photos consumed much of the small space inside the bag. He believed that after the war, he would continue to America, and his parents and family would meet him there.

The train rolled through what had been Czechoslovakia until a year before. The Germans declared Bohemia and Moravia, in the west, be made a protectorate of the German Reich. In the east, a German supported government in Slovakia declared independence and joined the Nazis in the war. Passing through the West Carpathian Mountains, Joseph saw the splendor of the High and Low Tatras and the Ore Mountains, which rose to altitudes as high as eight thousand five hundred feet. He marveled at the beauty of the snowcapped peaks and the sensation of traveling above the tree line. Yet while the splendor of nature captivated him, his thoughts stayed with Samuel and the rabbi.

During the trip to Budapest, Samuel lay on his stomach with ice packs on his back. The rabbi sat quietly holding an ice wrapped cloth against his face. The train stopped briefly in Kogice, the second largest city in Slovakia. Again their papers and travel permits were checked. At each checkpoint, the students feared another recurrence of Cracow station. Rabbi Stok spoke Yiddish, Hebrew, Polish, Czech,

Hungarian, Russian, and German, and this helped at each checkpoint by allowing him to speak with the police and soldiers in their language. Arriving in Budapest, the students looked to the future as Cracow became a memory.

Carrying their suitcases through the streets of Budapest, Joseph's first impression was that this was a beautiful city. The Danube River calmly flowed through the city, dividing it into two sections, Buda on the west side and Pest on the east side. The air smelled fresh. Cargo ships and passenger steamers plied the river, moving into and out of the docks. The majestic parliament building stood silhouetted against the Danube. The extravagant Buda Castle, built by Bela IV in the thirteenth century for protection against the Mongol attacks, seemed to cover an entire hill on the Buda side. Gently rolling hills and heavily wooded forests cast a graceful charm around the castle. Decorated bridges stood in parallel formation across the Danube, and the famous Margaret Bridge connected Magrit Island to both sides of the mainland. Tall church spires rose mysteriously in the fading light. Pest was flat and not as pretty. He noticed the large crowd of people on the sidewalks and absorbed the sounds of the city from bicycle riders, streetcars, and automobiles. After having traveled four hundred miles sitting on an uncomfortable wooden bench, it felt good to be walking. Thinking of his parents, Joseph reflected on how much he missed them.

Walking through winding narrow tree-lined cobblestone streets, the rabbi made a mistake in reading the directions. Winded and lost, he stopped. People passed by, glanced briefly, and continued on their way. Joseph smelled the sweet aroma of flowers planted in the window planters. Faces peered down from balconies above the streets.

Stone canopies sculptured with eagles, birds, or nymphs decorated the tops of the buildings. An elderly man in a heavy black jacket sensed their predicament and stopped to offer them directions. Weary from their long train ride, they finally arrived at the white and red brick faced Dohany Street Synagogue. Its two towers soared above the surrounding buildings, and its sculptured facade and large windows were compatible to the Byzantine Moorish style of its architecture. It seemed like a Moorish Mosque rather than a synagogue. Joseph entered and saw the largest synagogue in Europe, one that could accommodate three thousand people. He wandered down the long aisle peering at the stained glassed windows and the flickering of light through them. Built in 1859, a plaque commemorated its Viennese architect, Ludwig Forster. He focused his attention on the altar, decorated with a Star of David on a canopy, gold-sculptured decorations, and two large candelabras on either side of the ark.

Rabbi Stok had arranged with the rabbi of Budapest to provide lodging and food for the night. In a smaller building adjoining the synagogue, the students placed their belongings and then prayed the Maariv service, the evening prayer. This prayer, originated by Jacob, the patriarch of exile, was to show children that the night might be the epilogue to one day, but it is a prologue to another, even better day. Joseph returned to the room he shared with three others and wrote a letter to his parents.

> *Dear Momma and Poppa,*
>   *My first day away from you was a challenge. As it is stated in the Torah in the*

chapter Vayigash, "Do not become agitated on the way." I restrained myself during the dangerous moments of this journey, and our group arrived safely in Budapest. Yet what I witnessed today could be the beginning of an impending darkness. I remember learning in the Torah when God spoke to Jacob in night visions. The night of exile was about to begin. I feel the same is about to begin for me in my exile away from you. I know that God will be with me and I have no fear. I am concerned about your safety. You may be in danger as are all the Jews in Poland. I miss you very much and doubt whether it was a good idea to leave you despite what was said in the telegrams. I feel badly that I did not stay home during this time of crisis. I feel torn because of the conflict in me of following the telegrams' messages and my desire to stay with you. I miss you. Please send my love to my grandparents, aunts, uncles, and cousins. I look forward to the war ending quickly and all of us being reunited in Chemelnick. I will write often, knowing that each day will take me further from you. I pray that you, Momma, have a speedy recovery, and that God reunites us as he did Jacob and Joseph in the Torah.

Your loving son,
Joseph

The next morning, a light rain beat on the windows and, like a mist, covered the streets. Joseph did not notice the rain as he ate breakfast. His concern was how to mail the letter he had written. The sealed, unstamped letter was in his jacket pocket. Without having Hungarian currency and no time to find a post office, he decided to impose on the rabbi of Budapest. Joseph entered the rabbi's office. The rabbi was in his mideighties, and his heavy, slightly hunched body was dropped into an armchair. The walls of his office were dull, the sparkle of the paint having faded over the years. A round, heavyset face, filled with wrinkles and lines, emerged from under swollen eyelids.

"Good morning, Rabbi," Joseph greeted. "I would like to thank you for your hospitality. It is very thoughtful of you to shelter us for the night."

The rabbi of Budapest forced his eyes to open wide, and his lips parted and a faint voice replied, "You are most welcome, but you know, it is normal to extend kindness whenever one can." The rabbi continued speaking on the virtues of helping one's fellow man. Joseph let him speak without interrupting. When the rabbi stopped, Joseph told him how he remembered his father and mother and the pleasant times they shared together. The rabbi answered, "Memories are what has happened in our lives, and we hold on to them. But what we will do today and tomorrow becomes our future, and that is more important than the past."

"I will remember that," Joseph said, then he added, "May I ask a favor of you.

"Of course, anything," replied the rabbi.

"I know how busy you are especially in these times."

"Please, please," interrupted the rabbi. "Tell me what it is you want."

"I need to mail this letter to my parents. I do not have Hungarian money or stamps, but I will gladly pay for the stamp. Will you be so kind as to mail this letter?"

The rabbi accepted the letter and replied in a soothing voice, "Of course I will, and you do not need to give me any money. When you are away from your family, for them to receive a letter from you is comforting."

Joseph offered the money, and the rabbi held up his hand refusing it.

"May God be with you."

"Thank you, Rabbi. I will always remember your kindness."

"Kindness," the rabbi said, "is the generosity of humanity. It is helping a friend, a family member, a stranger. Rather than just talking of love and kindness, one lives his life with them, and your single kind act tips the global scale towards goodness. Kindness is something that people remember. You might say that an act of kindness becomes a future memory."

A Hungarian student entered the office, a look of agitation and worry creased his face and forehead.

"Excuse me, Rabbi," he said slightly out of breath. "I do not mean to disturb you, but you must come with me." Ignoring Joseph's presence, he continued, "Please forgive me for interrupting you. Tragic news is on the radio. Please come quickly, Rabbi. We do not know what to do. This will be a matter of life and death, especially for the group that arrived from Poland last night."

The rabbi pulled himself out of the armchair and followed the student. Joseph followed them into a study hall. The wooden floors were in neglect, and flakes of missing plaster dotted the walls. A brown wooden radio sat on a card table against a wall with dozens of students standing around it. The English accent of the radio broadcaster was distinct, and he delivered the news in an unemotional, sharp voice. Static made it necessary to listen carefully since some words were garbled. The voice announced, "This morning, May tenth, Winston Churchill succeeded Neville Chamberlain as prime minister." A pause. "On the war front, German Luftwaffe bombed the city of Rotterdam in the Netherlands. Early assessments report that the city has been destroyed. I repeat that the port city of Rotterdam has been destroyed by Nazi bombing." A pause. "In further war developments, German Panzer divisions have invaded Belgium. The expectation is that Belgium will capitulate shortly, placing France in grave danger. The French have relied on the Maginot Line in the east for its defense and is presently vulnerable to a German offensive through Belgium to its north. The Maginot Line will be of no defense for France." A pause. "Continuing the war report on this day, it appears the borders throughout Europe will be closed wherever Germans control the country. Without proper papers, crossing frontiers will be dangerous. Further updates on the war will be made throughout the day. You are listening to the *BBC* from London, England."

CHAPTER 3

Budapest to Belgrade

The wagon wheels needed an oiling. An irritating squeak sounded each time the wheels turned as they rolled through the ruts in the road. The idea of using the wagon to escape from Hungary was decided that morning at the Dohany Street Synagogue, based on news of the German attacks in Holland and Belgium. Bouncing from side to side inside the old circus wagon, Rabbi Stok and the students sat cramped together. The wagon was assembled with wood, including its top. The red, white, and blue hand-painted lettering of insignias and the circus name on the outside were faded and smeared. Sitting on a thin flat wooden bench, the students felt every bump jostle their bodies.

"Riding the train to Budapest was a joy compared to riding in this creaky old wagon," Mordechai blurted. To show off his knowledge, he added, "Someone told me that before the Great War, we might have enjoyed the comfort of riding in a wagonette, a light four-wheeled carriage, some with a top. Wagonettes were the vogue of Budapest with their crosswire seats in the front and two lengthwise seats facing each other at the back. It seems to me that the discomfort of this dilapidated circus wagon is like riding on the back of a camel."

"You know too much about everything," Joseph replied, "but at least it is good to hear your voice rise above the squeaking wheels."

Streams of light squeezed through the openings in the side boards. At the rear of the wagon, the large opening allowed in light and fresh air. Joseph sat in the rear and studied from a book. A student named Zev sat with his eyes closed, his childlike face covered in shadows, and his long skinny legs, looking like tent poles, tucked under the seat. Zev studied at the yeshiva because his family demanded it. Wanting to leave Poland, Zev imagined a new life in Shanghai without anti-Semitism. Avi, a grimace on his face, his lips pursed tightly, paid no attention to the others. Avi worried about everything. His friends teased him that he worried enough for everyone. Levi, with his deep voice, hummed a melody and stared off into space. He enjoyed singing in Hebrew and Yiddish, and his voice carried above all the others during services. He, like Joseph, was short and thin, his small beard covering a soft, smooth face. The students either talked quietly or sat in silence, fearful that this journey to safety would fail.

The four horses strained pulling the heavy wagon as it headed south toward the Yugoslavian border. Before leaving Budapest, the rabbis calculated that the trip would take two days to Belgrade, a distance of two hundred fifty miles. They assumed giving bribes to the border guards would allow for their passage through the Hungarian and Yugoslavian borders. Instead of taking their suitcases from

Budapest, each student had a sack filled with essentials for the journey: clothing, food, a canteen filled with water, money, photographs, and prayer books. In their pockets were ropes to fasten the sacks to their backs.

Dark storm clouds moved east, covering the red-orange glow of the impending sunset. Earlier in the day, the wagon bypassed the city of Kecskemet and traveled through Szeged, the last city before the border. Near the border, drivers and passengers stood outside of their cars, the engines off, waiting for the slow moving line to creep forward. As the line moved, they pushed their car a few feet toward the border. The Hungarian guards examined passports and visas thoroughly. Before approving anyone's exit, a transfer of money was made to the guard, who brought it to a Zsandar, a member of the Hungarian Gestapo. The Zsandar smiled and gave his approval to proceed.

The circus wagon reached the front of the line, and two guards approached and walked around it. They examined every passport and visa. A clean-shaven guard, in his early twenties, skinny like a scarecrow, with a long face, blond hair, and clear blue eyes with a wild look in them, approached Rabbi Stok. The rabbi offered him the bribe money. As he accepted it from the rabbi, he yanked the rabbi's hand, causing him to fall to the wagon floor.

"Get up, you dirty Jew bastard," ordered the guard. "Out of the wagon. I want you to show my friends how Jews dance. We need some entertainment. It gets boring out here doing the same sort of cruddy work day after day."

Rabbi Stok struggled down from the wagon. His face was expressionless, his eyes cast away from his tormenters, daring not look at the guards, fearing one of them would make this a personal affront against the rabbi rather than against Jews in general. The guards vacated their posts to watch, and the line of cars and wagons stopped moving. The guards sang an Hungarian folk song designed for a peasant dance and began clapping and stomping their feet in rhythm to the song. The guard yelled at Rabbi Stok, "Dance! Dance, you filthy swine!" He laughed with the bravado of showing off to his friends. Rabbi Stok began to dance, trying to keep pace with the melody. The singing and clapping grew faster, and people who had been waiting in line came to watch.

The students sat in solemn silence, watching the rabbi being humiliated, dreading what might happen to them. Joseph noticed the scowl on Samuel's face, his brows contracted in a sullen, angry manner. Joseph remembered Samuel telling him about the argument he had with his parents. Samuel did not want to leave for Shanghai. They insisted that, for his safety, he go, arguing that no one could predict when the war would end or how it would end for the Jews. Away from his parents and his four younger brothers and sister, Samuel now embraced the attitude that most things do not matter when you are away from those you love. Joseph realized that Samuel allowed his emotions to overwhelm his logic. Looking at Joseph as though he did not know him, his eyes darted from guard to guard like daggers thrown at a target. Joseph moved his hand up and down signaling Samuel to be calm. Samuel edged his way to the front of the crowd.

"Faster! Dance faster, old man!" yelled another guard. "We have not had this much sport in weeks."

Winded and barely able to catch his breath, the rabbi's round face grew red, his gray hair in disarray, and his eyes staring up to heaven. To enhance the festivities, the guards began firing their pistols and rifles into the air. Totally exhausted, Rabbi Stok slumped to the ground, laying there like a large sack of potatoes.

"Get up!" yelled the blond-haired guard. He fired his pistol into the ground near the rabbi and then placed it back in his belt. "Get up. The entertainment is not finished until I say it is finished."

The guards and the people laughed at the scene, more at the humiliation of the rabbi rather than at his dancing. Samuel jumped to the ground and ran to the rabbi to lift him. The guard yelled, "Hey, Jew boy, since you are out of the wagon, let us see you dance. You have more strength and can do better than the old man."

The storm clouds grew darker and drifted closer. In the distance, bolts of lightning flashed across the sky. Gusts of wind chilled the air.

Disregarding the prior warnings of Rabbi Stok, Samuel looked the guard in the eye and, with hatred boiling in his breast, spurted, "Why do you torment him? He is old. He is weary from a long journey. He gave you the money you wanted. What more do you want? He caused you no harm."

Watching in shock, Joseph was speechless. He remembered the admonition of Rabbi Stok, "Do nothing, say nothing, and do not look them in the eye no matter what happens." Samuel had disobeyed. Modechai shivered in fear, his face reflecting the disbelief of what was happening.

"Dance, you kike bastard," threatened the skinny guard, his voice filled with anger. The fun of humiliating the rabbi had ended for the guard, and now the scene changed to having fun with this Jew who had dare to speak back. Walking to Samuel, the guard dragged him away from the rabbi. "Get up on your feet. Let's see you dance."

He signaled the other guards to start singing the same folk song. It started to drizzle, yet no one seemed to notice. "Get up and dance," the guard ordered, kicking Samuel in the leg. Samuel rubbed his leg and glared at the guard standing over him. A loud clap of thunder broke the confrontation. Flashes of lightning lit the sky followed by thunder bellowing like cannons being fired. Suddenly, Samuel sprang from the ground like a leopard pouncing on a zebra. He grabbed the guard around the chest, knocking him to the ground, and punched him in the face. A small cut, trailed by blood, broke through the guard's cheek. Rolling in the dirt, the guard twisted out of Samuel's grip as they wrestled on the ground. During the scuffle, Samuel reached into the guard's belt and grasped his pistol. The guard grabbed Samuel's hand with both of his and twisted it as they fought for the pistol. The gunshot shattered the night air, sounding like another clap of thunder. Samuel fell backward, the pistol in his hand. The guard clutched at his stomach, moaning in pain. Circles of blood stained his uniform. Samuel pointed the pistol at the guard, the look of revenge in his eyes. Hatred replaced logic. The guard raised one hand in front of his face and pleaded, "No, no, don't shoot. We were only having some fun."

Another clap of thunder drowned out the shot. The guard fell backward. Two bolts of lightning flashed across the sky. Samuel fired again, and the guard died, blood oozing from his mouth and nose. The crowd ran back to their cars and wagons, and the guards ran for safety, ducking behind rocks and wagons. The rabbi climbed back into the wagon, and it started moving. Lying on his stomach, Samuel shot at the guards and wounded one. The guards fired back, and a swarm of bullets, like hail, struck and killed Samuel. During the chaos, the wagon moved toward the Yugoslavian border as the driver cracked his whip, urging the horses to quicken their pace. When the Hungarian guards realized what was happening, they began shooting at the fleeing wagon. Bullets ripped holes in the wagon cover and shattered wood, causing splinters to fly in the air. A sharp cry of pain, like a wounded animal, tore through the wagon. Seconds later it stopped, and a body fell over Joseph's legs as Joseph lay huddled on the floor. Overwhelmed with a fear he had never experienced before, Joseph trembled from the fear of dying. Closing his eyes, he began to pray. The wagon bounced and bumped along the rutted road and seemed close to overturning. Racing from the Hungarian border to the Yugoslavia border, the wagon ride seemed to last for hours but the incident lasted less than two minutes.

At the Yugoslavian border, the wagon stopped, and everyone climbed down. Trapped by the weight of the body slumped over him, Joseph pushed himself up from the floor and looked down to see Mordechai. Mordechai, Joseph thought, *the one with the most potential, the one to continue his family's name, the one who was to become a scholar of the Torah and Talmud, and the one who now lay dead.* Joseph turned him over and saw dead eyes staring back at him. In two days away from home, Joseph's once-calm existence was shattered by fear and killings. Trembling, he thought about his father warning him of the harsh realities of the world that he might face. *He was right*, thought Joseph, *and maybe he was right that I should not have left home*. The thoughts lingered, and a feeling of sadness crept into him.

"Are you all right?" Emil, the driver, asked. Emil had a rugged face with deep crevices, a cleft chin, and a nose that looked like it had been broken. Not having shaved for days, dark stubble filled the crevices and hid the dust on his dirty face. His clothing was frayed and torn in places, and his jacket was stained with grease and dirt marks. A brown cap covered his uncombed dark curly hair.

"Yes, yes," Joseph answered, "I am fine."

"Climb down. Only two are unaccounted for, and you are one of them."

"The other is here with me. I need help."

"Is he hurt badly?"

"It is Mordechai. He is dead," stammered Joseph, wiping tears away with the sleeve of his jacket.

"Come down. We will take care of him later. First we must be inspected by the border guards." Joseph moved his hand over Mordechai's eyelids, closing them, and covered his face with an empty burlap bag. Jumping from the wagon, Joseph walked toward the border guards. They examined his papers, said nothing, handed them back, and waved him away.

"Where is Rabbi Stok?" Joseph asked.

"Over there," pointed Emil. "He was wounded during the shooting."

Rabbi Stok sat on the ground, the students gathered around him. One of the students, Benjamin, wearing his frameless glasses over his blue eyes and with a stoical expression, cleaned the wound and wrapped a bandage around the rabbi's left arm. The bullet had passed through the fleshy part of his arm, missing the bone. Blood seeped through the bandage. Benjamin's long, nimble fingers quickly fastened a sling by placing the rabbi's arm in the cloth and then tying it behind his neck. The rabbi smiled at the comfort the sling brought him.

"Even in times of adversity," the rabbi said, "be thankful to God for any favor he bestows on you, even a sling for a wounded arm."

"Rabbi," Joseph said, "I am distressed to have to tell you that Mordechai has been killed. He is in the wagon. Shall we bury him here?"

Rabbi Stok looked upward and mumbled, "Dear God, it was not supposed to be this way. Already we have lost two boys, Samuel and Mordechai, and we have been on the road for just two days. Tell me, please dear God, did we do the right thing by leaving Poland?" After a minute of reflection, the rabbi turned to Joseph and said, "No, we bring him to Belgrade, and we will bury him there. Come, we must go."

Benjamin, who stood a head taller than the rabbi and with a full head of bushy blond hair, lifted him to his feet and guided him to the wagon. Part of the bench was cleared for the rabbi to lie down. Mordechai's body was covered and placed under the driver's seat. Joseph, Levi, and Avi volunteered to stand as there was no place for everyone to sit. "I do not mind standing," said Joseph. "It shows respect to Rabbi Stok."

Moving south through Serbia to Belgrade, the wagon trudged along the broken road, the squeaking wheels sounding like the shrill squawk of a crow calling its mate. The squeak grew louder as the wagon bounced and wobbled along. Benjamin watched as the rabbi dozed, making sure he did not fall from the bench. After a while, Zev, Meyer, and Abraham exchanged places with Joseph, Avi, and Levi. After sitting cramped in the wagon all day, it was a relief for them to stand and stretch their legs. In their yeshiva studies, the students were taught to be optimistic. Although some students came from poor families, they had maintained the confidence of continuing their future in Poland, where Jews had lived for eight hundred years.[*]

After the day's tragic events, a bleak skepticism settled upon the students. They paid scant attention as the wagon rolled through the cities of Senta and Novi Sad in Serbia, never imagining the savagery that would befall the Serbian people by the Nazis and the Croatians. Years later, they would hear of the one million four hundred thousand Serbians who were murdered.

Suddenly the wagon tipped to one side, and Rabbi Stok rolled off the bench. With the wagon tilting, Joseph, Levi,

---

[*] Beginning in the early twelfth century, Jews fled from Germany into Poland. Until the sixteenth century, they lived in safety, protected by Polish leaders like King Boleslav V and Casimir III the Great. The first pogroms erupted against the Jews in the early sixteenth century, but the worst one, instigated by the Cossacks, occurred in 1648. Since then, cruel anti-Semitism prevailed in Poland with its Jewish population numbering three million three hundred thousand.

and Avi tumbled into Zev, Meyer, and Abraham, knocking them down. In the darkness, there was a moment of panic.

"What happened?" someone shouted.

"Get off me, I can't breathe."

"Is the rabbi all right?"

"Move slowly so you do not hurt anyone when you stand."

"What happened? I was dozing."

"I do not know."

"The wagon lost a wheel," Emil said. "It will be okay after we fix it. But for now, you must get out and reduce the weight inside."

Safely on the ground, Joseph saw one rear wheel next to the wagon and the wagon supported by the three others.

"I need some help," said Emil, his body lean from a lack of food. "The wagon must be lifted so the wheel can be replaced. I have bolts to secure it."

Having been quiet on the entire trip, Isaac took command of his fellow students. Tall, muscular, and with a deep voice, he commanded authority. His classmates obeyed his dictates. Directing them to help the driver, Isaac's voice was mellow and friendly. The students followed the driver to the side of the fallen wheel.

"We will lift together," Emil prodded, removing his shaggy-looking jacket. "When the axle is lifted high enough above the ground, I will put the wheel on. Get a good grip and bend at your knees for maximum strength."

The students stood on both sides of the axle, trying to get a firm grip on the wagon. The driver commanded, "Ready, set, lift." The students slipped in the dirt, and some fell. The wagon did not budge.

"We will do it again," said Isaac. "Pray first and then dig in your shoes to hold the ground. If we do not get this wheel on, we spend the night here, not in Belgrade, and we are close to the city." Glancing at his classmates, he saw that they were not in strong physical condition. "I suppose we spend too much time studying and not enough time exercising."

"Who has time for anything but studying?" Avi said in a bitter voice. "Our life is all about studying, studying, and more studying. Look at where we are."

Isaac ignored his comments. "All right, we do it this time," Isaac encouraged, his lean, angular body braced against the wagon.

Emil dug in his heels, his toughened hands on the wagon, and snapped, "Ready, set, lift." The wagon moved upward. "Higher, more effort." He stepped away from the wagon, ran to the wheel, and lifted it to fit over the axle. "Not enough clearance. A few centimeters more," he pleaded.

Down came the wagon with a thud. Emil glared at the students, annoyed at how weak they were. "Empty everything from the wagon, even the body from the front seat."

Joseph turned to Rabbi Stok. "What do you suggest we do with Mordechai? Should we bury him here or wait until we reach Belgrade?"

Rabbi Stok spoke with difficulty as the bullet wound and the fall from the bench increased his pain. "Try one more time to put the wheel on. If it fails, we must bury him here."

The students emptied the contents of the wagon.

"Now when I say 'Ready, set,' you take a deep breath and bend your knees," Emil instructed, his eyes glaring at them in frustration, "and when I say 'lift,' use all your strength for a few seconds, and I will put the wheel on. Concentrate. If we fail, no one will rescue us until morning."

"Let's do it," said Levi, his voice bellowing like a foghorn.

Walking to the bare axle, Emil moved the wheel closer to it, rubbing dirt on his filthy hands. "All right now, let us give it a go. You want to be in Belgrade soon. This is your chance to help yourselves."

Joseph murmured a prayer, *Dear God, please help us lift the wagon.*

"Ready, set, lift."

The wagon stayed still. "Lift! Lift! Lift!" shouted Isaac, straining as he and the students struggled to lift the load. The wagon barely moved.

"God, give us the strength," said Isaac. "Everybody lift when I count to three. One, two, three." The bare axle moved up and cleared the ground with enough room to replace the wheel. It seemed like magic. Emil moved quickly, lifting the wheel, and in one swift motion placed it over the axle. Securing it in place, he commended the students on their efforts. While he secured the wheel to the axle, everyone rested. Emil worked without complaint as though everything that had happened was just a normal part of his job.

Isaac sat on the cold ground, his eyes filled with exhilaration. Dirt and splotches of dried blood covered the scratches and cuts on his hands. Pouring water from his canteen, he cleaned his hands. Glancing upward toward the cloudy sky, he murmured a prayer of thanks.

Avi sat next to Joseph. Avi lived in conflict, knowing what God expected of him and yet having difficulty in living that way. Thus his hazel-colored eyes showed fear and uncertainty. "What will become of us?" he asked. "I have prayed with all my heart and with all my soul, and still Samuel and Mordechai are dead and we struggle to survive. Is this God's way of helping us on our journey to China?"

Joseph looked at his friend, observing his black coat, black shoes, dirty hands, and mud-covered fingernails. Joseph remembered Avi as being one of the neatest and cleanest of all the students. They became friends in the yeshiva in Warsaw, Avi being from Lodz.

"Remember when we study the Exodus," answered Joseph, "God told the Jews to make small prayers but to continue their journey. We must do all that we can to succeed, and if our efforts are insufficient, then we must make longer prayers. We chose to make this journey. There was not much else we could do other than stay and face the Nazis. I pray for the safety and good health of my family, and that I see them again when the war ends."

"What about Samuel and Mordechai?" Avi asked. "How do we tell their parents? It is the worst thing a parent can experience, the loss of a child." He shook his head and looked away from Joseph. "Two days away and two of our friends have been killed. Would it not have been easier to have risked death with our families at home?"

"Remember the telegrams from Brooklyn?" Joseph asked. "We followed their advice. As for telling the parents of Samuel and Mordechai, it will be difficult. I suppose that Rabbi Stok will write them. How he goes about telling them the tragic news is something that I would not like to think about. Their grief will be unbearable, and they will doubt the wisdom of their decision in allowing their sons to leave. This will be a tragedy they carry for the rest of their lives."

It was after midnight when the wagon arrived in Belgrade. Everyone was exhausted and dozing, unaware of crossing the Danube River and passing the huge Kalemegdan Fortress. The architecture of the city reflected life as it had been one hundred years earlier. Stopping in front of the synagogue, Emil saw it was dark and knocked on the door. The once-magnificent decorative brick facade was faded, and dirt covered the gray walls. He waited, and shortly the wooden door was opened just a crack, and a skinny young man's face peeked out. "Who are you?"

"I am bringing the students from Budapest," Emil replied, the lines in his face sagging from a lack of sleep.

The man opened the door wider, and Emil noticed his pug nose, messy hair, and the night shirt he was wearing. "Oh, yes, we expected you earlier. Is everything all right?"

"Not quite. We had a bad time at the border. One of the boys was shot and killed. The rabbi was wounded and needs a doctor. Anyway, we are here. Where do you want us to stay?"

"Come in, come in, I will get some candles. Electricity is rationed, and there is none in Belgrade this late at night. Wait here, I will go back to the dormitory and get more candles. I will return in a minute."

They stood huddled in the cold, damp synagogue and waited. Joseph reflected that when one waits during a time of urgency, minutes seems like hours. Three men approached from the rear of the sanctuary, each carrying four candles. As they handed one each to Joseph and the students, another man headed for the doorway.

"I will fetch the doctor," he said. "It might be a while, but I will bring him here as quickly as I can." He hurried into the dark street illuminated only by the rays of moonlight seeping through the clouds. Isaac, Avi, and Joseph sat on a bench. Isaac was bedraggled. The glint in his brown eyes was dull, his clothing splattered with dirt and mud, and dried blood mixed with mud caked his hands. His large frame slouched against the wall, his eyes focused on the rough wooden floor. Avi, a dazed look in his eyes, rubbed his hands, trying to rub the dirt off of them. He used his index finger nail to remove dirt from under his fingernails.

"Joseph," Avi said in a voice of resignation. "We made a mistake leaving home. Two of our friends are dead, Rabbi Stok is wounded, and the Nazis are destroying country after country in Europe. What chance will we have to escape?" He paused and in a pious voice continued, "When we left on the train yesterday, I made certain to say the traveler's prayer. I emphasized the beginning, which reads, 'May it be Thy will, O Lord our God, and God of our fathers, to cause us to walk in peace.' There has been no peace on this journey."

Isaac started to say something then changed his mind. Joseph stood and began pacing and mumbled to himself. Looking at the sheer solidarity of the synagogue, Joseph was impressed with the brownstone with gray baubles, surmounted by Stars of David at the top. Dark wooden seats clung to the walls, and lamps emerged from shields above.

Isaac's frustration forced him to shrug his shoulders and, for one of the rare times in his life, remain speechless.

"Listen," said Joseph, "things happen that are bad, but we do not know what God's plan is for the situation. Sometimes we never know. There is a big picture to everything, and naturally, man wants to know everything and to have a reason why everything happens. For every difficulty, man wants to know the solution in advance. This satisfies man's emotion but not necessarily his logic. Today's sad events happened for a reason, but we do not know why, only God knows. So we make the best choices we can, yet God determines the outcome."

"Look at today's sad events," said Avi, his hands gesturing with every word. "Plan or no plan, two of our friends are dead. Their parents will recite prayers, and during their bereavement, they will not know how to comfort themselves. The price for our freedom is unseemly high." He grasped his chin between his thumb and index finger and in a skeptic tone exclaimed, "How are we supposed to get to Shanghai from here? The borders will be closed everywhere. We will be hunted like animals in the jungle and killed. We will not accomplish our goal of reaching safety, and at the same time our parents and families will be grieving for us."

Feeling exhausted, Joseph wanted to console Avi, but there were no words left in him. Avi held his face in his hands and shook his head in despair.

"We are trapped," muttered Avi. "We cannot return home, and we cannot reach China. We will be hidden here until the Nazis find us." He removed a small prayer book from his coat pocket and flipped through several pages before stopping to read and pray.

That night, before going to sleep, Joseph wrote a letter to his parents.

> *Dear Momma and Poppa,*
>
> *I write to you from Belgrade. I am well other than being tired from sitting in a crowded wagon for hours without being able to get out and walk around. The trip has been difficult, and there was tragedy along the way. I am sorry to have to tell you this, but Samuel and Mordechai were shot and killed, and Rabbi Stok was wounded. A doctor is caring for his wound. He will be unable to travel any further. Early tomorrow morning, I continue the journey to Shanghai, not yet knowing who will be leaving with me. I think some of the group will stay here in Belgrade. This seems dangerous to me because the Croatians have had ethnic feuds with the Serbians for centuries. Now the Croatians fight on the side of the Germans, and they will seek retribution against the Serbians. Papa, remember when we discussed the Book of Genesis and the concept of free choice and Divine Providence? It seems clear to me now. Each of the students in the yeshiva had a choice, to flee from Poland or to stay. Our group chose to go. We made the choice of our own free will. Yet after two days*

of travel, two friends are dead and the rabbi is wounded. Divine Providence knew the results of our choices before we did.

I pray that you are well and that Momma is feeling better. I will write again as soon as I have the chance.

*Your loving son,
Joseph*

Early the next morning, stillness filled the two-hundred-year-old synagogue. The usual morning prayers, talking, and banter were absent. Joseph and Avi entered the sanctuary and saw it was dark. The lights were off and the draperies drawn.

"What is happening?" Avi inquired.

"I have no idea," Joseph answered. "I must find the rabbi and ask him to mail my letter. I will meet you in the kitchen in a few minutes."

Avi walked to the kitchen. Isaac and Benjamin sat at a lopsided wooden table sipping weak tea from a glass. Other students, Emanuel, Saul, Abraham, and Meyer, huddled together on an unpainted, splintered bench nibbling on bread and drinking warm, boiled water. Avi's nose wriggled, and his upper lip twitched, a sign of nervousness. He went to Saul, a small, frail fourteen-year-old boy, the youngest in the group, who looked even younger than fourteen. Saul had large blue eyes, sandy-colored hair, a round smooth baby face with a sallow complexion, and no facial hair. As Avi approached, he noticed that Saul's face was red and that he had been crying. Trying to be cheerful, Avi said, "Good morning, Saul. What is the matter?"

"I cannot go. I am sorry," Saul blurted.

"What do you mean?" Avi asked.

Saul took a deep breath and let out a sigh before he continued. "It was decided that I stay here in Belgrade and maybe even try to return home. Emanuel, Abraham, and Meyer will stay as well. We are the youngest in the group, and after what has happened during the first two days, it will be safer to stay behind and try to return home. After all, it cannot be any more dangerous or any worse if we do not continue to China."

"Who decided this?"

"Rabbi Stok and the four of us decided. The doctor said that the rabbi will not be able to travel and needs time to heal from the gunshot wound. Also, Rabbi Stok said that before anything else is done today, we must bury Mordechai. His body was made ready by the students from here."

"Yes, we must bury him," Avi agreed. His mind raced between the two thoughts, one of burying Mordechai, the other about the possibility of the trip to Shanghai being canceled. He paused then asked, "But what will happen to us?"

"I do not know," Saul replied. "I pray that God protects you as you continue on your journey, and that you arrive safely in China."

"Thank you, Saul." Avi looked into Saul's eyes and studied his face. "This is a time in my life that I will remember always. Oftentimes a person knows when something or someone will become a future memory. These past two days, you and all of the students will be a memory for me. I pray that we meet again after the war."

"We will," answered Saul. "We will. Maybe in Poland, maybe America, maybe Palestine, but we will, we will."

Avi wanted to believe it, yet he knew how many times in life you meet someone whom you want to see again and become better acquainted with and it does not happen. *Is it the schedule of our lives?* he wondered, *or the distance between people that allowed the moment of a new friendship to pass? People do not meet by chance. They meet because of Divine Providence.*

Joseph approached Avi, his face tense, the muscles of his jaw locked, his teeth biting on his lower lip, and his eyes bulging wide open.

"What is it, Joseph? What has happened?"

Joseph found a piece of bread and tore it apart and began to eat it. With his mouth full and his eyes focused on the bread in his hand, he grumbled, "The rabbi told me that we cannot leave. The borders are closed. There is no transportation for us, no trains, no wagons, no bicycles, nothing. We can never make it to the boat for its scheduled sailing to China. He said that we are trapped and that it would be difficult and maybe impossible to return home."

"How can God let this happen?" Avi asked. "Only three days away from home and we are trapped. We cannot continue to Shanghai and cannot return home. We are trapped for who knows how long. What are we supposed to do, wait here for years until the war ends?"

Joseph rested his chin in the palm of his hand as he chewed on the bread.

Isaac came to their table, dark rings under his eyes from a disturbed night's sleep, and his clothing wrinkled and dirty. His usual cheerfulness was dissipated. "I heard the news. It is not very encouraging."

Before he could continue, Avi put his index finger to his lips to silence Isaac and pointed to Joseph, who was now in deep prayer. Joseph swayed from side to side with his head moving upward and then down and his lips moving without any sound coming forth.

"Please, Joseph, enough praying. We must plan," interrupted Isaac.

"Calm down," Joseph said. "I have been praying and thinking, and I may have found an answer."

Avi and Isaac drew closer to hear every word.

"First," Joseph continued in a confident voice, "God did not make anything happen to us. The killings were done by evil men. The ongoing debate is where free will and Divine Providence overlap. In life, sometimes you are feeling on top of the world, and at other times you are speeding downhill seemingly out of control. Today, we must make new decisions. It seems we are told to stay here for the duration of the war, but I have figured out a way to escape and reach Shanghai."

"Tell us," exclaimed Isaac. "I welcome good news and a way out of here."

A gleam shone in Joseph's eyes. His voice rose as his conversation became an announcement. "We are leaving tonight. We will make it in time to catch the boat and be in Shanghai on schedule."

In a voice of defeat, Avi said, "There is no transportation. We have borders to cross. Nazi sympathizers will be looking to kill anyone trying to flee. How can we possibly succeed?"

"Quiet," ordered Isaac. "That is enough of your gloom. Stop worrying because worry will not improve the outcome and it may actually ruin the journey. Let's listen. If his idea sounds good, we will try it. It is better than staying here where we have guaranteed failure."

"Tonight, after we leave," Joseph continued, "we will travel on foot. Every night, we will run as much as we can and walk when we have to. During the day, we will sleep. No one will be searching for us during the night. Benjamin, Levi, Zev, and I are leaving here for Shanghai. We can travel twenty or twenty-five miles a day. Maybe we might even ride a train to the Bulgarian border or even into Sofia."

"We can never make such a journey," exclaimed Avi. "Even if no one hunted us, the trip itself is too strenuous."

"Avi, you think about too many things at a time," Isaac said. "Just consider the first step, which is to leave tonight. It sounds possible to me, and I think we will make it to the ship on time."

Joseph looked at Avi and, seeing the despair in his eyes, said, "Jews survived for forty years wandering in the desert. We can surely survive for a week in Bulgaria."

CHAPTER 4

A Decision

Before going to their rooms, Joseph told them how to dress and what to bring. A short while later in the reception hall, Avi appeared wearing a black jacket, a brown cap, black shoes, and brown trousers. He waited nervously for the others, his arms folded in front of him. Benjamin and Levi appeared, dressed similar to Avi except for differences in colors. Each carried a suitcase. Benjamin's blond hair was hidden under the dark-green cap. Being overweight, carrying the suitcase was a strain and caused him to lean sideways. His blue eyes were sad and appeared larger than usual through his glasses.

"I hope we ride part of the way," Benjamin said. "Carrying this suitcase for a week would be too much for me. The books in it weigh many kilos."

Levi had a high forehead and a receding hairline and looked older than his age. "Avi," Levi said, "we will make it? I mean, we will survive, won't we?"

"Stop worrying," replied Avi. "Worry, worry, worry, that's all you do. No, that is all Jews do."

"Well, there is much to worry about, isn't there? And aren't you the one who worries the most?" asked Benjamin.

"No, I do not know about these things," Avi replied in an abrupt manner. "Life is in God's hands. We do the best we can along the way. And as for worrying, what does it accomplish? Nothing. Yes, I worry too much, but if you are able to do something about the situation, you do the best you can. If there is nothing you can do, it's in God's hands, and there is nothing to worry about. Do not waste your energy on worry."

"So why do you worry?" Levi asked.

"Naturally," answered Avi, "everyone would like things to work well. When there is uncertainty, people fear the result, and worry is an expression of that fear."

"You make sense, and I know you are right," Benjamin said in a serious voice. "Maybe it is genetic. My parents, especially my mother, worry about everything. With all of the uncertainty before us, I worry what will happen to us, and what may happen to my family."

Joseph walked into the room, and the conversation stopped. Benjamin, Avi, and Levi stared at him in shock. Before they could utter a word, Zev, another student, entered the room behind Joseph. Zev, a lanky teenager with a narrow neck, an oblong-shaped head, and brown eyes that squinted as he spoke, said, "I am ready to go."

Noticing Joseph, Zev blurted, "What have you done? You're appearance is different. I would not recognize you in Chemelnick."

"What did you do to yourself?" Avi asked.

"Why have you changed you're appearance?" Benjamin inquired.

Joseph stood before his friends wearing a pair of dark-gray pants, a navy-blue shirt, a dark-gray jacket, black shoes, and brown socks. He resembled most men in Belgrade or Sofia. Over his shoulder, he carried a pack with a belt around it that could be fastened securely to his back making it easier for him to carry.

"You look like a secular guy going on a trip," Zev stated. "This adventure will surely be a future memory for us to tell our children and grandchildren someday."

Isaac's voice bellowed from the hallway, "Are you ready to go? I am."

Isaac carried two suitcases and a knapsack filled with books draped over his back. He was oblivious to what was happening. "I borrowed the extra suitcase from Meyer," said Isaac. "He is going to stay here and said that he probably would not need it anymore. I am sorry to be late." Isaac scanned the scene before him. "Why is everyone lounging around? We have to leave soon. I checked the weather. It will be good tonight. No rain."

Joseph smiled at his friends, his eyes bright and clear. He undid the pack over his shoulders. Checking the time on his watch, he looked toward the large windows covered with heavy draperies and nodded to himself and let out a sigh.

"It is very simple," Joseph began. "Remember I told you what to wear and what to bring on the trip? I said to dress to look like everybody else and to pack lightly.' It is for our safety. Our main priority is to reach Shanghai and survive the war. I spoke to Rabbi Stok, and he said it is all right."

"Joseph," Isaac said, "this is not clear to us. What is the purpose of your clothes?"

"Please let me explain," began Joseph. "You all know of the telegrams received from America, actually from Brooklyn. They told us that we must flee from Poland because of the fear of the Nazis. We have chosen to flee and to survive. If we do not survive, then we may as well have stayed in Poland, at home with our families, and taken our chances with the Nazis. But we did not stay." Joseph began rocking his head forward and back as if questioning himself about what he was going to say next. "Already two friends have been killed, and Rabbi Stok wounded," Joseph continued. "We must succeed on this journey, not just for our survival, but for the sake of our families. After the war, we must be able to say '*Hineni*, I am here.' The Germans will lose because evil eventually loses no matter how well it conquers at the beginning of its treachery. It has been this way throughout history."

Sitting with a clenched fist covering his mouth, his voice fell to a whisper, as he looked into the eyes of each friend.

"This will be a strenuous journey," Joseph added. "Nothing worthwhile in life is easy. That is why many fail at what they do. Throughout history, many Jews have forsaken Judaism. We responded to the telegrams because we struggle for Jewish continuity. That is why we must be successful."

He stopped speaking, and the room was still. No one knew what to say. Joseph leaned forward, hesitated, fidgeted with his fingers, and began speaking in a tone that no longer was a friend speaking to a friend but rather the authoritative tone of a teacher lecturing his students. "In Jewish law, health and safety take precedence over everything else. We say that it is acceptable to eat on Yom Kippur, the holiest day of the Jewish year, if someone's health requires it. Yet in reality, we are taught that this can happen but never does. Jews do not eat on Yom Kippur. This is one of those times when our survival comes first. If we travel looking like religious Hasidic Jews, we have no chance to reach a safe haven. Our only chance is to dress and appear like everybody else, and then maybe we will survive."

Joseph gave a short laugh and corrected himself. "I mean prevail, not just survive. Rabbi Stok not only agrees but he is the one who suggested it. That is why I said what I said to you about dressing like everyone else and packing lightly. Return to your rooms and lighten your loads. We may be in for a rough trip and will not have the strength to carry heavy suitcases. It is your choice. Rabbi Stok said each person must live in his own way and be responsible for his decisions. You may do as you wish, but please decide quickly."

Benjamin's sad eyes became sadder, and he sat still, his heavy body sagging deeper into the chair. Here he was, a teenage boy, being forced to make decisions that would be difficult for men who were older and wiser. One part of him said that he should never have left Poland and the other part said there was no choice. A telegram from Brooklyn. A mandate from Hasidic headquarters in America. How could he not go? And now what must he do to survive and stay alive? That is what Joseph meant when he said survive—he meant to stay alive through this ordeal. Anger flashed through Benjamin's eyes as he thought of how much he hated the Germans. He was frightened of the future. Tears streamed down his cheeks. He pulled a handkerchief from his pocket and wiped them away. As more tears fell, Benjamin whimpered, "I want to go home now, but I am not going home. I am going to Shanghai. No matter how long it takes, no matter how hard the ordeal, I will survive. I will make my parents proud of me, by becoming the doctor they always wanted me to be."

Joseph went to Benjamin and put his arm on his shoulder. "May God protect all of us and our families in this perilous time," comforted Joseph.

Benjamin tilted his head toward Joseph. Turning to the others, with tears still in his eyes, Benjamin blurted out, "You heard what Joseph said. Well then, let's get going. We have to catch a boat to China."

CHAPTER 5

Belgrade to Nesebur, Bulgaria

Late that night, they boarded the train to Sofia, Bulgaria. Without their black coats, black clothing, and full beards, they blended in. The police at the station entrance, the police patrolling on the platforms, and the conductors on the train seldom glanced at them. Instead of carrying suitcases, each carried a pack filled with necessities, food, clothing, a toothbrush, a razor, soap, a prayer book, a photograph of their family, a writing pad, a pencil, and the ticket for passage to Shanghai. Around their waists, hidden in a zipper compartment in the underside of their belts, was their money. The steam engine train rolled along the tracks. The whining and clacking of the wheels and the swaying of the cars felt like the rocking of a cradle. Joseph and his friends slept sitting in their seats. Dawn was breaking as the train rumbled to a stop at the border. Joseph, Avi, and Isaac were awakened by the commotion of border guards coming through the train to check every compartment as they inspected identity papers. Joseph nudged Benjamin, Levi, and Zev to wake up.

"Do not say anything unless a guard asks you a question," whispered Joseph. "If you must answer, then answer in a word or two. No explanations. And do not look anyone in the eye. Understand?"

Rubbing the sleep from their eyes, they nodded. The sounds in the corridor moved closer. A large head poked inside the compartment. Its face had an extraordinary large mustache, long sideburns, and a shock of black hair under a green military cap.

"Papers, papers, and hurry up about it," he ordered.

They handed him the papers. Flipping through them quickly, he returned them to Joseph. "Are you all traveling together?" the guard demanded.

"Yes, sir," stammered Joseph.

The guard smirked and curled his bottom lip, nodding, his face embracing a smug smile.

"Sir," the guard mimicked mockingly. "Now aren't you the gentleman. Where, tell me, might you all be going?" He looked at Zev, and Zev trembled, unable to utter a reply.

"To Sofia," Joseph quickly answered.

"How do I know that you are telling me the truth?"

"We have no luggage," Joseph replied, "only a sack with a few essentials."

The guard smiled, enjoying this game of tormenting these young men. Another guard walked past and motioned that they must move along. The long mustache twitched in agitation. Preparing to leave, he stopped and turned to Joseph.

"Tell me one more thing, young man. It seems that your names on the papers are Jewish. You are not Jews in disguise trying to flee, are you?"

Challenging his glare, Joseph looked into the guard's eyes and without hesitation replied, "Of course not, we are not in disguise."

Still smirking, the guard flicked a hand upward in a gesture of "That's enough" and walked out of the compartment.

"How could you say what you did?" Zev intoned.

"I said what I said because I had to," Joseph replied. "That guard was looking to make trouble. And I did not lie if that is what you think. After all, we are not in disguise, just dressed differently than we are accustomed to dressing."

A feeling of relief overcame them, and they laughed that the threat of danger had passed.

Forty miles past the border, the train arrived in Sofia, the capital of Bulgaria.* "Our goal is to reach Nesebur within one week," said Isaac. Isaac had not spoken much during the trip, seemingly going along with whatever was decided by the others. As he spoke, his intensity caused his friends to focus on what he was saying. His narrow eyes, the narrow nose, the angular chin, the high cheekbones, strained as he continued. "A mistake can cost a life. This last part of the trip to the ship will be dangerous without us adding a mistake. Take nothing for granted. Assume that every man, even if he is not in uniform, is a Nazi searching

---

* Standing at the railway crossroads of the Belgrade-Istanbul routes, Sofia dated back to its founding by the Romans in the second-century CE. Sections of Sofia contained large sections of Roman remains, walls, paved streets, and artwork. For five hundred years, the Bulgars lived as serfs under Turkish rule until their successful uprising in 1912. Now as King Boris II signed away the citizenship of the Bulgarian Jews and allied Bulgaria with Hitler and Nazi Germany, Jews in Bulgaria lived in fear.

to hunt you. And when you see Nazi arm bands, do not flinch or react. Your life depends on it."

"Also," Joseph added, "I think we should split up. Instead of traveling as we have, in a group of six, let us divide into three pairs. We will be less conspicuous that way, and we will meet on the ship next week."

"Even if we do that," Benjamin asked, "how will we get to Nesebur?"

"By car, by wagon, on foot, any way we can," Joseph affirmed. "Trains do not run often from Sofia to Nesebur, and we must learn if tickets are available for the next train and whether the train will arrive in time for us to board the ship. No matter how, we must find a way.

"But I do not know anything about such things," said Levi. "I came on this trip and thought that Rabbi Stok would look after us. My parents told me that the journey would be safe and I would return to Poland after the war."

"After the war, we will all return to Poland and greet our families," Zev assured them. "That is why we must store our memories with all that happens to tell them about it."

"I propose the following pairings," Isaac interrupted. "Joseph, you go with Zev. Avi, you go with Benjamin, and I will go with Levi. How does that sound? This way, one of the older goes with one of the younger." No one objected. "Good, it is settled. Now let us be on our way."

"We will meet again, won't we?" Zev asked. "I do not want to be shot the way Samuel and Mordechai were." Sadness swept his brown eyes as they scanned the floor. "I am frightened. Every day, I feel that I face death. I suppose that is what evil brings to the world, fear and killings."

"Stop talking like that," Isaac said. "Everything will go well, you will see. And worrying does not accomplish anything except more anxiety for all of us, and we have had enough anxiety on this trip for a lifetime."

"I cannot stop worrying," Zev said. "I guess that it is an inherited trait because my mother and my grandmother worry all the time about everything. Can you imagine that when my mother cooks soup, she worries whether the soup will be too hot or too cold when it is served?"

"Discard that part of your inheritance, Zev," Isaac chuckled. "We have enough to confront with the Nazis in Bulgaria."

They left the platform in pairs, each nodding a goodbye.

It was early morning in Sofia, and a cloudy mist hung in the sky blocking the sun. Bicycles lined the streets and sidewalks and were the main transportation for going to work. In Bulgaria, cars were a luxury, and gasoline expensive and scarce. By midafternoon, the workers ended their day, allowing time for a large dinner with their family and time for a nap. Walking through the streets, they noticed the Turkish influence inculcated during the five hundred years Turkey controlled the Bulgars. Many buildings were architecturally designed with a Moorish flair. The city, however, stood in poor condition caused by neglect. It was common to see houses with broken windows in need of painting, streets disintegrating into potholes with large gaps where bricks used to be, and garbage piled in open bags strewn on the streets.

"This is a shabby city," Zev commented. Zev was in his late teens and had the appearance of one who does not age because of his baby face. Adding to his youthfulness was the fact that he needed complete explanations of what was happening, like a child asking his parent why. "It is the worst place I have ever seen. It is dreary, depressing, dirty, dingy, and disgusting."

"Five words beginning with the letter *d*," Joseph answered, "and each of them a criticism about Sofia. Considering that you have not been to many cities, you are quick to judge. Anyway, we are not here to visit, merely to pass through. Maybe we can find the synagogue and get help there. Also keep in mind that no matter how discouraging it seems about us reaching Shanghai, we must pray and hope for the best."

They walked at a brisk pace, trying to blend in with the citizenry of Sofia. Zev trembled at the sight of uniformed police wearing arm bands with swastikas. The police passed without noticing them.

"I was scared. I thought we would be stopped," Zev said, his face contorted in fear and helplessness.

"Stop being gloomy," Joseph asserted in an intense tone. "No more fear, and stop your incessant worrying. I have enough on my mind not to have to listen to that from you. It does not help us at all. We have something to accomplish, and we will accomplish it."

"I'm sorry."

"I did not mean to be harsh, but you must tell yourself to be tough and that we will be all right."

Ahead of them, they saw a man dressed in black Hasidic clothing. Quickening their pace, they walked to within a few feet behind him. Speaking in Yiddish, Joseph said, "Do not turn around, we may attract attention. Please tell me where the synagogue is."

The man stopped and turned around. Joseph stared at an old, shriveled face, covered with an unkempt beard, and green eyes that had experienced great suffering. His tattered clothing hung loosely on his skinny body. Looking at Joseph and Zev, the old man started to cry. Without uttering a word, he motioned for them to follow. Trailing at a distance, they walked at the old man's hobbling pace. Twenty minutes later, in a dilapidated part of the city stood the synagogue. Joseph imagined that decades ago, this had been a magnificent edifice. Age and lack of money caused its former elegance to decay. The building was decrepit. Tiles on the roof were cracked, and many were gone. The front doors were broken and splintered, the door handles and locks missing. Large panels of wood shuttered the windows, and paint peeled from the facade.

The old man crossed the street and walked around to the side of the building. Joseph and Zev followed, stopping at a wooden door that opened below the street level into a basement.

The old man knocked on the door four times, hesitated, knocked twice more, waited, and knocked once. He looked at Joseph and Zev, his eyes filled with tears, and said, "May God bless and protect you during these terrible times." Standing at the door, Joseph and Zev watched him limp to the front of the synagogue, turn right, and disappear.

"Maybe this rabbi can arrange transportation to Nesebur," Zev said. "We are only a few hours away by car or truck. If we arrive early in Nesebur, we could spend a few days resting while we wait for the ship to sail."

A shutter boarding a window creaked as a sliver of light penetrated the darkness inside, and then the shutter creaked again as it closed darkening the interior. The door opened, and Joseph and Zev saw the rabbi of Sofia stooped over, like a hunchback, emaciated, wearing clothing that was once finely tailored but now was shabby with tears, holes, and worn thin spots. The rabbi's eyes commanded attention with their warm, penetrating gaze. Speaking in Yiddish, he welcomed them to enter. They descended a flight of stairs and were led into a room in the basement. Two small light bulbs hung from a cord attached to a ceiling beam. Both bulbs were lit, yet the room seemed dark. Moisture on the walls and ceiling, combined with the smell of rotting floorboards, filled the room with an odor that made it difficult to breathe. Although the weather outside was warm, the room was chilly. On a table under the light bulbs were books for prayer and Jewish study. The books were torn and the pages stained. A piece of stale bread and a dirty cup rested next to the books.

"Who may you be? And what brings you here?"

Zev swallowed hard at the sight of the rabbi, shocked to see a rabbi in this poor condition. To him, rabbis were examples for the community, in what they taught, what they said, how they lived, in everything they did.

"Good day, Rabbi. I am Zev Kravitz."

"I am Joseph Shalosky. We come from Poland and need help to get to Nesebur, and from there travel by ship to Shanghai to escape the Nazis."

"Please sit," offered the rabbi. "Tell me the latest news about the war, about the world outside of Bulgaria. News is difficult to receive here. The government blocks the important news. Our physical lives are under their control."

Joseph told the rabbi about the German advances and the danger the Jews faced. After he finished, the rabbi sat silently, staring at his hands contemplating what to reply. Speaking in a raspy, deep voice, the rabbi commented, "It will be worse than anyone can imagine. Life for Jews in Bulgaria is terrible, and the Germans are not yet here. I was trained to be the spiritual leader of this Jewish community. I gave sermons, performed the rituals, and tried to educate the congregation. That has all ended." He shifted his gaze toward the light coming through the cracks in the shuttered windows. "Today, God has given me the opportunity to help you. I must do what I can and pray that it is sufficient."

"We will be grateful for that," Joseph replied.

"You followed an old man here?"

Joseph nodded.

"The man who led you here," the rabbi continued, "they beat him. The Nazi thugs beat him and injured his head and damaged his brain, and he was not the same ever again."

The rabbi ran his tongue around his mouth, trying to make saliva to moisten it because the hoarseness was irritating his throat. After a long breath and a gesture of helplessness by throwing his arms in the air, palms up, he continued, "Do not ask what the old man was like before they beat him, it will only cause you grief, and there is enough grief. You must try to see a bright future even at times like these. Too many people emphasize the negative things and fill their life with despair. They believe in an adverse result. Throughout Jewish history, there have been tragedies, and we often dwell on them rather than celebrate the continuity of the Jews for millennium."

The rabbi started to cough, like he was choking. Worry lines creased Zev's brow as he looked from the rabbi to Joseph and back to the rabbi. Without hesitation, Joseph looked through the dimly lit room, located the bathroom, cleaned a dirty glass, and brought the rabbi a glass of water. The rabbi sipped the water.

"I am all right," the rabbi said. "The dampness does that to me. It is not good for my lungs. You ask yourselves, why do I stay here? There is no place for me to go. Until now, the Nazis tolerated me and left me alone. If I go to live with a Jewish family, I place that family in danger. The risk is great." He finished the water, and his hand dropped to his side with the glass in it. "The longer the war continues, the worse it will be for the Jews in Europe. Here the Nazis will treat us as the Egyptians did during the time of Pharaoh. Jewish homes will be marked, restrictions will be placed on Jews traveling, and phones will be disconnected cutting off communication. We will be expelled from schools and thrown out of work. There will be more, and it will terrible."

"Can you come with us?" Zev asked.

"Yes, I would like that," he answered, "but I am too weak to make the journey."

Joseph's mind raced back to his home. He pictured his mother. She was weak, worn down by her illness, and not strong enough to travel on this journey. *Who knows, maybe she is better off staying in Poland and taking her chances there. If the war ended quickly, everyone would be saved.*

"The world will let us be killed by the thousands," the rabbi continued.

Joseph opened his sack and placed food on the table. "Here, you will need this."

"Yes, I need the food, but I am ashamed that I must take it from your meager supply. Please tell me how I can help you."

"We need transportation to Nesebur."

"Oh, yes, you told me that. I am forgetful these days. Age often does that to one's memory. When I was active, I remembered everything." The rabbi shifted to another topic. "Boris, that is, King Boris has troops wearing swastikas on their arm bands. If they find a Jew, they can do with him whatever amuses them. It is awful. My congregation has gone into hiding because several of them have been tortured, and many killed. The police do not imprison Jews because they would have to feed them and do not want to. Their barbarous behavior is random."

"That does not happen in Poland," Zev insisted.

"I pray that it stays that way, but with the Nazis in control…" the rabbi's voice trailed off, and his eyes stared blankly ahead without focusing on anything.

"We had better go," Joseph said. "Goodbye, Rabbi. May God protect you."

The rabbi returned to the present and directed them. "Go to King Boris Place, not avenue or boulevard, and find Sofia Shalom Trucking. The code is 'Rabbi Levi from the moon.'"

"Rabbi Levi from the moon?" repeated Joseph in a questioning tone. "What does that mean?"

The rabbi smiled, displaying stained teeth mixed with spaces where teeth had fallen out. "In Jewish mysticism, 'Rabbi Levi' is a walled plain in the fourth quadrant of the face of the moon, about fifty miles in diameter."

"Is that true?" asked Zev.

"Yes, that is a fact. Not many people know or have ever heard of this, but it is true. Rabbi Levi exists on the moon."

"Thank you very much for your help," responded Joseph as he shook hands with the rabbi.

"Thank you," Zev said. "I do not suppose we will ever meet again, but I shall always remember you."

"Only God knows whether we will meet again. Until such time, we will leave it in his hands."

"In all of the excitement, we do not know your name," said Joseph.

"I am Rabbi Senesh, Solomon Senesh. I am sorry for not introducing myself properly when we met. I wonder whether it is my age or the world we live in that causes my memory to fail. I want to remember, but often it is easier for an old man such as me not to remember to survive during these terrible times. Sometimes we remember too much, and then memory causes suffering over things that happened and cannot be undone."

Rabbi Senesh held his head in both hands and with an agonizing cry began to weep. Joseph and Zev stood still, watching this once-proud rabbi suffer. Through his tears, Rabbi Senesh's muffled voice gasped, "Now go and be well. Survive for all of us."

Joseph and Zev took several steps backward in deference to the rabbi before turning to leave. As they turned, two men in dark-blue gendarme uniforms, pistols in their belts, stood in the shadows blocking the doorway. One was burly and fat and had a twisted smile on his face. His name was Rezo. Having served time in jail for assault, he was released once the war started and given a position on the police force. The other was short, with thick horn-rimmed glasses, a large pockmarked face, and a broad, ugly nose. His name was Willie. The dark shadows on Willie's face made him look grotesque. Fellow police considered him the most sadistic man on the force. Zev and Joseph shivered in fright.

"Well, well," Rezo smirked, "what have we here? Looks like a couple of kikes, but you can never tell."

"Can't you tell from the stink?" Willie added. "Them bastard Jews all stink to hell. Why were they ever put on this earth to stink it up and torment the likes of us?" Willie shot a glance at his comrade. A shudder ran through Zev's body as he took small steps backward, nearly tripping in the dark.

Rabbi Senesh stood and said in as loud a voice as he could muster, "You are not supposed to enter this synagogue. That was the arrangement agreed upon by the chief gendarme."

The two men laughed, ignoring the rabbi's words. Looking at Joseph and Zev, Willie said, speaking in Bulgarian, "You are Jews, aren't you? I mean, you do not look Jewish, but you must be, or you would not be here. Of course you could lie and tell me you are not Jews, but that would be hard to believe since you people lie and cheat all the time. So what is your story? Let me hear before we take you for a walk to the park."

Joseph, not understanding the language, looked to the rabbi for a translation. The rabbi, trembling where he stood, translated the gist of what was said. Joseph, trying to act bravely, took a step forward toward Willie with the horn-rimmed glasses and ugly nose. Speaking in Yiddish, Joseph spoke to Willie in a polite, firm tone, and the rabbi translated.

"You are very observant in what you said," Joseph said.

Willie liked the compliment and smiled. Rezo grimaced.

Joseph continued, "We were walking in this neighborhood to bring food to the rabbi. He is old and needs food as you can see." He pointed to the table with the food on it.

Before the translation was completed, the fat Rezo, noticing the food, went to the table and grabbed it. Zev was aghast. He blurted out, "You are stealing the rabbi's food." Rezo, not understanding what was said, began to laugh, his large belly rolling up and down. Zev controlled his urge to jump at him.

"You kikes make me laugh," Rezo said. "Is it that you kikes are funny or are you just dumb? We do whatever we want to Jews here. Just be glad that we are not like the Germans or you would be dead already. And you little boy," speaking to Zev, "do not raise your voice to me again or I'll cut your tongue out. Now let's go for a walk to the park. Rabbi, you can stay. You are too old to have any fun with. We have a treat for these two outside. Now move your Jewish asses and fast."

The rabbi translated that they must go with these policemen, omitting the obscenities. Zev and Joseph were pushed up the stairs and shoved into the daylight. Two more dark-blue uniforms stuffed with sadistic-looking policemen waited outside. One of them said to Willie, "What took you so long? We are tired of waiting."

"Stop your complaining," he replied. "It is not easy finding Jews these days. They hide from us, but we are going to have some fun with these two. They brought food to the rabbi. Want some of it?"

"No food. Let's get on with the fun, and then we can get a bottle and have a few drinks. I need a drink."

"Me too," said Willie, the sunlight reflecting from his horn-rimmed glasses. The pockmarks on his face appeared larger in the daylight.

The policemen attached large yellow Jewish Stars of David to the back of Joseph and Zev's jackets. The stars covered most of their jackets. The police paraded Zev and Joseph through town to the park. People stopped and stared at the spectacle, smiling at this humiliation of Jews. Outside the park, a wet brush with worn bristles was handed to Zev.

"Start scrubbing the walk, Jew boy," ordered Rezo as he munched on the food that he had stolen from the rabbi. "Clean it nice. Make it shine like silver and gold. You know about silver and gold, don't you? That is all you Jew bastards know, money, money. And no shirking or else you'll feel my boot."

Zev understood the meaning of what was said, took the brush, stooped to his knees, and began scrubbing the walk. Joseph watched helplessly, a policeman on either side of him. Zev scrubbed until the brush dried out, and then the brush was wet again from a faucet, and the scrubbing continued. Sweat covered Zev's back, neck, and forehead. People watched the humiliation of the two Jews.

"Your turn soon," growled a policeman to Joseph. "Watch your buddy closely, and you will learn to scrub better than he does." He and the other policeman laughed at what they considered these funny insults.

Joseph knew he was being ridiculed but did not understand what was said. With a look of dismay in his eyes, Joseph watched Zev suffering as he scrubbed the sidewalk. Joseph's mind drifted away, far away from Sofia. In less than a second, the brain can remember episodes in one's life. Joseph remembered his home and his mother and father greeting his return from school with hugs. Dinner was cooking in a pot on the stove. The pleasant aroma of the onions and garlic mixed in with the vegetables and potatoes floated through his memory. Remembering his parents caused him pain. The delightful gleam in his mother's eyes and his father's encouraging gaze strengthened him during this time of fear. Cupping his hands over his face, he let his head slump. He closed his eyes and began praying silently as he swayed back and forth.

People surrounded the scene. A father, with his son on his shoulders, stood near the front of the crowd. "Look," he said to his son, "those are dirty Jews, the ones who control the banks. By the time you grow up, there will not be any more of their kind in Europe."

Rezo smacked his burly belly with his hands like he was clapping on his stomach as he gloated. He moved closer behind Zev and prodded him with kicks to his buttocks. The crowd became an audience at a spectacle, and

Rezo pretended to be the star of the show. Every time he kicked Zev, Rezo made a funny face and jumped up and down, and his audience laughed. Zev scrubbed hard until the brush was dry and then handed it to Rezo. He wet it and returned the brush to Zev. As the show of humiliation continued, the policeman who had been standing alongside Rezo wiggled through the crowd carrying a pail of water. Approaching Zev, he emptied the bucket of water on him, shrieking like a hyena as he did it. The crowd roared with laughter as though they were at a circus.

How much longer would this go on? Joseph worried. *How much more could Zev endure?*

After being drenched, Zev kept his head down and continued scrubbing. The crowd inched forward, and the circle around Zev, and Joseph shrunk. Rezo stood behind Zev, still kicking him to the amusement of the crowd. After he stopped kicking, the policemen joined the crowd and laughed with them. It was like a cadence of kicking, stopping, and laughing. After each round of kicks, the laughter grew louder, and the crowd began shouting, "Scrub harder, Jew bastard! Scrub harder, Jew bastard!"

Rezo kicked Zev harder than usual, and Zev fell from his knees on to his stomach. "Get up, kike! Get up and scrub!" Rezo bellowed.

Zev rolled over, and instead of being on his knees, he squatted with his back to Rezo. He took the brush and tossed it up in the air. All eyes followed it skyward. During that diversion, Zev twisted around in a split second, and like a lion chasing a gazelle, he leaped at the fat policeman's belt and grabbed his pistol. A hush fell on the crowd like the quiet at a funeral. Joseph was aghast, his mouth opened, but no words came out. He realized what was to happen would be a tragic future memory if Joseph lived to remember this day. Willie and his comrades reached for their pistols.

The first gunshot shattered the stillness of the late spring morning. Birds stopped chirping and fluttered skyward. Rezo screamed in agony, clutching his stomach, as blotches of blood soaked through his shirt, turning it red. He fell to his knees near Zev. Pain caused his eyes to bulge like a grotesque mask, and gasps replaced his voice, sounding like those of a dying animal. Zev fired again, and the bullet passed through Rezo's nose and hit the back of his head. Blood gushed from his face and head, and he fell sideways, coming to rest on his side. A puddle of blood spread over the freshly scrubbed sidewalk.

The crowd screamed in panic and fled toward the exit gates. The father, with the boy on his shoulders, was knocked to the ground and trampled by the rampaging crowd. The police shot at Zev, and piercing-hot flames of bullets struck his shoulder, legs, and chest. Shrieking in pain and with blood oozing from the wounds, he rolled over and shot Willie, watching him fall dead on the walk. With the pistol empty, Zev fell back as bullets ripped into him with terrible violence. His breathing fluttered, and he gasped for his last breaths. He saw his father, wearing a prayer shawl, praying with his eyes closed. He saw his mother wearing an apron cooking in the kitchen. He felt himself falling into a pit. A bright white hazy cloud appeared, then everything was blurred, and his pain stopped.

CHAPTER 6

A Future Memory in Sofia

One of the policemen who shot Zev walked to Zev's body and with the front of his boot turned him faceup. Zev's eyes were closed like a child taking a nap. His body was covered in blood except for his face. The policeman's broad nose was bleeding from a cut, and blood trickled down his face. Throughout the chaos, Joseph had moved off the walk toward the shrubbery and stood still. The other police watched. Walking to Joseph, he wiped the blood off his face with the back of his hand. He pressed the pistol into Joseph's back and pushed him in the direction he wanted. Joseph knew no pleading or begging for mercy was possible because no common language existed between them. A strong hand on Joseph's shoulder signaled him to stop at the main entrance to the park. Surrounded by a high decorative steel gate, the park entrance had a grassy area lined with flowers and shrubbery shaped in a semicircle and bordered by shade trees. The midday sun had reached its peak directly overhead and cast shadows at Joseph's feet. Joseph was forced to sit on a brown wooden bench inside the entrance to the park. An obelisk, a four-sided shaft made of stone with a monolithic pyramidal apex, stood beneath an oak tree. Behind it, hidden from view under a bush, were a pick and a shovel. With smears of dried blood on his face, the policeman removed the tools and dropped the shovel near a bench and searched the ground with the pick looking for a soft area. Locating one, he struck at it several times. Throwing the shovel toward Joseph, he motioned to start digging. Removing his jacket, Joseph picked up the pick and chipped at the earth until the soil was loosened. Taking the shovel, Joseph dug for an hour until he was knee-deep in the hole. His arms and back muscles hurt, and his forehead ached from lack of water. The policemen watched in boredom, drinking vodka. Whenever Joseph stopped to catch his breath, the policeman gestured for him to continue. As the depth of the hole reached Joseph's waist, he stopped digging and tossed the shovel out of the hole.

"More," the policeman grunted in Bulgarian. Placing his pistol at his side, he rubbed his grimy hand across his unshaven face and grinned with a glow of satisfaction, looking at his buddy. They both swigged more vodka. After digging two more hours, Joseph stood chest deep in the hole. Large blotches of sweat covered his shirt and pants. Using pantomime, Joseph gestured that he wanted a drink. The policeman filled a container and brought it to the hole. As Joseph reached for it, the policeman poured the water on Joseph's head. The policeman grinned and walked back to the bench mumbling.

The amount of dirt mixed with small stones grew into mounds around the hole. Each shovel full became more strenuous because the hole was deeper and the piles of dirt higher. Daylight turned to dusk in the hole as the mounds blocked the sunlight. Exhausted and near collapse, Joseph wiped the sweat from his forehead and eyes.

A mean, sadistic look spread over the policeman's face. Raising his pistol, he pointed it toward Joseph and fired. A small pile of dirt near Joseph's head flew into the air, and some landed on his face and head. Joseph stared at the policeman in anger. The policeman motioned to Joseph to dig faster. With his remaining strength, he dug deeper. The muscles in his arms and shoulders sagged with fatigue, and his back hurt. The policemen sat on the bench and watched. Anyone who stopped was waved away.

When the depth of the hole covered Joseph's body except for his head, the policeman signaled to stop digging. Joseph began to climb out of the hole and saw the pistol aimed at him. The policeman took the shovel from Joseph and tucked his pistol into his belt. The policeman shoveled dirt into the hole as Joseph looked up at him. He dropped the dirt carefully, one shovel full after another, not allowing any to land on Joseph's head. The dirt wrapped around his feet and legs and filled in around his body. Instead of being shot, he was being buried alive. More dirt filled the hole covering his hips and chest. His hands and arms were trapped against his body. Breathing became labored as the dirt pressed against his chest. The policeman shoveled until Joseph's shoulders were covered and only his head remained above ground.

The policeman returned the pick and shovel to its hiding place and sat on the bench to catch his breath. Other passersby stopped to look, but the police chased them away. The policeman placed a yellow Star of David on the ground in front of Joseph's face and placed the packs of Zev and Joseph on each side of Joseph's head. Stretching out on a bench, he stared at what he had done and smiled. After a few minutes, he walked to Joseph, grimaced at him, and spit on his head, and he and his buddy walked from the park.

Joseph was being crushed by the weight of the dirt pressing against his body. Thirst scorched his throat and lips. A splitting headache just above his eyes caused intense pain, and he closed his eyes to relieve the pain.

Dozens of Bulgars of Sofia came to see if the rumor was true, and to their delight it was. Here was the spectacle of a Jew buried up to his neck and helpless. Their reaction was to humiliate him. Stones, dirt, rotten fruit, and sticks were thrown at the head sticking out above the ground. The benches filled as people watched the show, some drinking beer, and others eating snacks.

Blood oozed down Joseph's face, the drops resting on his upper lip or dripping into his mouth. With his mouth dry, it was an effort to spit out the blood. The minutes passed excruciatingly. After a day that seemed to last forever, the afternoon sun fell in the west, and shadows swallowed the park entrance. With the elongation of the shadows, the people drifted away and returned home. The park was nearly empty of people. Birds chattered in the trees and searched the grounds for crumbs of food.

At dusk, it was time to close the park gates. The gatekeeper, an old man with a gray beard who walked with a limp, shuffled to the gate with a set of large brass keys in his hands. He saw Joseph's head sticking up from the ground but paid no attention to it. Instead, he noticed a middle-aged woman wearing a dark-brown coat, with a flowered scarf on her head. She looked as if she had been an attractive woman twenty years earlier, but deprivation and sorrow had changed her appearance. Lines creased a once smooth forehead. Dark-brown eyes, like bright buttons, gleamed from her narrow face. Sitting on a bench, she and the gatekeeper locked eyes. Across from where she sat, two men in their late twenties or early thirties sat on a bench with their legs crossed. One of the men had straight hair, deep-set dark eyes, and a narrow, angular chin. He looked angry. The other man was built like a lumberjack with short, strong arms the size of a tree trunk. He wore a black cap over long curly hair. The gatekeeper motioned to the woman that it was time to leave. She ignored his gesture. He limped toward where she sat. Pulling up her coat's collar to hide most of her face, she said, "You will do me a big favor, and I will pay you something for the favor."

The gatekeeper smiled and scratched his beard and replied, "I suppose it depends on the favor, but give me a moment. First I must lock the gates."

"That is the favor," she answered. Her voice was soft as she continued, "Close the gates and make it look like you locked them, but do not lock them. Leave them unlocked until we finish our job here."

"I do not understand. Not lock the gates but close them as though they are locked. I could lose my job. I will stay until you finish what you want, and then I will lock the gate."

"No, that will not work. You could be in trouble, and I do not want you to be part of that risk. It will be enough if you just do what I ask." She moved closer to him and lowered her voice, "How will anyone know? It will soon be dark, and people who pass will not look closely at the lock. I promise to lock it when I leave."

"Why do you want to stay here?" the gatekeeper inquired.

She nodded to the head sticking up from the ground. "For him. We are going to dig him up and free him. No human should be treated like this."

The gatekeeper gazed into her eyes and saw the intensity of what she was about to do. He thought that if they dug up the Jew, that would be fine with him, but if he refused her request, maybe the two young men would beat him.

"Okay, okay, I will do it," he said.

She handed him a bank note. He stared at the amount and stared at her. She handed him another note. He smiled at her in thanks and placed the money in his back pocket. He returned to the gate and pretended to lock it. Looking back, he next turned away and walked home.

The woman motioned to the two men, and they removed short-handled shovels from under their coats. Looking around the park, she made certain it was empty of people. She removed a canteen of water from her purse and, kneeling at Joseph's head, allowed a few drops of water into his mouth. Joseph licked at it slowly because it was uncomfortable to swallow. The woman poured water on her handkerchief and wiped his face. Hardened streaks of blood could not be wiped off.

"It is all right. We will remove the blood stains after you have a bath. How horrible to treat another human with such contempt and hatred. Have they no shame?"

Being careful not to hurt Joseph, the two men began digging at the far sides of the hole and slowly removed one shovelful of earth after another. As they dug, dirt fell away from Joseph, and the pressure eased on his body. He tried speaking, but no words came forth. His mouth was dry, and his head throbbed from the headache. He tried smiling to express his gratitude, but even that simple task was difficult.

The woman encouraged the men, "Dig as carefully as possible. This man has suffered enough and does not need another injury. Even if it takes an extra ten minutes, we will run the risk with the police rather than hurt him."

The men dug in silence. Checking the gate, she saw that life outside the park was quiet, and that they had not been spotted by any passersby.

"Just a while longer," she assured Joseph.

Joseph looked at her, and his eyes fluttered and then closed as his head fell toward the side. The men stopped and stared at Joseph. The woman placed a hand against Joseph's neck and felt his pulse. Turning to the men, she whispered, "He is okay. He just passed out. We must get him out of here."

The men grabbed Joseph under the arms and tried to lift him out of the hole. His body budged, and earth fell away, but enough dirt kept his body trapped. The men dug faster, and additional piles grew around Joseph. With his upper body clear and only his legs buried, one of the men stepped into the hole and lifted Joseph up to the arms of the second man. Lying on the ground, Joseph gained consciousness and sipped the water offered to him. The men refilled the hole and patted it smooth with their shovels, making it look like the ground around it.

"Are you feeling better?" the woman asked Joseph. He nodded. His eyes were watery from the pain and the ordeal as he gazed at the three strangers. *They must be angels*, he thought, *sent from heaven to save me*.

"Will you be able to walk?" He nodded again. "Good, let us go."

Joseph tried to stand and fell back on the ground.

"We will have to carry him. Let us make it seem like he is drunk. Maybe he will be able to walk later," she added.

She locked the gate, and the four of them did their best to blend in with the pedestrians on the street. Supported by the two men, one on each side of him, Joseph struggled to gain control of his leg muscles. He staggered along, looking, to their relief very much, like a drunk. It was dark, and the working day had ended. People rushed home, others strolled to a café or restaurant. The affluent relaxed in a mineral bath. A cool spring wind blew through Sofia, making the national flag of Bulgaria flutter atop the opera house flagpole.

CHAPTER 7

Three Angels in Sofia

The apartment consisted of two small rooms, one a plain bedroom with faded green carpet, the other a living area, crammed with an old black sofa, four brown wooden chairs set around a circular table, another smaller table with a radio on it, a standing lamp with a torn lamp shade, stained and cracking linoleum, and a kitchen set against the wall. The kitchen sink was sandwiched between a woodburning stove and an ice box. The toilet and bath were halfway down the outside hall, in a room slightly larger than a closet, and shared by the four families living on the floor.

    They placed Joseph on the sofa, and the woman offered him a glass of water. With trembling hands, he gripped the glass and sipped until he drank it all. Two more glasses of water alleviated his thirst and the dryness in his throat. Slowly and with deliberation, he looked around. Everything was strange, and his ordeal exhausted him. Confusion mixed with fear overwhelmed him. Before him stood Ruth, a weary, middle-aged woman with wisps of gray appearing in her dark-brown hair, her face more wrinkled than the old framed photo of her with a man, probably her husband. She saw that he was recovering and smiled at her two sons. Joseph forced a smile at the taller son, Samuel. He turned to the other son, named Michael, who still wore his black cap, and he saw a handsome face with wide blue eyes possessed by a sense of independence. Joseph forced himself to sit up, holding his hands by his sides to steady himself. He stood, took a few steps, and sat back on the sofa.

"Who are you?" asked the woman. "Why did they bury you? What are you doing here?"

Joseph stared at her and did not reply.

Michael interrupted, "Momma, what if he speaks another language and does not understand what you are saying?"

A bewildered look crossed Ruth's face. She assumed Joseph was Bulgarian because it was common for the fascist police to treat Bulgarians with cruelty. She brushed away some strands of hair that had fallen in front of her eyes.

"How can that be? We are in Bulgaria. There is a war on, and you believe that this young boy who looks like he is no more than fourteen or fifteen years old came here from another country alone?"

"It is possible," replied Michael.

"Anything is possible, but this is unlikely."

"Speak to him in another language."

"All right, I will try." She took a deep breath and rubbed her cheeks with the palms of her hands. "Welcome to Bulgaria. May God bless and protect you."

First she spoke in Romanian, then Hungarian, repeating these sentences twice in each language. Joseph did not understand.

"Hello, how are you?" he asked in Yiddish.

"You speak Yiddish," she replied. "I do not speak as well as I used to because I have not spoken it for a long time. Please speak slowly. It will return to me."

Joseph replied in a weak voice but one filled with joy. "Of course I will. At last, a language I understand. Thank you for saving my life. I am sorry that I could not introduce myself properly. I am Joseph Shalosky. I am traveling from my home in Poland to Shanghai." With anxiety in his voice, he added, "I must reach Nesebur in time to board the ship for Shanghai."

"You are traveling alone?" she inquired. "Oh, excuse me for not introducing ourselves. My name is Ruth, and these are my sons, Samuel and Michael. They do not speak Yiddish. That is my fault, and I am sorry for it. You see, here in Bulgaria, it is dangerous to be a Jew. Assimilation is easier, to be like everyone else. They killed my parents because they were Jews. My husband died in the hospital because there was no medicine to cure him. But all that was a long time ago. Anyway, our last name is probably too difficult for you to pronounce, so let us call each other by first names. Please continue."

"I am sorry to hear of your losses," Joseph replied. Pausing, he studied each face then continued, "Today I am accompanied only by God. I started the trip with many friends. Some stayed behind in Budapest for fear of the rest of the journey. Others were killed during our escape." He bowed his head. "I mourn for them. May their souls be bound in eternal peace." Lifting his head, he spoke calmly, "This trip is a mission that I was directed to take by the head rabbi from Brooklyn, New York. How could I refuse such a request? Yet look what has happened to me. I was buried and left to die, and you saved me like three angels sent from heaven." His voice choked, and he covered his face.

"Are you all right?" she asked, filled with anxiety.

He removed his hand from his face. "I am almost okay."

Ruth asked, "Would you like something to eat?" Without waiting for a reply, she added, "Wait, I will get you something."

"I would like something plain, because I eat only kosher."

"I could say this is a kosher home or was a kosher home, but kosher food is nearly impossible to find."

Joseph changed the conversation and asked, "Why did Bulgaria align with the Germans?"

"As an ally of Germany," Samuel replied, "Bulgaria hopes to recapture Macedonia from Yugoslavia and Thrace from Greece. These provinces were stripped from Bulgaria after World War One."

"How many Jews live here?"

"Maybe fifty thousand, but most are not religious. They dress and act like everyone else and blend in with the other minorities here like the Armenians, Turks, Greeks, and Gypsies."

Pouring hot tea for Joseph, she looked haggard as strands of hair fell on her face. She spoke in a voice filled with emotion.

"King Boris and the patriarch of the Bulgarian Orthodox Church support the rights of all citizens, yet Jewish shops are closed, Jewish homes are marked, Jewish travel restrictions exist, and Jewish children cannot attend school. My sons have been fired from their jobs and now work doing odd jobs for people we know. With the three of us working, we have enough money to live. We considered going to Hungary, but that will not help us. The head of Hungary, Admiral Horthy, controls his Arrow Cross troops, better known as the Eaters of Jews, and Jews fear for their safety. Why do you cry? What I tell you is sad, but they are facts. We learn to live with them." Her eyes narrowed to a squint, and with a pleading voice asked, "What other choice do we have?"

Trying to regain his composure, Joseph said, "I am nineteen years old, and in all my years of learning since I was six, I see war and suffering and do not comprehend why humanity succumbs to evil. I want to believe our future has hope."

"I do not know," replied Samuel. "No matter where we live, it is temporary, even if temporary means many years. Jews have lived in Poland for seven hundred years, and look how the Poles discriminate against Jews now. Hitler brings out the worst in people." Ruth translated for Joseph to understand.

"I remember reading about the Soviet revolution in 1917," she said, rubbing her cheek. "Socialists envy anyone who has an advantage over another, regardless of how it was achieved. This was the foundation upon which the Communists took control of Russia. Hitler uses this emotion of envy against the Jews. He conjured up many supposed injustices perpetrated by Jews at the personal level, and this helped turn the German people against the Jews. It also roused the latent envy in those who sympathized with the Germans. And when these envious people saw that the Jews possessed ambition, an ambition which motivated Jews to work hard to achieve success in education, the professions, and as shopkeepers and merchants, the envious were roused to frenzy with the feelings of 'Why not me?' The perpetrators of envy passed onerous laws against Jews, confiscating their property, imposing work, education, and travel restrictions upon them, and imprisoning their leaders and intellectuals. The great diversion from personal failure and government failure was fulfilled. The envious had found someone to blame for their failures. Their warped conclusion in the extreme would be the destruction of Jews by death, their death being the elimination of envy and the resolution to atone for the failures of the envious." Ruth paused. "Excuse me for that diversion. I am sorry, my mind wandered. This day has been stressful and violent. Our lives have become stressful and violent. There is no peace."

Joseph fell back in the chair, his hand covering his eyes, and spoke, "This morning, my friend Zev was shot. The police humiliated us because we were Jews. We had just left the rabbi's quarters in the synagogue. Zev lost control as they harassed us. He grabbed one of their pistols and shot two of them dead before the other two shot him. That is why, I suppose, they wanted me to die a tortuous death. You are my guardian angels. It seems that Divine Providence has a plan for each of us, and I hope that mine is to survive. Reaching the ship in time is crucial for my survival."

"What is your plan to reach Nesebur?" Michael asked.

Joseph avoided an answer and instead asked Ruth, "How did you know what was happening to me, and why did you save me?"

Ruth was tall, her dark-brown hair worn back and held with a barrette and wrapped around her face. Her dress hung straight down as she paced the room nervously, rubbing her hands, and then pressing them against the course material of her dress. "I left my work a few minutes before lunchtime, and hurried to reach my sons," she spoke rapidly. "I wanted them to know that I may be fired. In my hurry, I cut across the city by going through the park. I rarely go to the park, much less through it. As I approached the entrance, I saw a man digging a large hole, and a policeman stood nearby with a pistol pointed at him. I raced through the park and found Samuel and Michael at work tilling a field. I told them the news and what I had seen in the park, and that we must free this man. The rest, you know."

She translated it to Samuel and Michael.

"I suppose other Jews might have helped you," said Samuel, "but it fell upon us to be your angels."

"I guess," she added, "that it was luck that I saw you there."

Joseph looked at Samuel, Michael, and Ruth. "Again, with all my heart, I thank you for saving my life. As it states in the Talmud, 'To save a single life is as though you saved all mankind.' From my perspective, it was not luck that saved me, it was Divine Providence. Think of the events that preceded my rescue, and to me it was all directed by the hand of God."

Joseph waited for her to finish her translation before continuing, "As for my plan to escape, it has failed. Now I just rely on God to help me survive by my wits. Already I have taken much of your time and I must go. Did you by any chance save my pack?"

"Do not despair," Ruth answered. "A long time ago, I learned a saying from a famous rabbi named Luzz something or other."

Joseph interrupted with the name, "You mean Rabbi Moshe Luzzatto."

"Yes, I think that was it," she continued. "He said that 'All that befalls us in the world, the good as well as the bad, are tests.' You are being tested just as we are. You were saved because God's plan is for you to reach Shanghai, but you are in no condition to leave. Look at you." Her motherly admonition reminded Joseph of his mother, and his mind drifted back. He remembered the scarves his mother wore to cover her hair. They were dark colors, blue, black, or brown. "Stay until you are stronger. Anyway, you cannot travel by day. Search parties are out looking for Jews trying to flee. You must travel at night and hide during the day. Yet it is far to Nesebur. How will you reach the ship in time? There is no safe transportation for you."

"I will run. Yes, that is it, I will run," Joseph responded. "I will run at night and rest during the day. That way, as you say, I will be safe. Before I go though, I would like to ask you a favor."

"Yes, of course, what is it?"

Joseph spoke slowly, allowing Ruth time to translate what he was saying. "I need to write a letter to my parents, and I would like you to mail it for me. I must let them know where I am and that I am all right. I want them to know what has happened on my journey. As I write, I explain myself to them, and by doing this, I hope they understand why I left home. One day, the memories of my life with my father and mother as well as the events that I write them determine my identity. Someday, my childhood in Poland, my parents, this journey, and you saving my life will be future memories."

Ruth left the room and returned with a sheet of paper and an envelope. Samuel, with his narrow angular chin breaking into a smile for the first time in Joseph's presence, extended his pen to Joseph.

"Thank you," Joseph replied, grasping the pen. "I will write later."

Exhausted from the day's ordeal, fatigue overwhelmed him, and Joseph lay on the sofa and fell asleep. An hour later, he awakened and looked around the apartment and for several seconds did not remember where he was. After being shown the toilet and bathtub in the hallway, Joseph soaked in the tub's hot water and scrubbed with a washcloth to remove the encrusted dirt on his skin.

Joseph awoke the next morning alone in the apartment. Ruth, Samuel, and Michael had left for work. A note on the table said to wait in the apartment until they returned. Next to the note was food and what earlier had been a hot glass of tea. Joseph said his morning prayers and thanked God for restoring his soul. He washed his dirty clothing in the kitchen sink using the scrub board that he found underneath it. Tonight he planned to start running to Nesebur. After eating, he cleared the table and began to write.

FUTURE MEMORIES

> *Dear Momma and Poppa,*
> *I pray that you are blessed with good health and that Momma is feeling better. This is the third letter I am writing, this one from Sofia.*

Joseph stopped writing because the ink bottle was empty. Searching to find another one, he noticed the framed photographs filled with faded pictures of a husband and wife standing with their family in front of a farmhouse, a young couple with two small boys seated on a sofa, of a man in an army uniform with medals on his chest, an old couple standing in front of a house holding hands, and a young child with ribbons in her hair, photographs displayed to preserve memories.

He found a pencil with an eraser and continued writing.

> *I wrote you from Budapest and Belgrade. During these days, I have traveled many kilometers towards Nesebur. Last night, in Sofia, I stayed with a kind family, Ruth and her two sons, Samuel and Michael. They helped me survive a bad situation. Zev was killed by Bulgarian police in Sofia yesterday, but this family saved me.*

He read what he had written and erased the last two sentences. He did not want his parents to know the bad news.

The ship sails in six days from Nesebur. It is two hundred fifty kilometers away, and tonight I will begin on foot to arrive in time because there is no other transportation. I expect to meet Avi, Benjamin, Isaac, and Levi there. I am afraid of the uncertainty of this trip, yet my clarity of purpose gives me confidence to move ahead.

I am sorry that I left Chemelnick, because I miss you and the family and the world that I grew up in. I should be bearing the same burdens and struggles that you are enduring. You wanted me to stay, but after I received the second telegram, I felt that I had to go. Please forgive my decision, and do not be sad. Sadness dulls the heart and weakens the spirit.

Give my greetings and my love to my grandparents and the rest of the family. I know that you are writing to me, and I hope to read your letters when I arrive in Shanghai. I love you and look forward to the time when we are together again.

Your loving son,
Joseph

Dusk settled over the city, and dismal dark-gray clouds hung in the sky. A breeze chilled the air. Samuel and Michael walked several paces in front of Ruth and Joseph. They passed the Royal Palace and the sixteenth-century Banya

Bashi mosque. Joseph did not bother to notice either of these structures, his mind preoccupied with his plan for escape and his prayers to see his parents and family again. The cobblestone streets ended at the edge of the city. The four continued walking on a rough road until they entered the forest.

"Stay in the forest and keep the road on your right," advised Ruth. "Follow this road east. Always go east, and you will reach Nesebur and your ship."

"Yes, yes," Joseph replied, "I remember, and I have the map that Samuel drew. With God's help, I will arrive in time." He handed Ruth the letter and pleaded, "Please mail this for me." She nodded and then translated to Samuel and Michael. After she finished, a stillness invaded their hearts, and no one spoke. During times of final farewells, or terrible grief, or great joy, the heart becomes unable to transmit to the brain what it wants to say. But at moments of such stillness, words need not be spoken for the heart is capable of speaking through the eyes. Joseph looked deeply into each face and focused intently. He wanted to remember their eyes and the lines around them, their smiles, and their tears, and to preserve these in his memory, like a camera snapping photos. He knew these faces would become future memories.

Ruth took a handkerchief from her pocket and wiped tears from her eyes. Samuel and Michael stared at the ground around their feet.

"The way life goes," sobbed Ruth, her eyes filled with pain, tears streaming down her face, "means that this is a final farewell between us. We will never see each other again." Her tears fell faster than she could wipe them away.

"You have our address, and I know that you will write, but only God knows if we will still be at this address and if we will survive this war to read your letters. And if there are reasons you do not write, we will know that sometimes you will think of us. When you do, please say a prayer for our souls. Go on your way, Joseph, and may God protect you on this journey and for the rest of your life."

Samuel hugged Joseph with a strong grip. Michael took hold of Joseph's hand and shook it. Joseph looked at each face and studied it again intently.

"Why," Ruth asked, "do you stare at us like that?"

"I have no photograph of you," Joseph replied. "I must always remember what you look like, for you restored me to life from a certain death. I must keep your images clear in my brain, and when I think back to these days in Sofia, I will remember each of you. You will become part of my future memories."

CHAPTER 8

To Nesebur

Ruth, Samuel, and Michael watched Joseph disappear into the night. He did not look back as it would have been too painful. The night was cool, and he heard the wind rustle the treetops. Crickets chirped in the woods, and the shrill call of a night bird pierced the silence.

Joseph started running through a much-traveled narrow path covered with large ground ferns. A sense of terror ran through his body. Fighting vigorously to calm his nerves, Joseph kept repeating, *God will protect me.* The moonlight cast enough light for him to weave his way through the forest. Struggling up hilly terrain, Joseph ran until he was winded and then slowed to a walk. Catching his breath again, he continued running. Occasionally he spotted the headlights of cars on the road, reassuring him that he was staying on the right trail.

After a while, his legs became heavy, and it felt like sacks of potatoes were attached to them. Stumbling over a rock, he fell, his weary legs not responding quickly enough to avoid the fall. His side began to hurt from exhaustion.

Stopping more often to catch his breath, Joseph panted for air. Although the trail was firm, he fell again, tripping over a tree root. His calf and thigh muscles ached. At school, there was limited time for exercise, and Joseph spent the exercise time studying. Running for his life through the forest, he suddenly understood what it meant to be in good physical condition. Exhausted, he began to walk, plodding over slopes and rocks. He concentrated on each step, thinking only of the next step, and not concerned about seeing the end of the trail. He had faith that he would succeed and thought, *This trek is like life, goals being achieved one step at a time.*

Moving through the canopy of the forest, Joseph suddenly fell for a third time. He had not noticed the uneven patch of ground that caused his feet to fall out from under him. Getting up was an effort. The forest grew darker as the moon's light failed to penetrate the thick foliage. Sounds of birds whistled through the forest. A chill from the night cold stung his eyes and nostrils. The rustling trees stood like dark-brown giants bending anonymously over him. Stepping over a fallen log, he saw small animals darting across his path. Joseph maintained the walking and running pace until the first rays of sunrise filtered through the forest. By now, completely exhausted, he found a hollow in the earth, sheltered by trees and ground ferns, and he crept into it. Covering himself with his coat, he lay down and went to sleep.

He lay in a deep sleep until the sounds of men singing awoke him. A Nazi patrol of five men walked on the road. Wearing helmets and dressed in faded green uniforms, they carried rifles over their shoulders and pistols on their belts.

Fear paralyzed Joseph. He remembered what happened to Samuel, Mordechai, and Zev. The thought of their killings unsettled him. He lay motionless on the soft earth, peeking out at the patrol, and now convinced why he had to stay still during the day and only travel in the dark. He tried to sleep again, but many things ran through his mind, keeping him awake.

On the second day, his pace was slower. He was weary, and most of the food that he brought with him was eaten. Praying and studying from the three books he carried filled the daylight hours when he was not sleeping. He pleaded with God that he and his family have a safe deliverance from the impending disaster being cast over Europe.

On the third night in the forest, Joseph heard voices ahead of him. Fearing that they were thieves, he stopped running and proceeded carefully through the brush and trees until he saw a clearing and six men sitting around the smoldering embers of a fire. In the dim light, Joseph could not see them clearly. The chattering of their voices became distinct as he moved to the outer edge of the clearing. They were speaking Yiddish, and Joseph did not want to startle them. They could be carrying guns and think he was a thief or a Nazi. He called out just loud enough for them to hear, "Please help me. I need help."

The six stopped talking and ran for cover, hiding behind trees and rocks. Two of them had pistols in their hands.

Again, Joseph cried out, "Please help me. I mean you no harm."

A tall, lanky man wearing a shabby dark-brown jacket and brown pants with tears in several places shouted back in Yiddish toward the unknown voice, "Step forward with your hands up in the air. Walk slowly towards the fire. I have a gun aimed at you."

Joseph obeyed and stood in the center of the clearing. A man in his early twenties approached him. Everything about him was narrow, his face, nose, chin, and eyes. His brown eyes were bloodshot from lack of sleep, and black semicircular rings hung under them. An unkempt beard covered his face. The pistol was leveled toward Joseph.

"You speak Yiddish?"

"Yes," Joseph replied, afraid to say anything else that might anger this man.

"Why are you here? How did you get here? Are you alone?" The questions came quickly without waiting for a response.

"I am Joseph Shalosky from Chemelnick, Poland." Joseph lowered his hands to his sides. The fear disappeared as he saw the uncertainty disappear from the eyes of the man pointing the pistol at him. "I am going to Nesebur to catch the boat for Shanghai. I am fleeing from the Nazis."

"To Nesebur. Ha-ha-ha, you will never make it to Nesebur on foot unless your boat leaves in a month." The others laughed too. "Are you alone?"

"Yes, now I am alone. My friend Zev was shot in Sofia," Joseph replied, "and I come from there. A group of us left the yeshiva in Poland seeking refuge in Shanghai. This is my third night of traveling. I am tired and hungry. Who are you?"

"We are a group of the resistance fighting the Nazis in Bulgaria. If you do not know our names, you will not be able to identify us if you are caught. If they catch you, they will torture you for information, and you will have none to give." The gentle manner changed as he abruptly questioned Joseph. "If you are from a yeshiva in Poland, then why do you appear the way you do?" He aimed the pistol at Joseph. "Perhaps what you tell us is a lie and you are a spy. You look more like a spy than a yeshiva student."

"May I sit? I am very tired," asked Joseph.

"Answer me first. We cannot risk a trap and be caught by the Nazis. That would be the end of all of us."

"I asked the rabbi in Budapest if I could change my appearance to help me survive, and he agreed."

Wind rustled through the darkness of the trees, and the air felt cold. The hoots of night owls could be heard mixed with the chirping of other birds. The red glow from the dying embers faded, and the fire died. Weariness overwhelmed Joseph.

"May I sit please?" Joseph asked again.

The leader lowered the pistol, shrugged his shoulders, and nodded. Joseph sat. "Most Jews who flee use other routes," the leader said, "and Nesebur is not one of the escape cities." Before he turned and walked away, he said, "Wait a minute, I will get you some food."

Joseph ate the potatoes and cabbage and left the meat because it was not kosher. He decided to become a vegetarian during his journey to China. This way, he would not be concerned as whether the meat or poultry he was offered was kosher.

Looking carefully at the group, he recognized that they were only a few years older than his friends and were risking their lives by fighting the Nazis. He wondered, *How long can they survive like this?* His thoughts were interrupted when he was offered water.

"Thank you," he said and drank quickly and finished a second cup without stopping to take a breath.

The group assembled away from Joseph, and he struggled to make out their conversation.

The leader turned to the group. "What do you think? Is he really a Jew fleeing, or is this a clever way to betray us? Consider that he appears from nowhere, claims to be running for two days towards Nesebur from Sofia, says he is a yeshiva student from Poland but does not look like one, he could be a clever infiltrator from the Nazis."

A tough-looking, blond-haired man said, "Test him. Ask him something about Sofia and see his response." He zipped his jacket closed and put his hands in his pockets as the night breeze stiffened.

"Okay. Let me think. I will sit and talk with him and discover the truth."

The leader returned and sat next to Joseph. With his cap off, Joseph saw curly brown hair above a narrow forehead. The squinty eyes bore through him but in a friendly way. "Are you okay?'

Joseph nodded as he swallowed the last of the food.

"You don't like meat?"

"I do like it," Joseph replied, "but it is not kosher, so I cannot eat it. For this journey, I will eat only fish, vegetables, and fruit, assuming I can get any of it along the way."

The leader rubbed his hands together to keep them warm. "What you are trying to do is admirable. People react differently to the same circumstances. During this war, some people will stay home and hope for the best. I predict they will be slaughtered. They refuse to see the facts. They cannot face the truth. They deny reality, the reality of what is happening throughout Europe. They believe that as terrible as things may get, it will not affect them. It will be over in a short while and life will return to normal." He ran his hand across the stubble of his beard. "Others, like us, will resist and fight and maybe even die. And a few like you will flee with the hope of surviving and continuing the future we dreamed about. I suppose we all do what is best suited for each of us."

"Will I survive?" Joseph asked. "I pray every day that I will, but only God knows. How do I reach Nesebur in time for the boat? You said that at the pace I am running, it will take many days to get there, and I have only a few remaining."

"If you had this plan to escape," the leader asked, "and you knew the distance between Sofia and Nesebur, then why is it that you are struggling through the forest in a hopeless pursuit of reaching Nesebur when you must know there is no time to catch the boat?"

Joseph did not look up. He sat on his hands to warm them as a chill ran through his body. A restless wind whistled through the tree tops.

"My plan is to reach the boat in time. I did not know that I was moving slowly through the forest. You see, after my friend Zev was shot in Sofia and the police tried to kill me too, I did not want to risk going to the place where I could receive a ride to Nesebur."

"What place are you talking about?"

"Sofia Shalom Trucking."

"You know that company?" the leader pursued. "Where is it located?"

"At King Boris Place," Joseph replied.

"And what else do you know about getting a ride?"

"I was to say 'Rabbi Levi from the moon.'"

The leader turned to his group and in a loud whisper said, "He is okay. He knows 'Rabbi Levi from the moon.'" He turned back to Joseph. "That's good. You go to sleep now. In the morning, I will arrange for you to get to Nesebur in time for the boat."

"Yes, I need to sleep badly. I am very tired."

"You have been telling us the truth, but we had to be certain. If you were a clever spy, all of us could have been betrayed and killed. But you knew the code that Rabbi Senesh gave to us, and that means he trusted you. If he trusted you, then we follow his trust. In the morning, I will make the arrangements. It may take a while, but you will be on the ship to Shanghai."

"After what you told me, how will that be possible? You said the distance to Nesebur is greater than I can run in the few days remaining before the ship sails. Yet you, whose name I do not even know, tell me casually that I will be at the ship in time. In Sofia, a family of angels saved my life, and now without sounding heroic, you simply state that everything will be okay. Are you an angel too?"

"Please don't get carried away with all of that angel stuff. After all, every time a person does a good deed does not make him an angel. Good people just act that way because it is the right thing to do. Without performing good deeds, we lose our humanity, and once we lose our humanity, our loss of civilization will not be far behind. Enough talk. Get some sleep. It will not become much colder than it is now." He turned and walked away.

After putting on a sweater under his jacket to stay warm, Joseph lay down. He looked up to the dark evening sky. "Thank you, dear God, for the blessing that you are about to bestow on me." And he went to sleep.

Early the next morning, the group marched through the woods, staying out of sight of the road. They moved silently on paths seldom used and crossed streams rushing with water from the spring snow melt. Crossing a stream, Joseph slipped, and his foot sunk ankle deep into the icy water. He shook his foot and kept on walking. The sun pierced the trees, casting shadows dark and deep on the forest floor. Tiny green shoots sprouted from the awakening buds. After four hours, the group stopped to rest and eat. Joseph had not noticed that a small village was sitting atop a hillside about a mile away. The leader pointed to one of the youngest in the group and said, "It is your turn. Go to the village. You know what to do. We will wait for you here exactly one hour from the time you reach the road. If you are not back in time, you know where to look for us. We will continue heading east." The two men synchronized their watches, bid each other a goodbye with the wave of a hand, and the young man ran toward the road leading to the village. Sitting on a large smooth rock, Joseph pulled his writing pad and a pencil from his sack and began writing a letter to his parents. The others rested or talked to one another in whispers.

Dear Momma and Poppa,
   I do not have much time to write a long letter. I pray that sometime later today, I will be on my way to Nesebur to board the boat

for China. Several people in Bulgaria have risked their lives to save mine. It seems that through both good times and sad times, we build our memories, and I want to always remember these angels, as I call them, who saved me. This journey away from you, away from the ones I love, has been filled with danger. But please I beg you, do not worry, I am fine. I have survived with the help of God. I even manage time to study. When the war ends, I will return home, and we will be reunited. I eagerly wait for that time. Momma, I especially look forward to tasting your delicious beets again. I miss you all very much. I will write again as soon as I have the chance, but I will be further from home and the letters will take longer to reach you.

Your loving son,
Joseph

He addressed the envelope, carefully folded the letter, placed it inside, and sealed it. He kissed the envelope before going to the leader and asking him to mail it. The leader agreed and refused the money Joseph offered for the stamps.

Joseph smiled kindly and said, "You are a good man. I will pray that you survive the war."

The leader opened several of the snaps on his jacket as the morning air grew warmer. "Who knows? We'll see. I do what I must. Someone has to defend the good against the evil. After all, you do what you must to survive and perpetuate Jewish continuity. You and I have made choices."

Joseph peered into the sharp gaze of this man, only a few years older than himself. He recognized the strength and conviction that carried him through this battle with the enemy. Could this have been the brother Joseph never had? Here stood a man without a name, only the identity of leader, to protect himself from discovery.

The leader continued, "If people like us do not denounce evil deeds, it is not because we accept them, it is because we are defeated. I refuse to accept defeat. You and I battle the Nazis, the fascists, the Arrow Cross, or whatever they are called in a particular country in different ways. If we are lucky, we will both prevail. You know what Winston Churchill said, 'We will never give up. We will never surrender.'"

He studied the man's face. It was pale and covered with stubble. His dark hair was uncombed and greasy. He seemed somehow anxious and uncertain, with fearful eyes. His body seemed frail, and his physical presence contradicted the strength and conviction he had heard moments before. Although Joseph believed that it was in God's hands, Joseph felt they would never meet again, and that this man's effort to save Joseph's life was already sinking into memory. *How many future memories must I store?* Joseph said to himself.

The hour passed slowly. Waiting impatiently for someone or for something to happen changes one's perception of time. Fifty-nine minutes after the young man headed to the nearby village, the leader spoke to the group, "Let's go.

Something delayed him, and we cannot wait. We will try another village later this afternoon."

"Wait," interrupted Joseph. "Give him just another five minutes. I know he will be here."

"That is against our rules, and you are a stranger and not one to interfere. You do not understand the consequences of a mistake in judgment here in the forest. We are being hunted every day, and we must remain cautious."

"Please wait just five minutes. I know he will return. I can feel it."

"You believe that because you are religious that you know things we don't." In a display of hesitation, he put his right thumbnail in his mouth and gnawed at it. Everyone noticed the uncertainty. They also saw an emotional quality unknown to them in their leader. "Fine, we will wait the five minutes that you ask, but not a second more."

"Thank you," Joseph said, and he began to pray. Five minutes passed like a blink, and the young man did not appear.

"Okay," said the leader. "I gave you five minutes, and now we must go with you or without you. Let's move, everybody."

Joseph's disappointment was apparent. His shoulders sagged under the weight of his pack, and his head drooped. He said nothing as he trudged through the forest with the group, thinking that the port at Nesebur seemed to move farther away.

The early afternoon sun rested directly above the forest and created long shadows of the trees on the forest floor. Like ghosts, the group disappeared into the shadows and just as quickly reappeared into the sunlight. A clearing emerged, and from the top of the hill, they saw a village less than a mile distant on the near side of the road in the valley. The village appeared like a relic from another century, with houses made of unpainted mud bricks, dilapidated roofs, tiny windows, crumbling chimneys, and low entrance doors where one had to stoop to enter.

"My turn," commanded the leader turning to the group. "Wait here. Stay together and keep an eye on me. And while I am away, I do not want a blemish to remain in your thoughts about this man," he added as he pointed to Joseph.

He walked away at a quick pace and shortly entered the village and disappeared from sight. Joseph opened his prayer book and read quietly, his lips moving. Deep in prayer, he paid no attention to time. A stirring of the men around him shattered his concentration. The leader was walking up the hill at a leisurely pace. When he reached the group, he smiled and said, "Today is a beautiful spring day, and we must enjoy a pleasant walk down to the village." His tone changed as he added, "It is safe, and there are no patrols in the area. Remember, we move as usual, two at a time, and allow space between each two. We are not a group coming down from the hills but rather a few boys returning from a walk. We must not attract attention." He scanned their faces for approval. "Okay. Let's go."

After the first ones left, the next pair waited two minutes to allow enough space between them. The others followed this procedure, until they assembled in a large barn on a farm in the village. The barn was bleak, its once-bright-red paint peeling and faded. The weather vane atop the roof was tilted and appeared like it would topple at any moment. A cow and a goat inhabited two of the stalls, and an overturned stool lay near the cow. Patches of straw covered the floors. A broken window was stuffed with rags to keep out the cold air. The ladder to the hayloft had missing rungs. Several beams were rotted, and the foul stench of the animal droppings permeated the air.

One of the men commented, "It is not like home, but this is better than sleeping in that cold, damp forest." The others agreed.

Stepping into the middle of the group, the leader addressed them solemnly. "We can stay here for a day or two and can use the bath at the house at night. Please bathe quickly to save the hot water for the next person." Quickly his face changed engulfed in sadness. "Now most important, please give your farewells to Joseph. Just as we have left our families to fight, Joseph has left his to fight for their continuity and for Jewish continuity. Wish him well and remember him, for this is probably the last time you will see him." The leader stopped, sighed, and in deep reflection added, "Life is filled with too many last times. We do not know when it is going to be a last time, but this time we do."

Each man shook Joseph's hand and either patted him on the shoulder or gave him a hug. Joseph was crushed with emotion as he bid them farewell. Joseph and the leader walked toward a gas station at the edge of the village. Joseph asked, "Now that I am leaving, it will not matter if I know who you are. Please tell me, what is your name?"

The leader gave him a quizzical glance and smiled, his eyes relaxed and sparkling for the first time since Joseph had met him. "Reuben is my name, and yes, I am Jewish.

None of the group knows that because some are Jewish and some are not. I organized them to fight the Nazis, not to become involved in religious squabbles. With them, I even use a different name so they do not know my identity if they are picked up by the secret police."

"You are the brother I never had," Joseph said in an endearing tone. "In the Torah, the section of *Vayeishev*, Reuben is the oldest of Joseph's brothers. The brothers stripped Joseph of his tunic made of fine wool and cast him into a pit filled with serpents and scorpions. It was Reuben who intended to save Joseph, and so the past repeats itself here as you intend to save me."

"I do this," said Reuben, "not because I am religious. I help you because it is the good thing to do. If the situation was reversed, I know that you would help me. Someday, you may be helping people who are strangers. When you do, I hope that you will remember me."

In an emotional tone, Joseph replied, "Reuben, you will always be a part of my memories."

They arrived at the gas station. It was covered in dirt. Nothing was paved. A ramshackle wooden one-room house acted as the business and home of the one man who ran the station. Two blue pumps stood in mud and dirt.

A four-wheeled gray panel truck pulled into the station and stopped at the pumps. Dents in its side panels, rusted bumpers, and almost bald tires showed the truck's age. An old bearded man hobbled from the shack and asked the driver how much gas he wanted and then began pumping. The driver walked to Reuben and spoke to him briefly, and Reuben answered with a nod. After this exchange, the driver went to the outhouse behind the shack. Reuben motioned to Joseph to get in the truck. Joseph wanted to say goodbye again, but having done this earlier, he knew it was time to go. The driver returned, paid for the gas, started the engine, and the truck pulled away. Sitting in the front seat, Joseph twisted backward and waved to Reuben. Reuben waved back and watched the truck head for the road to Nesebur.

Joseph introduced himself to the driver, and the driver smiled at Joseph. The driver appeared to be in his late thirties or early forties, with wide round bulging eyes and a face shaped like a pumpkin. Speaking in Bulgarian, he tried to engage Joseph in conversation, but Joseph did not understand, and Joseph spoke in Yiddish then in German to the driver. The driver shrugged, not comprehending. For the rest of the drive, they were quiet as the truck rumbled along the bumpy road.

Driving along the valley with the Balkans to the north, the mountains extended for more than two hundred miles across central Bulgaria ending at the Black Sea. Twenty passes crossed these mountains, including Shipka Pass.[*]

At Sliven,[**] a small town on the main road, the truck stopped for gas. Joseph calculated that it was about one hundred kilometers to the port. Looking at the sky, he saw dark gray clouds of smoke floating skyward from the stacks of the textile and woodwork mills in the town.

Joseph dozed as the truck rolled west to the Black Sea. In his slumber, he dreamed that he heard voices in distress, but they were not clear. Were they his parents speaking? He

---

[*] In 1877, a great battle took place during the Russo-Turkish war for Bulgarian independence.

[**] In Sliven in 1834, the first factory was built in Bulgaria.

saw them standing in the doorway as an enormous black cloud, like a tornado, raced toward them. Joseph tried to tear away the cloud and shout a warning, but he could not speak and failed to warn them. The dream scene brightened into a white background. He saw his grandparents sitting at the kitchen table in their home crying. Quickly, the scene darkened, and he heard a voice shout, "Dear God, what will become of us? Is this the last time we will see you?" *Who said that? Was that my grandfather?* Blackness covered the dream, and thunder rumbled in the distance. "Run, Joseph, run," whispered a voice. *Who said that? Was that you, Papa? What is happening? I cannot move.*

"Help me, help me," Joseph mumbled aloud in his sleep. "I want to see my parents. Please, God, help me." Joseph felt a push against his shoulder. The driver was pushing his shoulder to wake him. Joseph's mouth was dry, and droplets of sweat were on his face and neck. He thanked the driver and then opened his water can, drinking several sips. Approaching Nesebur,* the truck reached the top of a hill, and Joseph viewed the town below. Nesebur appeared like a town protruding into the Black Sea. The truck entered Nesebur through an opening in the fourth-century stone wall surrounding the town. Broken or missing stones punctuated the wall. Rolling over cobblestoned streets, they passed old timbered houses, fifteen Byzantine churches dating from the fifth through the seventeenth centuries,

---

* Nesebur, developed in the year 513 BCE as the Greek trade port of Mesembria, sits on a small rocky peninsula. The Black Sea is unique because its deepest regions have no oxygen in the water. Without oxygen, this condition preserved ancient wood belonging to sunken ships that transported salted fish, similar to salt cod, from the Black Sea to Greece. The trade occurred between the third and fifth century BCE.

and the Archaeological Museum, where ancient ruins filled the rooms.

That afternoon, a ship docked in Nesebur. Workmen unloaded cargo, carrying bags or boxes on their backs or using wheelbarrows or hand pulled wagons. The driver gestured to Joseph that this was the ship to board. They shook hands and said goodbye, this time knowing what the other was saying. Joseph studied the driver's face for a moment and then left. *Another memory, another last time,* he thought.

At the dock, Joseph reunited with his friends. Isaac and Levi related that they arrived the day before after having traveled by train part of the way and hitchhiking the rest. Avi and Benjamin looked bedraggled, their faces dirty, their clothes torn, and cuts on their hands. Avi explained that from Sofia, they were given a car ride most of the way but were let off when the driver had to turn south about forty kilometers before Nesebur. For the past two days, they trekked through the forest, traveling at night to avoid the patrols on the road. A group of resistance fighters fed them and gave directions to the port. Joseph wondered if this was Reuben's group but knew there were many resistance groups hiding in the forest.

"We kept going," added Benjamin, "running as much as possible, and arrived here before dawn this morning. Where is Zev?"

Joseph relayed the story of how Zev died in Sofia and how Joseph was saved by the Ruth and her sons, Michael and Samuel.

Levi interrupted and said, "Another one of us dead. How many more will die? Was it worthwhile to leave our families to die in strange lands? Who will ever visit Samuel, Mordechai, and Zev's gravesites? Their families will not even know where they are buried." Turning abruptly, he walked away from the group.

After hours of waiting in long lines, they boarded the *Burkas*. Standing on the deck, Joseph gazed upon the tranquil green-blue colored sea. He studied the workmen in the port and the flurry of activity. He remembered the people who saved him during the past few days. With tears in his eyes, he remembered Samuel, Mordechai, and Zev and whispered, "Too many goodbyes."

CHAPTER 9

Nesebur to Asian Seas

The morning sun sent shimmers of glitter off the minarets and domes of Istanbul. Appearing first was the Blue Mosque, followed by the Sultan's Palace, and then the four needle-pointed minarets of the Hagia Sophia Mosque built in its dark-red masonry. The ship steamed into the port of Istanbul.* Joseph watched in fascination. All his studying had not prepared him for a world outside of Europe. Being accustomed to small-village synagogues, the fortress-like size and majesty of the dome of the Hagia Sophia Mosque overwhelmed all the buildings surrounding it. Standing on one of the seven hills of Istanbul, this masterpiece of architecture greeted the traveler sailing to or from the Black Sea. Joseph had finished his morning prayers earlier and stood at the railing observing the scene. He had read that Istanbul was the former capital of the Byzantine Empire for one thousand years and the Ottoman Empire for five hun-

---

* Istanbul was founded by the Greeks in about 660 BCE. It straddles the Bosporus at the entrance to the Black Sea and is the only city in the world to be built on two continents, Europe and Asia.

dred years, and that Emperor Justinian built the Basilica of St. Sophia between 532 and 538, and later the Basilica became a mosque. The *Burkas* docked, and the passengers were allowed four hours to visit.

Joseph avoided visiting the mosques and did not have time to visit the Topkapi Palace. Instead he wandered along the narrow lanes of the Grand Bazaar and Spice Bazaar. The wares from the Moslem world and Asia inundated the Grand Bazaar. He was overwhelmed seeing merchandise that he had not realized ever existed. In the Spice Bazaar, the burlap bags stuffed with spices enveloped his nostrils with aromas that sometimes were pungent and caused him trouble breathing.

As he surveyed the strange surroundings and what seemed to him the even stranger people wearing clothing he had never seen before, the Turks looked at him, a westerner, as someone who definitely did not belong there. Divided into three parts, Joseph stayed on the Stambul part, the peninsula between the Marmara Sea and the arm of the Bosporus. The brief four hours did not allow enough time to go to the Beyoglu, which included the suburbs of Galata and Pera, and Uskudar,[*] formerly called Scutari and standing on the Asian side of the Bosporus.

After having the cargo loaded and the ship fueled, the *Burkas* untied from the dock and moved at a steady pace on the Bosporus to begin the journey across the oceans and seas separating Europe from China. Joseph studied during his days aboard ship as the *Burkas* traversed the eastern Mediterranean Sea to the Suez Canal. Passing through the

---

[*] In Uskudar, at a hospital during the Crimean War from 1853 to 1856, the British nurse Florence Nightingale tended the wounded.

canal into the Red Sea, all one could see was desert, the desert of Arabia to the east and that of Egypt to the west. The Red Sea led to the Gulf of Aden, passing Yemen and Somalia and opening into the Indian Ocean. The Maldives appeared like sandbars in the ocean, being just three feet above sea level. At Columbo, Ceylon, the *Burkas* unloaded cargo and refueled.

After days at sea, Joseph had little interest in this port, especially since the passengers were not permitted to disembark. All he could see from his brief visits on deck was tropical forest. During the day, the deck was hot because in this region of the world, located a few degrees north of the equator, the average year-round temperature in Columbo was eighty-one degrees Fahrenheit. On this day in port, it was hotter. In the evenings, after praying the *Mincha* and *Maariv* services, Joseph went on deck. He liked the smell of the salt air and felt comforted by the ocean breezes. The clear fresh sea air revived him from his restless routine of studying in a cramped cabin. Standing at the stern of the ship, he watched the trailing wake made by the engines as the ship churned through the sea. The firm white waves at the bow dissipated as they moved farther from the ship and blended into the dark blue sea.

How the water in the ocean reflects life, he thought. *Man's life was like a wake in the water, the ripples reaching places and people both known and unknown. As man strives to move forward, tides and currents, both in constant motion, cause shifts, and man must adapt to these changes.*

Joseph realized that as he moved closer to the safe haven of Shanghai, he was moving away from his past, away from his family, away from his friends, and away from those he loved. He forced his memory to retain images of the way they looked, the sounds of their voices, and the smiles on their faces. He knew they loved him and missed him. Tears swelled in his eyes as he remembered that in the Book of Psalms it says that "God preserves all our tears." Sensing a significant transition in life, a feeling of emptiness swept through him because he knew that Chemelnick had become the past, the past of his childhood. He fought to retain that past, for in it, memory is irrevocably stored, and he desired to live in that life again. The family planned that after the war they would be reunited, and Joseph's departure would not be the last time they saw each other. Joseph kept faith there was purpose in what he was doing, to give his life meaning to fight for survival. Realizing he could no longer change his circumstances, Joseph understood that he would have to change himself by adapting to this different life that was just beginning.

During the day, temperatures reached close to one hundred degrees. Occasionally heavy torrential rains broke the heat and high humidity. As soon as the rain ceased, the temperature soared again. Joseph never experienced heat this intense, and studying became difficult. He discovered an opening under a hanging canvas crate cover where he could sit out of the sun and reduce the heat. Wiping perspiration from his face and neck, he noticed the ship's change of direction as it sailed from the Indian Ocean, into the Strait of Malacca, a narrow body of water between the Malay Peninsula and Sumatra. Jungle-covered mountains, dense forests, plantations of rubber trees, and miles of beaches made up the terrain of the Malay Peninsula. From the Strait of Malacca, the ship traveled thirty kilometers upstream to the confluence of the Kelang and Gombak rivers to the city of Kuala Lumpur.*

The activity in port appeared chaotic. Hundreds of workers moved about in every direction like ants bringing food to an anthill. Workers scurried with bags either on their backs or carried on long poles extended over their shoulders. Laborers pushed wheelbarrows filled with loaded burlap bags. Languages Joseph never heard spoken were being shouted among the laborers unloading and loading the *Burkas*. Malay, Chinese, English, and Tamil intermingled through the port. Joseph had arrived in Malaysia, where there were no Jews, only Muslims, Buddhists, Hindus, Confucianists, and Christians.

The next stop for the *Burkas* was just north of the equator at Singapore. Entering the harbor, British Navy warships rested at anchor as part of the British Naval bases in Singapore and Sembawang. The base was considered an impregnable fortress. Its guns, however, were aimed in the wrong direction. Fortified against attack from the sea, in a little more than one year, Joseph and the rest of the world would learn that the Japanese would attack through Malaya, and the British garrison would be forced to surrender.

The *Burkas* departed from the port and entered the Strait of Singapore. The strait, being one hundred eight kilometers long and seventeen kilometers wide, ran between the south coast of Singapore Island and the Indonesian Riau Islands, linking the Strait of Malacca to the South China Sea. Joseph was fascinated and in awe of all he had

---

* Kuala Lumpur, founded in 1857 as a tin mining town, means "muddy river bottom." In 1895, the city was chosen as the capital of the Federated Malay States.

seen and the amounts of geography and history that he was learning. In the yeshiva, learning consisted of studying the Torah and the Talmud, and each learning day lasted for twelve hours. There was no study of world geography or history.

Finally the *Burkas* turned north and away from the intense heat of the equator. Moving along the China coast, the ship passed between Hong Kong to the west and the Philippine island of Luzon to the east. Approaching Formosa, in the East China Sea, a festive air spread among the passengers. A sense of imminent safety from the terrors of the war caused an atmosphere of relief, relief from the anxiety that they would not reach their safe haven away from the horrible war. Passengers stayed on deck for longer periods of time, most speaking about how much longer it would be until they arrived in Shanghai. Their feelings of joy were soon crushed.

Near the waters around Okinawa, shouts reverberated throughout the ship.

"What is it?" Joseph asked.

"Japanese approach our ship. See their boat. We are doomed," a passenger answered.

Peering out to sea, Joseph watched a Japanese patrol boat, its flag showing a blazing-red sun set against a white background, closing in on the *Burkas*. The boat, armed with machine guns and cannon, cut swiftly through the sea. The captain of the *Burkas*, sensing the predicament, cut the engines to allow the Japanese boat to come alongside. Joseph watched as a brief conversation, complete with hand gestures, ensued between the Japanese commander and one of the officers of the *Burkas*. Obeying Japanese orders, the

Burkas changed course and followed the patrol boat toward Japan. Melancholy stifled their previous joy, and Joseph and the passengers watched in solemn silence as the coast of China receded in the distance and soon disappeared over the horizon.

The *Burkas* was escorted to Kobe,* a city on Osaka Bay, at the eastern end of the Inland Sea. Japanese soldiers armed with rifles and fixed bayonets boarded the ship and forced the passengers to disembark. Joseph heard snatches of comments like, "It is happening again here, just like with the Germans."

Canvas enclosed trucks transported the passengers to detention camps consisting of an open plot of land surrounded by ten-foot-high barbed wire fences. Guard towers manned by Japanese soldiers watched the detainees. Hope quickly faded for the passengers as they either sat on the bare ground or stood, all the while staring at the barbed wire fence. Sitting close to the fence, Joseph took his prayer book and began to pray for God's help. He prayed for his family, his friends, and himself. Joseph believed that whatever happened was in God's hands. There was no need to worry because what man was able to control, he should control, and what was beyond his control was in God's hands. Many passengers, not possessing this faith, became depressed. In their minds, internment behind barbed wire fences had never been a possibility. Throughout the jour-

---

* Kobe was renowned for building ships for the Japanese Imperial Navy. It was also famous for producing the best sake, or rice wine, in Japan. Prior to the war, Jews arrived in Kobe, and the Japanese sent them to Shanghai. Japan wanted to rid the country of westerners. By 1937, four thousand Jews had departed from Japan and moved to Shanghai. After Kristalnacht on November 9, 1938, in Germany, thousands of Jews fled to Shanghai.

ney, the narrow focus was refuge in Shanghai and a respite from the war. They had been counting the hours until they arrived in their safe haven. Joseph thought, *Man proposes, God disposes.*

Unknown to Joseph and the passengers, visas to enter Japan had been obtained through Jewish organizations from a place thousands of miles away from Kobe and nearly halfway around the world. Oftentimes, events that appear bad bring good results. The city of Kaunas* was an industrial city in Lithuania and the capital of independent Lithuania until 1939 when it was annexed by the USSR. The Soviets renamed the city Kovno.

The intent of opening the consulate was for Consul Sugihara to spy for Japan by collecting information about the military movements of the Soviet and German troops. At this time, the German army had invaded and conquered Poland, triggering the start of World War II. In March 1940, the Soviet army conquered Finland, and in May, they took control of Lithuania. In June 1940, France surrendered to Germany. In September, the Germans began bombing England, and on September 27, the Axis Tripartite Pact was signed by Germany, Italy, and Japan.

---

* In November 1936, Japan and Germany signed the Japan-German Anti-Comintern Pact directed against the Communist International (Comintern) and specifically the Soviet Union. In case of an attack by the Soviet Union against Germany or Japan, the two countries agreed to consult on measures to safeguard their common interests. Three years later, in the autumn of 1939, Chiune Sugihara was sent by the Japanese government to Kaunas to open a consulate. Consul Sugihara was a handsome man with fine features. He had a round face with a sharp straight nose, eyebrows dark and full, piercing eyes filled with a warmth of friendliness, wide lips accentuated his mouth, a head full of soft wavy hair, and a gentle personality beaming through to all who knew him. More important, he was a kind man, and kindness motivated the decisions he made in his life.

Fleeing the onslaught of the Nazis in Poland, Jews fled eastward into neighboring Lithuania. By the summer of 1940, thousands of Jews gathered at the gates to the Japanese consulate in Kaunas asking, pleading, and begging for transit visas. Consul Sugihara believed that the issuance of visas to Jews might be considered a hostile act by Japan against Germany pursuant to the Japan-German Anti-Comintern Pact. Seeing the plight of the refugees at the consulate's gates touched his conscience. Sugihara telegraphed Japan requesting permission to issue transit visas to the Jews. One of Sugihara's cables read, "Hundreds of Jewish people have come to the consulate here in Kaunas seeking transit visas. They are suffering extremely. As a fellow human being, I cannot refuse their requests. Please permit me to issue visas to them."

The Japanese government denied his request. The cable Sugihara received read, "Concerning transit visas requested previously, stop. Advise absolutely not to be issued to any traveler not holding firm end visa with guaranteed departure from Japan, stop. No exceptions, stop. No further inquiries expected, stop. K. Tanaka, Foreign Ministry, Tokyo."

For days, torn between his conscience of doing what was humane and his loyalty to his government, Consul Sugihara defied the orders received from Tokyo. Quoting a Japanese proverb, "Even the hunter cannot kill a bird that comes to him for refuge," he sent two more cables requesting permission to issue visas. The Foreign Ministry replied both times again with an emphatic no. Their third cable read, "The Foreign Ministry is opposed to hundreds of foreigners passing through Japan for reasons of public security."

In July 1940, the situation worsened. The Soviets told Sugihara that they wanted him to close the consulate by August. On August 23, the Soviets and Germans signed a nonaggression pact. That same day, Lithuania was annexed by the Soviets, and the Japanese were ordered to close their consulate. Chiune Sugihara had no time left. The Japanese foreign office ordered Sugihara and his family to evacuate immediately.

His wife, Yukiko, supported his decision, and to her it was like watching calm water gently flowing over shimmering stones in a stream. The Foreign Ministry would fire him, and he would forfeit all chance of promotion and thereby end his career in government.

The following morning, defying his orders to evacuate, Consul Sugihara announced to the Jews waiting outside the Japanese Consulate that the visas will be issued. The crowd began to rejoice, some started to pray, and others hugged and kissed their family members. Consul Sugihara allowed the Jews to enter the consulate through the garage, one Jew at a time entering his office. He issued each visa by hand as there were no printed ones where he could simply complete the empty spaces. These transit visas would allow the bearer to enter and stay in Japan for up to thirty days before continuing to his final destination. The end visa stated that the final destination was Curacao, a Dutch island located in the Caribbean Sea.

For four weeks, working from eight in the morning until late in the evening, Sugihara attempted to write at least three hundred visas a day, but a lack of paper and ink prevented him from reaching that goal. Jews volunteered and assisted him with the issuing of the visas. A German Lithuanian, desiring to save Jews, worked in his office too. With their help, Chiune Sugihara issued two thousand one hundred ninety-three visas. A visa was sufficient for one family. A Jewish organization obtained many of Sugihara's handwritten visas. Approximately six thousand to seven thousand Jews were saved through Sugihara's enduring efforts. Many Jews did not obtain his visas and stood outside the consulate, tears in their eyes, as Sugihara and his family finally departed. Soon after they left Kaunas, ten thousand Lithuanian Jews, one-third of the Jewish population of Kaunas, were rounded up, taken into the fort overlooking the hills of Kaunas, and shot by German murder squads.

At his departure, Sugihara said, "I will never forget the look of despair on the faces of the Jews who did not get visas as we left our consulate. Tears welled up in my eyes, and I apologized to them in my mind as I asked for their forgiveness."

CHAPTER 10

Japan to Shanghai

In the Japanese detention camp, Joseph, Avi, Isaac, Levi, Benjamin, and the rest of the students lived in one large room. During most of the day, the Japanese forbade the detainees to go outside. Joseph and the students studied from sunlight to sunset. A few times a day, Joseph would walk around the room for exercise. Greasy soup was the only food served to them, the soup being barely edible.

"Will this nightmare ever end?" asked Avi in an agitated voice. With his loss of weight, his cheeks had shrunk into the sides of his face, making it seem like his eyes were bulging. Avi viewed life through the prism of the moment rather than what might be. "We were supposed to go to Shanghai, to study until the war ends, and then return to our families. Instead, look where we are. We are prisoners in Japan, isolated in one room without decent food and no hope for release."

"We must pray harder," Joseph interrupted.

"Praying is good up to the point of starvation, then what?"

Trying to calm him, Joseph sighed and folded his arms, and admonished him. "In the Torah, section *Vayeishev*, Joseph, the son of Jacob, was imprisoned for twelve years although he was innocent. Making the mistake of placing his trust in the chamberlain, a fellow prisoner soon to be released, instead of in God, Joseph's prison sentence was increased by two years. The lesson to be learned at times like this is that having faith is vital."

"I do not see the connection between our predicament and the story you just told," sulked Avi.

"God determines everything Avi, don't you see? Just as God had Joseph imprisoned, he would cause him to be freed." Joseph began pacing, waving his arms enthusiastically as the words poured from his mouth. "If we pray as hard as we can, maybe God will grant us a miracle." He paused and scratching the back of his neck added thoughtfully, "Maybe we will be freed."

Avi rolled his eyes. "And if we are stuck here for who knows how long, then what?"

"Then we are stuck here and must make the best of it."

Avi shrugged his shoulders and gazed out the one tiny window in their room. "You are very optimistic. I wish I could be that way."

Malnutrition and famine ravaged the Jews in the camp, yet the Japanese guards ate rice at their meals, rice being a luxury because of its scarcity. Isaac's face had become elongated by his loss of weight, and dark rings hung under his eyes. The confidence that he had once exuded diminished.

Staring at the floor, Isaac moaned, "I have heard about those who have died."

"Why? From what?" asked Avi, looking intently at Isaac.

Shaking his head, Isaac added, "No medicine. No food. Some died from starvation, others from dysentery or typhoid. Children died too. I wonder how long we will last here."

Joseph looked up and ran his fingers through the small beard covering his shrinking round face. "Please, that's enough talking about death. Our time is better spent studying and praying."

Isaac replied in a beaten tone, "I pray with all my strength, and with all my soul, yet still we stay trapped here waiting to die."

"Pray harder. God will listen."

Isaac sighed and inched his way between the three-tiered bunk beds back to his bed and picked up his prayer book.

One morning, a Japanese guard entered the building, shouted words in Japanese, and threw a bundle tied with brown string on the floor. Isaac picked it up and untied the string that held a pack of mail. Quickly he read the names on each envelope, handing it to the appropriate student.

"How does anyone know that we are here?" Avi asked skeptically. "How does anyone know that we are even alive in Japan?

Isaac handed Joseph a letter.

"Think back to before we left," Isaac replied. "We completed forms, answering questions about ourselves and our families and what our plans of escape were. Those information forms were collected by one of the Jewish agencies, and that is how they know where we are."

Flipping through the letters, he removed several and placed them at the back of the pack. "Who are those for?" inquired Avi.

"Samuel and Mordechai," Isaac responded sadly.

Joseph, seeing the return address was his home, kissed the letter and, walking to his bunk, focused his memory on the faces of his father and mother.

Joseph read the letter slowly.

May 9, 1940

Dear Joseph,
  Thank you for your letters. Each letter helps elevate our spirits during a sad time in our lives. Since the war began, life will never be the same again. Oh, the killing, it does not stop. Germans are everywhere. What is worse are the Polish people who join in for the adventure of killing Jews and stealing everything of value from Jewish homes. The Germans allow them to do this.
  Food is scarce. Each day becomes another challenge for us to survive. We must survive, and we will survive until this horrible war ends. One day, we shall be reunited as a family again. Your grandparents suffer as do each of us, family and friends alike.
  Swastikas were painted on the synagogue doors and windows. A few days later, the hoodlums shattered the windows and they broke down the doors. They looted and burned the synagogue. Flames reached high into the sky. Brown smoke clogged our lungs. It was hard to breathe. By a mira-

cle, your father saved the Torah. Everything else was consumed by the fire. The people of Chemelnick struggle to survive this brutality and in other villages Jews suffer as well.

Wouldn't this be a good time for the Messiah to come?

No matter how difficult life appears at times, always have faith in God. He will protect us. Above all, you must live. You must survive. If we do not live through the war, I know you will carry our memory with you for all of your life.

Our precious son, we pray with all our strength, with all our soul, and that we will be together again after the war. Stay well, dear Joseph. Take good care of yourself. We miss you and we love you with all of our hearts.

*With all our love,
Momma and Papa*

Joseph read the letter again. Tears swelled in his eyes and trickled down his cheeks. He made no effort to stop them. He remembered his mother's face—the love in her eyes, the slight curve in her nose, her gentle mouth, and the wrinkles in her forehead. Joseph thought of her appearance as being that of an angel. Next his memory brought forth his father with his eyes filled with wisdom and love and his once-dark-brown beard now mixed with speckles of gray. *Is my memory correct?* Joseph wondered. *I should have paid closer attention. Maybe I am remembering it wrong. What I remember from my home and family, I may remember it differently in the future, if I remember it at all. Can that happen to me? I wish I could see them again and take closer notice. I was oblivious. My life was spent learning, and my family spent theirs working, as most people do, and we did not take enough time to notice the details of those we love and to store them away in our memory, to be recalled in the future.* Speaking aloud to himself, he said, "I want to be home."

The next morning, Isaac and Joseph stood in the office of the commandant of the detention camp. Through an interpreter, Isaac requested permission to travel to the US Consulate in Yokahama to collect the thirty-nine visas that the Lubavitcher rabbi obtained for them in New York. These visas would allow the group of thirty-nine students entry into the United States. The Japanese commandant, who had never seen a Jew before, was courteous and granted the request. The next morning, Isaac and Joseph departed from Kobe by ship on a nine-hour journey carrying folders filled with documents. Yokahama was the largest port in Japan and its second largest city after Tokyo.

"It is amazing that I received that letter from Brooklyn," Isaac proclaimed to Joseph. "Now we have a chance of reaching America and not having to go to Shanghai. Why should we go to Shanghai, for who knows how long, when we can go to America now? The rabbi has arranged it all. New York is the place to go." He smiled and with a gleam in his eyes added, "When the war ends, I will return home. I look forward to that day." Changing the subject, Isaac leaned over the railing and pointed to the sea. "Look at the color of the sea. It is blue farther away from the shore and two shades of green closer to the shore. I wonder what the color of the sea is around New York."

"I hope and pray you are right," Joseph replied with uncertainty.

After disembarking in Yokahama, a rickshaw, pulled along by an emaciated Japanese man wearing little more than a loincloth, carried them through the narrow dirt streets. The streets were crowded with people, rickshaws, bicycles, cars, and vendors displaying their wares. It was an atmosphere of seemingly disorder. The smell of the city contained a disturbing mixture of the aromas of food being cooked and sewerage. Joseph remembered what he had considered large crowds in Chemelnick on a Friday afternoon. Friday was the day for shopping for the Sabbath. Compared to the population of Chemelnick, Yokahama was gigantic. "I suppose it is all relative to what one is accustomed," he said to himself.

The flag of the United States of America with its forty-eight stars and red and white stripes blew gently in the soft breeze on the flagpole over the US Consulate. The consulate building was large compared with the surrounding Japanese buildings. Constructed of stone, it stood higher than the wooden structures in Yokahama. The facade was gray and covered with dirt and patches of mildew. The windows needed a washing. Eight steps led to the entrance doors, and two United States army guards.

Approaching the guards, Isaac spoke in the best English he could mutter. "We have an appointment with the consulate."

"Name?" the soldier questioned.

"Huh?" Isaac mumbled in confusion.

"What is your name?" the soldier repeated.

"Sorry. I did not understand. My name is Isaac Levy."

Joseph whispered to Isaac, "When did you learn English?"

"In my spare time," replied Isaac.

Scanning through a visitor's list, the guard ordered, "Go ahead inside," as he opened the door for them. Inside, a wide, long hall with doors on both sides opened into offices. The floors were marble and needed polishing. To the right was a broad staircase winding up to the second floor. In front of them, seated at a desk, was a young American woman in a military uniform. She motioned for them to come to the desk and gave them directions to the proper office. Entering the office, Isaac and Joseph sat and waited with a dozen other people. A low murmur of voices drifted through the waiting area and stopped whenever an American voice announced the name of the next person to be interviewed.

An hour later, their names were called, and Isaac and Joseph entered the office. An American, about forty-five years of age, dressed in a dark-blue suit, a white shirt, and a striped red tie, sat at his desk. He was heavyset with broad shoulders, clean-shaven, and his brown eyes appeared enlarged by the lenses of his eye glasses with their thin black frames.

Glancing at Isaac and Joseph, the American consul noted, "I have the request before me for thirty-nine entry visas into the United States. There are several questions I need answered regarding this group." He paused and gestured with his hand toward two chairs. "Please sit down."

Isaac and Joseph obeyed. "First, do you have parents living in Europe?"

"Yes," replied Isaac, and he translated for Joseph. Joseph nodded.

"What about the others in the group? Do they have parents living in Europe?"

"Yes, we all do. We are fleeing from the Nazis, and that is why we want to go to America."

The consul clasped his hands together and studied the faces of these young men. He looked out the window and watched the clouds drift slowly through the blue sky, all the time squeezing his hands together and then relaxing them. He had been in this position many times before, but it still bothered him to have to reject humanitarian requests for entry into the United States.

"Your request for the visas must be denied at this time. I am sorry."

"I do not understand," Isaac said in shock. "Why is this happening? Is there anything wrong on the applications? What are we supposed to do?" Isaac did not translate for Joseph, who watched the scene in bewilderment.

The consul repeated his denial and walked to the door waiting for them to leave. Isaac and Joseph sat stunned.

"Please," the consul said. "I am truly sorry. I am obligated to follow the policies set forth by the United States government."

"What is the reason that our request is denied?" asked Isaac. "Our lives may depend on these visas." Isaac made a fist and pressed it to his mouth, lost in thought. "In America," he continued, "our lives will be safe until the war ends. After the war, we will return home to our families.

No one knows what will happen to us in Shanghai. If these visas are denied, then at least, please, I beg you, give me the reason for the denial."

Biting his upper lip, he removed his glasses and stared into the eyes first of Joseph and then Isaac. "I will give you a brief explanation, although it is not required for me to do so." The consul turned away from Isaac and Joseph and speaking in a monotone said, "Under the administration of President Franklin Roosevelt, the policy is that if applicants have family in Europe and are of Jewish descent, then the request is to be denied. Until the war ends, European Jews are to be excluded from entering the United States." Looking directly at them, he added in an apologetic voice, "This is not my policy, but it is my duty to enforce it. My advice is that you go to Shanghai. After the war, if you change your mind and do not want to return home, apply again for an entry visa into the United States. One more bit of advice, go to Shanghai as soon as possible. I sense that war with Japan is imminent." Pausing, he concluded, "Sometimes life does not seem fair. This is one of those times."

"But please help me understand how this policy came into existence?" Isaac pleaded.

Pacing around the room, the consul looked out the window, started to speak, grimaced, and continued pacing. Finally, after taking a deep breath, he replied softly, "What I offer to you now is my opinion, to try to help you understand the reason you are being denied entry into the United States. Those who govern the United States and Great Britain decided that they will not make a concerted effort to save Jews during the war. They fear that if this policy was reversed, Germany and its allies will release thousands of Jews, forcing the United States to take in many, and forcing Great Britain to allow Jews into Palestine. Neither country wants to do that."

Joseph saw the dismay in Isaac's face. "Translate what is happening?"

Isaac translated quickly in Yiddish, and Joseph answered, "God must have a different plan for us."

Isaac sat stunned.

"Do you understand what I have said?" asked the consul.

Isaac nodded.

The consul led them to the door.

"It was good of you to tell us. I know it was a difficult thing for you to do. You are a good man," said Isaac.

Joseph spoke to Isaac, "May God bless and protect him."

Isaac translated. The consul said, "Thank you both."

The trip back to Kobe was thoughtful for Isaac and Joseph. "Divine Providence interceded in our life as it always does," said Joseph. "God wants us to live in Shanghai until the war ends. We told everyone that is where we planned to go, and that is where we will go. Going to America would have been a dream, but God has postponed that dream."

"Living in Shanghai will bring a life of hardship," replied Isaac. "Had we gone to America, life would have been much better."

"That is true for many. Yet I believe that the attitude one brings to the situation determines its outcome. We must not let fear overwhelm us."

"Suppose life in Shanghai is unbearable. What kind of attitude will change that?"

"Our attitude will not change the circumstance. It will change the way we look at things, and when we change the way we look at things, the things we look at change."

"I know that," said Isaac. "Why must we suffer as we have throughout history? Jews pray and have faith in God. We love him, and yet we suffer. That is a reality and not a difference of attitude."

"In our studies, we have learned that life is not fair. The consul told us that too. At those times, we must learn to accept the hurt and to accept the pain, but we must go on trying to seek joy, contentment, love, and fulfillment in life. If we do not do that, then what else is left us?"

CHAPTER 11

Shanghai, 1940–1941

On July 7, 1937, the Japanese declared war on China. Four months later, on November 9, the Japanese conquered the city of Shanghai. Four thousand Jews lived in the city. One month later, on December 13, in east-central China, the city of Nanking fell, and the Japanese conquerors showed no restraint in their brutality, cruelty, and killing of thousands of Nanking's residents. Nanking, 155 miles from Shanghai, had been the capital of Chiang Kai-shek's Nationalist government between 1928 and 1937.

The thirty-nine students from Poland arrived in Shanghai[*] on a typical summer day, hot, muggy, with torrential rains in the afternoon. Garbage floated in the river, and a stink emanated over the city as the rain mixed with the garbage in the streets. The pungent smell overpowered their senses. Isaac looked at the murky-brown water mixed

---

[*] Many Jews who had received visas in Kaunas did not use them, instead remaining in Lithuania. Their unused visas were collected by Jewish relief agencies and redistributed to other Jews. On August 14, 1940, a visa with the number 1,746, out of the 2,139 that Chiune Sugihara issued, arrived for Joseph Shalosky. Joseph was on his way to Shanghai.

with the garbage in the river and, with a feeling of resignation, said to Joseph, "Look at the difference between the color of this filthy water and the clear blue-green sea around Kobe. This river is a putrid-muddy color. I hope that this is not a sign from God of what awaits us in Shanghai."

"We will know shortly," replied Joseph flatly.

Stepping off the gangplank, Joseph stood in the most crowded city in China. Ostentatious office buildings and bank buildings stood above the skyline over the harbor on the Huangpu River. In Kobe, Joseph studied about Shanghai and China and learned that from the midnineteenth century, Shanghai grew into a densely populated manufacturing city. During its one hundred years of trade with the west, the Chinese offered special privileges to the foreign government officials and foreign merchants. By creating international settlements where foreigners lived, there existed a sharp contrast between the wealthy residences of the foreigners and the dismal poverty of the Chinese living outside the settlements.

Carrying their bags, the group walked toward the ghetto. Rickshaws with large wheels rolled past them in the crowded streets. Seeing the affluent, wearing their tunics made of silk, traveling in horse-drawn carts, reminded Joseph of Yokahama. He noticed that the commoner wore a dark-blue jacket made of cotton, thus class distinction was visible through the clothing. Hordes of dark-blue jackets crowded out other colors.

The Japanese controlled the city and quartered the new Jewish immigrants in the ghetto. One hundred thousand Chinese already lived there. The day after they arrived, they found their way to Mr. Zev Barlofsky's home. On a regular basis, Barlofsky gave money to Jewish refugees and had agreed to provide some to the three of them. Joseph and his friends were disappointed to hear that Barlofsky would not give them anything because he claimed that he provided enough already. Unknown to the three, that night, Barlofsky had a dream. In it, he pictured a rabbi with a long white beard who told him that he must continue to help the impoverished. The following morning, Barlofsky told this to the rabbi at the yeshiva, and the rabbi showed him a picture of the Lubavitch rabbi. Astounded to see the same face that had appeared in his dream, Barlofsky continued to give money to support the students.

Days passed quickly, and the students spent most of their time studying. One morning, Joseph peered through the dirty window in their narrow dimly lit room and looked at the gates surrounding the ghetto. Before becoming part of the ghetto, the building they lived in, along with most others, was situated in the poorest section of the city. The ghetto consisted of very old, decrepit wooden buildings constructed close to one another, causing the streets to be narrow. Neglect caused splintering, cracking, peeling, chipping, and filth to overwhelm the buildings, making them seem like they were about to collapse. Besides studying, his thoughts were riveted to two things: obtaining a permit to leave the ghetto until curfew and continuing to bribe the Japanese guards to allow food into the ghetto. The money for the bribes arrived regularly from Brooklyn, and even that money did not buy much food.

One morning, Isaac, Avi, and Joseph were in their room. Isaac, whose tattered clothing hung on him like a scarecrow, said to Joseph, "If we survive living in Shanghai, these terrible conditions will become a memory, an unpleasant one, and who wants a memory like this?"

"Pretend you are listening to a record," answered Joseph patiently. "On it, there are several songs. Suppose you do not like one of the songs, what would you do? You lift the needle and place it in the groove for the next song. It is the same with your memory. When you think of unpleasant things, skip over them. Play a pleasant memory."

Isaac shot a glance at Joseph and skeptically asked, "And how is that done?"

"Whenever an unpleasant memory comes forward," Joseph continued, "force your brain to remember a person or an event that you enjoyed. By doing this, it will stop you from being upset. Try to lock in that good memory. Maybe it is your mother's smile, or a celebration you attended, or the touch of your father's hand, or a delicious Sabbath meal. Another possibility is to remember the famous saying that 'this too shall pass.' For example, think back to our lives at the yeshiva in Natrusk. How difficult it must have seemed. First there was the entrance exam and the requirement to learn two hundred pages of Gemorrah. Next we forced ourselves to adjust to living at the yeshiva, away from our parents. It was difficult, and of course, we all complained there was not enough food. We compared their portions with those our mothers gave us. In the beginning, it seemed we would not be successful there. Do you remember?"

"Yes, I remember," said Avi with a sigh, his thoughts lost in memory. "I would rather forget what life was like living there, but it is instilled in my memory. Certain memories just stay with you no matter the circumstances." He grimaced trying to move away from that memory. "At the other yeshiva here in Shanghai, the one outside the ghetto, they have enough food not to go hungry. Rabbi Aaron Cuttler of the Vaad Hatzolah arranged for food for all of the students in Shanghai, but not for us."

"Why not us?" asked Joseph.

"We are Lubavitch, and he does not like Lubavitch," replied Isaac. "I wonder whether the chief rabbi of Shanghai, Rabbi Ashkenazi, knows what is happening."

"Think of the positive," said Joseph. "Do you remember what happened the day after we arrived? I remember that well, but that was months ago. His dream was Divine Providence. My dream is to leave China. As the war drags on, it seems I will be here forever." Rubbing his hands together, he fidgeted with his fingers before continuing. "When the war news arrives, it makes me miss my family more. I have mixed emotions, because I believe that leaving Poland was good, but being away from them is difficult. So I preserve my memories and pray that I see my family again. If it is not meant to be, then my departure from them will have been a last time, and in life, there are too many last times."

Isaac smacked his hands on his thighs and abruptly changed the subject. "The war news is not encouraging. A few months after we left home, I think it was in September, the Germans bombed London for the first time. Two months later, they destroyed the English city of Coventry."

Joseph interrupted, "That is enough about the war. Instead, concentrate on things you remember from your home. Focus your memory on happy details of good events. Since you have the feeling that this unsettled life will never end, think of those wonderful memories. The good memories will drive away the upsetting thoughts."

"How do you know all this?" asked Avi.

Shrugging his shoulders, he replied, "I do not know. It just comes to me. Only God knows."

Avi and Isaac resumed their studies. Joseph removed a letter from his pocket. It was wrinkled from having been unfolded and folded many times. Joseph read it again. It was in his father's handwriting. His father wrote in Polish and German. His mother wrote in Yiddish. During his months in Kobe, he received letters from his parents. In Shanghai, no mail arrived. He cherished each letter from his parents.

June 1, 1940

Dear Joseph,

I pray that this letter finds you well. Your letters to us are like messages from heaven. They give us encouragement that you, our only child, will survive.

I would like to tell you that life in Chemelnick prospers. I cannot. The war has brought horrors to our people throughout Poland. The Germans bombed the orphanage in Natrusk, the town where you went to yeshiva. It was the first town bombed. At the yeshiva, Polish thugs broke in and stole valuable items. They beat up the two guards and beat several of the students. The guards were unarmed. The government did not protect the Jews.

From Natrusk to Bialystok, the Germans bombed the Jewish towns and villages. Dead bodies lined the roads. What the planes did not destroy, the German soldiers did. They burned the buildings left standing after the bombing. Flames lit the night sky. The Germans use fire as their weapon of evil. Not only do Jews suffer. On May 13, less than one month ago, the Germans destroyed Rotterdam, the largest city in Holland. Imagine a city founded in the 13th century senselessly destroyed by the Germans.

The Germans kill Jews whether they are observant or not. And they do what they can to humiliate us. They shave the heads of Jewish women, calling the women animals on two feet. Jews are stoned whenever they go out to search for food, and food is scarce. I pray that this war ends soon, for how much more suffering must we endure. On our neighbor's shortwave radio, we heard that a few days ago the British Navy and an armada of small boats rescued their soldiers, about 225,000, plus 112,000 French and Belgian soldiers. This happened at a town called Dunkerque in France. Perhaps this is a sign that things will get better for us.

I do know from history that when tyrants or kings stand on the backs of Jews, they will not reign for long.

WILLIAM TANENBAUM

Stay well, dear son. As it is written, God should have pity on the child. Take good care of yourself. May God bless and protect you.

With all of our love,
Momma and Poppa

CHAPTER 12

Shanghai, 1943–1944

After the Japanese bombed Pearl Harbor on December 7, 1941, living conditions in Shanghai became worse for both Jews and Chinese. The winters were bitter cold and damp, and summers were very hot and humid. Later in December, another group of Jewish students from the town of Mir in Poland arrived in Shanghai. These students from the Mirer Yeshiva were famous for their mastery of the Talmud.

The harsh winter had taken its toll on Isaac. He appeared bedraggled, clothing in disarray, hair unwashed and matted on his head, and speckles of dirt dotted his forehead. His once-new suit appeared shabby after sleeping in it during the freezing winter nights to keep warm. Isaac, Joseph, and Avi worked as book publishers, supplying books to the students. The work space consisted of a small room, the size of a storage closet, illuminated by two light bulbs. Dark shadows drifted across the cluttered floor. A mimeograph machine, cartons filled with paper, books piled in corners, a wooden table, and crumbled, ink-stained paper made it difficult to walk in the room.

Joseph pleaded with Isaac and Avi to concentrate on book publishing and not on deprivation and suffering. He felt weary, and his loss of weight caused exaggerated lines near the corners of his mouth and under his cheekbones. Thinking of his parents weighed heavy on his mind, and he doubted whether he made the right decision in leaving. Joseph's thoughts returned to the present, and he spoke to Isaac and Avi with authority. "The students depend on us for books, and we are the ones in charge of printing them. Let's work and not think about other things or other places. I know how you detest this life here, but for me, it is the attitude one brings to the situation. I try to make the best of what exists here. My other choice is to be bitter and complain about things I have no control over. And of course, there are things that upset me, but it is best not to speak about them. No one wants to dwell on the sorrows of someone else."

"I suppose you are right," countered Avi. Looking disheveled and living in constant anxiety, Avi's eyes reflected sadness and were glassy because he had a cold. "I will try to change my attitude. I do not know why it is difficult for me to be more optimistic." He shook his head in doubt.

"Meanwhile," Joseph replied, "I think we should consider our job as publishers as beneficial to the students. The more difficult part is bribing the Japanese guards to permit us to distribute them. I often ask myself why we do this since we do not earn anything except ink-stained hands." Looking at his hands, Joseph smiled and continued. "The mimeograph machine doesn't print well all the time, and one day we will have no more ink for it, and when there is no more ink, we will do another job. After all, one must do the right thing, even when it is difficult or inconvenient to do. It is easy to be gracious when life is peaceful. The challenge is to do the right thing when you do not feel like helping."

"We will study and work and learn to wait patiently," Isaac said. "Remember what Ecclesiastes wrote, 'A season is set for everything, a time for every experience under heaven.'"

"I know," Avi agreed as he put his head down. Stammering, he added, "You know that I have faith in God, but I have such pain being here, being away from home. I miss my mother hugging me, and I miss the kind, loving way that my father spoke to me. I miss my sisters. I even miss the way they teased me. Continuing this life with the expectation that someday it will be better seems impossible for me. I would rather be home with my family and try to help them and to suffer whatever they suffer rather than be here publishing books."

Isaac and Joseph sat in solemn silence. Avi had expressed what they were thinking about but would not say. He forced them to remember their past life, a life that was no more, a life that was now a memory. Joseph covered his face with his hands and rocked back and forth, his mind far away from Shanghai. Isaac maneuvered between the cartons on the floor and went to the door.

"Time to change the mood," Isaac said. "Let's go for a walk."

Chaos prevailed in Shanghai after the bombing in Hawaii. Japan invoked harsher decrees against the Chinese and foreign residents. Passes were required to enter and leave the ghetto. They walked through the crowded streets to the Suzhou Creek, a tributary of the Huangpu River. On the way, they saw men pulling large wheeled rickshaws, some filled with people, others heavy with goods. In a rickshaw, a wealthy male passenger could be identified by the bald spot on top of his head and the small circular tuft of hair with a pigtail hanging down his back. Electric tram cars with people hanging out on all sides moved along the streets. Men stood in front of opium dens, soliciting pedestrians to enter. Coolies in workshops sewed swaths of cloth into clothing.

They watched as large ships and smaller craft headed toward the main river from the tributary. A crisp breeze chased away the bad odors of the industrial factories that dumped their waste into the Huangpu. Upriver from Shanghai, a large electric power station and a cotton mill used the river for dumping their waste.

"Do you know how this war started between Japan and China?" asked Isaac. Without waiting for a reply, he continued like a professor giving students a lecture.

"It began in 1932 after Japan invaded China. Japan sent troops to protect thirty thousand Japanese living in Zhabei, the Little Tokyo section of Shanghai. But the official war began on July 7, 1937, after the Japanese claimed that a Japanese sailor mysteriously disappeared. Their troops went on war alert, but the missing sailor reappeared, and Japan needed another excuse to start a war. The excuse happened after two Japanese military men in uniform were ordered to stop at the entrance to a Chinese military airfield. The Japanese refused to stop and were shot. The Japanese navy steamed up the Huangpu River."

"That's enough," interrupted Avi. "I am not concerned about history. I'm concerned about how we ever leave Shanghai and return home."

It began to drizzle as they explored different streets, each one bringing them new sights. Coolies carried goods in large baskets, each basket attached to a long pole, the pole carried over the shoulder. Umbrellas for sale hung on a line in stalls. Japanese soldiers, with bayonets fixed to their rifles, patrolled the streets. Joseph and his friends knew about the mistaken bombing of the Bund, when, one month after the war started, five Chinese bombers tried to sink the Japanese flagship, the *Idzumo*. The planes were shot down. Before they crashed, they jettisoned their shrapnel bombs, and one hit on the Bund and destroyed the Palace Hotel. Seven hundred died. Another bomb hit Frenchtown at the Great World Amusement Park, and two thousand three hundred died.

They continued walking toward the Hongkew section. Since December 7, the Japanese took control of the International Settlement, the French Concession, and reigned over all of Shanghai. The Japanese flag, with its distinctive bright-red sun on a clear white background, surrounded the perimeter of the International Settlement. One of the largest jails in the world stood near the corner of Ward and Chusan Roads, one block from the Oihel Moshe, the only Orthodox synagogue in Shanghai, and the center of Jewish refugee life. American and British sailors, who had surrendered to the Japanese, were held in the prison. A Japanese machine gun post, with its guns aimed at the prison, was set up near the steps of a European-style café. Three soldiers sat behind the guns.

"Remember before the war," asked Joseph, "when we would see Americans and British walking in the streets? They must be in hiding for fear of being captured and put in the concentration camps outside of Shanghai."

"You tell me not to worry," replied Avi, "and all you talk about is the war. I hear war history from Isaac and Japanese occupation comments from you."

Joseph looked at Avi, took a deep breath, and turned away.

The drizzle turned to a steady rain and sections of unpaved streets turned to mud as they walked quickly back to the Hongkou Ghetto.

Later that evening, Joseph wrote a letter to his parents.

March 11, 1942

Dear Momma and Poppa,
I miss you very much. I reread your letters often. Since arriving in Shanghai, I have had no mail from you. The last letters I received were in Kobe, and that seems long ago. I hope and pray that you are well. Life in Shanghai is bearable. As you may expect, since the Japanese entered the war, life is more difficult. At least, they let us struggle for ourselves and occasionally do not steal the shipments of food sent to us from Brooklyn, New York. I sent you a package of food. I paid a Japanese guard to ship it to you. He has done it for others. Messages

from America say that the packages arrive. I do not complain because I know what you suffer in Europe. I have learned how Jews in Europe suffer. Is it true about the killings and the concentration camps? I pray that it is a rumor, a bad rumor.

Our group of thirty-nine students study at the Mirer Yeshiva every day. Regardless of the hardships here, I pray all of the services daily, for no matter what happens, I will always maintain my faith in God and my belief in Judaism. Neither the Germans nor the Japanese will undo that.

Please keep writing here. Maybe I will receive some of your letters. I love you both and pray for your safety. I still look forward to the day we are reunited after the war. I always remember our life together, especially Momma's delicious Sabbath dinners and Poppa's loving smile. Again, I repeat how much I miss you.

Your loving son,
Joseph

One year later, the Japanese issued a decree declaring all Jews living outside the ghetto must relocate inside the Hongkou Ghetto within three months, and not after June 30, 1943. Life in the ghetto was worse than life outside it, and now those refugees who could afford to live outside became desperate to abide by the decree. Many traded larger, more comfortable houses for smaller, crumbling ones inside the ghetto. Failure to obey the Japanese meant being put in jail or being killed.

Learning about the decree, Joseph spoke to Isaac and Avi, "One never knows what life has in store. I take pity on their plight and believe the saying 'Man proposes and God disposes' is true. It seems that based on our knowledge and experience, we make choices and exercise our free will expecting a certain result." Speaking in an authoritative voice, Joseph continued, "Yet our ego and vanity prevent us from accepting the fact that many times the results are beyond our control. Man craves to be in control of his life. Just think of things you have planned and how often the results differed from what you expected. All of the refugees living outside the ghetto believed they were secure for the duration of the war. Many people claim unexpected results occur because of fate or coincidence or destiny or luck, but for me, it is all divine providence."

After June 30, 1943, Jews who did not move into the ghetto were imprisoned and held in the same cells with Chinese criminals. The cells were infested with lice and rats, and typhoid fever was rampant in the jail. Some Jewish refugees converted to Christianity and were allowed to remain living outside of the ghetto. In addition, the converts received fifty American dollars and a certificate stating they were Catholics.

Joseph learned about the conversions and said to Isaac and Avi, "Let us say a blessing for those who converted. I would not do it, but under these circumstances of hardship and suffering, I can see why some Jews do."

"You refuse to see the reality of what is happening here," Avi blurted. "It does not matter if the Jews are religious or not. All that matters is that Jews are being imprisoned or converted. I suppose that we should consider ourselves fortunate not being in either category." After outbursts like this from Avi, Joseph and Isaac said nothing.

Forced by the Japanese to move, the Mirer Yeshiva purchased two attached houses on Wayside Road. The common wall between them was broken and resulted in a yeshiva consisting of one large building. Services and studying were done in the auditorium on the second floor. Hundreds of students at the yeshiva used the prayer books and the books of the Talmud many times a day. The books were brought to Shanghai from Poland and, as they became frayed, caused more printing work for Joseph, Isaac, and Avi.

Isaac nipped at his thumb and despondently looked around the tiny printing room and gazed at the dark walls. "What does it mean when the breakdown of the prayer books coincides with the breakdown of the food supply? Remember after the attack on Pearl Harbor, kosher food was not available in Shanghai. Shortages existed for most food items, especially butter, margarine, eggs, fresh vegetables, fruits, and meat." Staring into Avi's eyes, Isaac gently spoke, "It is a difficult time for all of us, but we are better off in Shanghai than in Poland."

"God is testing our endurance," said Joseph in a whisper, his energy depleted by a shortage of food. "Just as Abraham was tested by God, who imposed painful and difficult trials upon him, we too are being tested. The Hebrew word for *test* literally means 'to be lifted up.' That means for every difficulty and every suffering that God throws at us, it is a challenge through which we can become spiritually elevated. I believe that one day this period of our life will be nothing more than a bad memory. After all, not all memories are good. It is just better to remember the good ones and not to dwell on the bad ones."

"May we live that long," Avi said. After having lost twenty-five pounds, his clothing hung on his body like a crumbled cloth bag, and his immune system was weakened. He coughed and quickly covered his mouth. The cough continued and had lingered for weeks. Life in Shanghai meant living without essentials, without medicine, without heat during the freezing winter days, without sufficient food, and without warm clothing. Avi added, "I have heard that Janovich died of a combination of tuberculosis and starvation. Many Jews here have committed suicide because of the terrible conditions."

"One must have faith in God, and then suicide is never a possibility," Isaac said. "Meanwhile, I try to remember simple things, like what it feels like to have a hot bath or delicious chicken soup. Just remembering these things makes me feel better. I thought that only big things mattered in life, and they would be the things to remember. Here I am in Shanghai, and now a hot bath and a bowl of soup would be a treat. I think of all the times that I took them for granted and did not pay attention to what is now a luxury in my memory."

Joseph remembered his walk yesterday and swallowed hard as the memories leaped forward. He saw Chinese families living in tents, their houses having been confiscated by Japanese soldiers. He heard children cry and saw many children not wearing clothing. The tents had no heat, no electricity, and no running water. Joseph thought, *During this winter, many of them will die.* He remembered the children and adults picking through garbage of the Japanese searching for food in the hope of finding a morsel to keep them alive one day more. Flooded streets contained dead rats. Joseph asked himself, *Will my future memories be filled with suffering, death, and emptiness?*

"Meanwhile, look at us," Avi whimpered with sadness in his voice and tears streaking across his face. "We barely survive here. We are like the Chinese outside the ghetto, no fuel for heat, hardly any food, toilets that do not flush anymore, and people dying from starvation or from freezing to death. I believed from the time I left Poland, that when the war ended, I would return home. I had no doubt of this, but very slowly the horrors of the war forced my belief to collapse. I started pretending that life would return to the way it was before the war. Hiding behind a mask of pretending, I knew life would not be the same again. Now all that remains is a dream, and I cling to it." Tears trickled down Avi's face. "The dream gives me hope, and hope gives me strength. Witnessing the reality of war, the illusion of returning home has ended." Tears swelled in Isaac's and Joseph's eyes. "Saying goodbye to my family may have been the last time I will ever see them."

"As Joseph always tells us," Isaac said with wet cheeks, "we must be strong."

"Tell us that at dinner tonight, Isaac," Avi replied, his voice trembling and tears in his eyes. "Remember to cut the bread extra thin so you can hold it up to the light and see whether there are any worms in it."

"That is enough," snapped Joseph, wiping tears from his face with the back of his hand. "You are both right. We must be strong, and we must do our best to take care of ourselves. This is our personal battle, our personal war, and we will win. Any man can, even under these circumstances, decide what shall become of him, both mentally and spiritually. He may retain his human dignity, even in Shanghai, under harsh and brutal Japanese occupation. It is our spiritual freedom, our belief in God, which cannot be taken away. This is not a moment for quotes, yet one quote from Nietzsche comes to mind, 'He who has a why to live can bear with almost any how.' It is strange the thoughts that pop up in your mind without knowing why. Yet if we follow that idea, our lives will possess dignity and hope."

The winter of 1943 brought with it the usual heavy rains drenching the city. The Huangpu River overflowed its banks, and because of inadequate drainage, dark-mud-colored water flooded Shanghai. Filthy brackish water poured into the ground floor of apartments, houses, office buildings, and stores, destroying shops, stalls, restaurants, and tents. Worst of all, bloated dead human bodies, having died from starvation, typhoid fever, cholera, tuberculosis, or viral infection, floated down the flooded streets. Floating in the floodwaters with the dead bodies were garbage and dead rats.

As the harsh, cold winter turned into spring, the floods subsided. The war wreaked havoc on the trees and plants, and few remained to bloom. Summer arrived accompanied by extreme heat, monsoon rains, and more flooding. The three years in Shanghai had taken its toll on their appearance. Avi dreaded looking at himself in the mirror because he looked like a ghost, his features sunken into his pale-white face. Isaac lacked energy, his eyes dull and listless, and his usual enthusiasm gone. Joseph resembled a shrunken dwarf because of the weight loss on his small body. Their struggle, like those of the Chinese, was for survival. After they obtained a permit to leave the ghetto, each one checked that the round metal blue pin was fastened to his coat. The pin, issued by the Japanese authorities, acted as a permit allowing them to move through Shanghai and was valid for one month. As they moved about the city, Joseph pondered, "Consider our lives in Shanghai as being a part of history, although not a pleasant part. In the future, you will remember these days and relate the story to your children and grandchildren. Your story will seem to them as ancient family history. One day, long after we have physically passed from this earth, there will be no one to remember us as specific individuals. Only the story will be remembered."

Isaac gazed at Joseph and felt the bond of friendship that was building between them. Smiling, Isaac said, "Let's continue walking. The weather is good today, and it is better than having those cold winter winds from the north freezing us through our clothing."

They walked toward the river in the direction of the Garden Bridge, an arched metallic structure with steel bands crisscrossing one another. Makeshift shelters cluttered the streets. Dead bodies lay in the road. They passed through the streets clogged with people shoving and pushing one another. The boys had learned that men who wore red tunic-like jackets were considered upper-class society whereas those in plain blue jackets represented the working class and peasants. In the 1937 battle for Shanghai, burned-out buildings stood as reminders that Shanghai was part of the war zone. Open-air stalls covered with large white sheets protected the goods for sale against the sun's heat and against the flies. Banners hung from windows and from stores announcing an election.[*]

Approaching the river, they saw streets filled with shanties built precariously on elevated slender poles above the ground. These one-room wooden huts housed entire families. Other makeshift shelters cluttered the streets. The stink of the sewerage, floodwaters, dead bodies and dead rats, and garbage inundated their smell. Often what sounded like moaning, but was really singing, reached their ears.

Avi weaved his way through the streets trying to observe everything in detail and make it stick in his memory. "I will never return to Shanghai again," Avi said.

"When you say you will not return here again," Joseph replied, "I say that is optimistic. We do not know if we will survive the war or whether we will ever leave Shanghai, and you already surmise that you will not return here. May it be from your lips to God's ears."

They laughed, something they did not do often. On the way back to the ghetto, they saw Chinese squatted on dilapidated seats that looked like benches without backs, talking to one another. A few were drinking hot tea. Passing food stands, they smelled the aroma of the food cooking, and for a few moments, the stench of the garbage and dead bodies faded.

---

[*] Chiang Kai-shek, formerly the leader of the Whampa Military Academy, won the election. His goal was to fight the Communists in China, not the Japanese.

FUTURE MEMORIES

That night Joseph fell into a deep sleep and dreamed that he saw his parents smiling. It was not clear where they were. A mysterious light surrounded them. His mother, Sophie, hugged him, a gentle hug around his neck. Gentle best described her in her treatment of people. Her eyes brightened whenever she performed an act of kindness. Joseph felt her warmth around his neck. She floated away, and his father, Jacob, came into view and hugged him. Joseph felt the power of his father's arms embrace his back and shoulders. His father's strength emanated through the home and in the synagogue. His devotion to his family and friends instilled his strength into them. His father floated into the distance toward his mother. The rest of the scene was void. All he saw were his parents. Words floated across the void, "If you want to accomplish a good deed, God will help you accomplish it. We love you. May God bless and protect you." As they spoke, a dark swirl of wind, like a tornado, swallowed them, and the dream became black. In the blackness, he vaguely heard what sounded like a whisper, "We love you," as their voices faded. Startled, Joseph awoke. Perspiration soaked his neck, shoulders, and forehead. He made a promise to himself that he would keep the memory of his parent's hugs and smiles forever.

CHAPTER 13

Shanghai, 1944–1945

The next day, Joseph skimmed through a recent issue of *The Shanghai Jewish Chronicle.* He learned that most of Europe was under Nazi control. Reflecting on the group that helped him in the forest in Bulgaria, he thought of their desire to stay and fight the Germans. *Were they captured and killed?* Using their knowledge and past experiences, they believed they were secure. That was their prediction of the future. *It is strange that we try to predict future events, but it is all in God's hands. Some people call it coincidence, luck, or fate, but I believe it is Divine Providence whatever happens. Why did I flee from my home and my family? Was it more courageous to fight or to flee? Everyone has reasons for choosing what he does and makes the best choice he can at the time.*

Another article attracted his attention. It announced the names of villages and towns destroyed by the Germans and what happened to the inhabitants. Joseph scanned the list, and toward the bottom of it read the name Chemelnick. A shiver rushed up his spine, and his heart raced faster. The article went on to explain the following:

The inhabitants of these towns and villages were transported like cattle in boxcar trains to Treblinka. Treblinka was a killing center, not a camp with barracks for sleeping. Chance for their survival was hopeless. Before boarding the cattle cars, the Nazis killed the local rabbi in each town and burned his body in the town square for every Jew to witness. In several towns, the Nazis forced the rabbi to dance naked with a naked woman before executing both of them in front of the Jewish prisoners.

Joseph was shocked. His breathing became uneven and deeper, and his pupils widened. Reading became impossible as his focus drifted back to his parents. He forced his mind to seek memories of them, and this made his heart smile as tears sprang from his eyes. He remembered his mother's way of babying him by allowing him to do whatever he wanted because he was the only child. He remembered the beets that she fed him, especially at times when food was scarce. He remembered his father's devotion for studying and how he learned to emulate his father's moral integrity. He remembered that our past illuminates us from the inside out.

Anticipating what the article would say next, Joseph's muscles tensed, and his hair bristled a bit. Thoughts raced back and forth in his brain. Confusion, anger, uncertainty, and emptiness engulfed him. He continued reading as his skin became cool and clammy. The article described that *many of the men were in weak physical condition, having done forced labor for many months, like shoveling snow in the winter. On the walk to the railroad station, the local Poles threw stones at the passing Jews, aiming to hit them in the head.*

Suddenly Joseph felt alert, tense, and nervous. His illusion about being reunited with his family after the war was fading away. Rivers of tears streamed down his face. He said a prayer for them, hoping that his family departed before the Nazi roundups. Although the news was dismal, he knew not to assume anything until he had the facts.

That night, Joseph dreamt about his mother and father. In the dream, their images were not visible because everything was black. In the darkness, Joseph heard their voices as though from behind a wall and far away. Straining to hear their words, he moved toward the emptiness. As the sounds became clearer, he heard them say, "We love you. We love you."

The dream continued, and Joseph sought to escape from the black to the light. Paralyzed by the darkness, he could not see or move. He imagined that he was living in Egypt, during the time of Pharaoh, and it was the ninth plague, the plague of darkness. Joseph pleaded that God allow him to see light again. Suddenly, Joseph heard a whisper say, "When the earth was empty with darkness, the original light was of an intense spiritual quality." His parents were ensnared by the wicked, those who are unworthy of enjoying God's light.

FUTURE MEMORIES

Joseph woke, and tears hurried from his eyes. Sweat covered his forehead, and perspiration soaked his nightshirt. Speaking aloud in the darkness of the night, Joseph said, "Momma and Poppa, I will remember you always. I will love you more every day. I will miss you more every day."

Old blankets hung over the windows to stop some of the cold winter wind from freezing the room. Unlike the Chinese, who wore tufted jackets to keep warm, Joseph and his fellow students wore old, thin clothing as they suffered through another bitter winter. Throughout the ghetto, plumbing pipes froze and often burst during frigid days and nights. Learning from the Chinese, Joseph, Avi, and Isaac wrapped the pipes in their building with thick bunches of straw and secured them with string to prevent freezing. Winter took its toll on everyone. At one point, the three of them attended funeral services for two students at the Baikal Road Cemetery.

The *Shanghai Jewish Chronicle* brought news of the world outside of Shanghai. Isaac supplemented the news by listening to German radio broadcasts. In doing so, he learned more about the war and conveyed the news to Joseph and Avi. Enduring weeks of the freezing winter, Joseph and Avi listened to Isaac as he conveyed the latest news. Hearing it caused them stress and shattered their emotions. Isaac gave the news with an intent look in his eyes that made him appear to be squinting. During the course of the winter of 1944 into the year 1945, Isaac's proclamations sounded like headlines, although some of the news was months old.

The Allies liberated Rome on June 4.
Two days later, another force landed in Normandy, France.
The Germans are retreating.
The United States Navy crushed the Japanese fleet in Leyte Gulf.
America's General Douglas MacArthur landed at Leyte in the Philippines in October, and that means the Japanese are in the same predicament as the Germans.
Roosevelt, Churchill, and Stalin met in November in Tehran to discuss strategy.

"I believe that the war will end soon and Germany and Japan will be defeated," Isaac concluded.

"From your lips to God's ears," Avi answered without the usual skepticism in his voice. The *Aufbau* newspaper, published in New York in German, was carried to Shanghai by travelers. It listed the names of those known murdered in the concentration camps under the Nazi code name Operation Reinhard. Joseph winced as he tried to stop from crying, handing the newspaper to Avi. "What is it? Why the gloom? There is too much gloom here. We should be happy. After all, Isaac said that the war will be over soon and we will return home."

Avi skimmed through the newspaper and began reading the seemingly never-ending list of names. Suddenly, he put his hand in his mouth and shrieked, a shriek like the cry of an animal caught by the leg in a trap. His eyes bulged, staring blankly at the page, and he began sobbing. Stunned by Avi's cry, Isaac and Joseph moved toward him, uncertain of how to react. A moment later, Avi slumped to the floor. Propping him up in a chair, Isaac quickly read through the list and saw the names of Avi's parents, grandparents, sisters, aunts, uncles, and cousins. Avi was the only surviving member of his family.

From that day, the trauma of their deaths affected Avi's personality. He became quiet and passive, drained of enthusiasm and energy. He functioned as one who was in an emotional coma. Muttering in a whisper, Avi often murmured, "I will remember them. I will remember them." He seemed unaware of saying this.

Everyday news arrived at the yeshiva informing the students and the rabbis of the murders of family members. It was beyond human comprehension and imagination and emotional capacity for them to accept as reality that everyone they knew—their father, mother, brothers, sisters, grandparents, aunts, uncles, cousins, and friends—were murdered, and the village they grew up in razed and burned. Sadness, grieving, pain, and emptiness enveloped the yeshiva. Condolences were given, accompanied by hugs and tears. In the yeshiva, times of mourning came frequently. Joseph anticipated the inevitable news, and one day it arrived.

> *Chemelnick was destroyed and its inhabitants carted away to Treblinka.*

Joseph dreaded this day and accepted the fact stoically. Sitting *shiva* (in mourning), he kept alive the hope that his family had escaped and survived. His mind fluttered, remembering first his aunt Miriam. In her early sixties with soft gray hair, a narrow face with high, slanted cheekbones, and a thoughtful look in her eyes, she always brought him special gifts at Chanukah. His memory floated to Uncle Abraham. He was a few years older than Momma and had a soft fine brow, nose, and jaw and would take him on walks when he was a child. *Strange*, Joseph thought, *how one remembers people or events that have not surfaced for years. It seems that memories are stored in a bucket and need only to be brought to the surface again.*

Isaac heard nothing about his family and prayed for their survival. He hoped for the best but feared for the worst. For Joseph and the students, it was beyond all logic how one endured the suffering of these losses. Joseph's entire past was destroyed, physically gone forever, only remaining in his memory.

On occasion, brief respites of joy entered the yeshiva. At the Oihel Moshe Synagogue, Joseph, Isaac, and Avi attended a bar mitzvah, where a Jewish boy, age thirteen, is recognized as a man. Entering the synagogue, Joseph spoke to Isaac and Avi, a note of sadness in his voice.

"This bar mitzvah shows that Judaism has survived this tragic war. The Allies will soon be victorious, and the remnants of the surviving Jews will carry the heritage and values of our ancestors to future generations. If we ever overcome the pain and emptiness of our loss of our families, we shall tell our future generations, those yet to be born, of our memories from before the war. We shall relate to them the goodness and kindness of their grandparents and great-grandparents. Our memories must be focused today to be vivid in the future."

FUTURE MEMORIES

It was 1945, and the war was in its sixth year. The Japanese in Shanghai were low on gasoline, and without it, they attached charcoal burners to the rear of their vehicles, with the burner using charcoal as its fuel. The Japanese employed forced labor of adults living in rooms facing the street to dig foxholes as part of their plan to defend Shanghai in house-to-house fighting. The Japanese did not allow for the rains and the floods that would render most foxholes useless. When the rain came, it lasted for ten days, accompanied by intense winds. For that reason, houses in Shanghai were constructed without basements because of the flooding.

Isaac declared, "The war will end very soon. I just know it. I feel it in my bones."

"Predicting the future is only for prophets," Joseph replied. "Most humans are not prophets although they like to believe they are. An educated guess is all that man possesses, and just as often as he is correct, he can be wrong."

The next afternoon, Isaac joyfully announced, "The war is over in Europe. Germany surrendered unconditionally two days ago, on May 7, at Reims in France."*

"Who knows, maybe you are a prophet after all," answered Joseph.

In the ghetto and in Hongkew, the Allied victory was a time for quiet celebration. No one dared celebrate openly for fear of upsetting the Japanese, whose ally had just been defeated. For many, there was no celebration, as uncertainty about their relatives' survival in Europe overwhelmed them.

In the confines of their room, Isaac and Joseph placed one hand on the each other's shoulder and began dancing to a tune they hummed. Avi sat glumly nearby and watched. As the dancing continued, Joseph reached out and grabbed Avi by the hand and forced him to join in their circle of dancing. With smiles on their faces, each one remembered his family and pretended to be happy on the outside but was sad on the inside. Joseph kept his hope alive that his family survived. Remembering them brought him emptiness and pain.

The dancing stopped. "We will go home?" Avi asked, like a child asking his parent a question.

"Avi, my dear friend," Joseph replied, "we have no homes or families. All that is left to us is our memories. Preserve your memories because that is all you will have in the future."

Avi cradled his head in his hands and cried. Isaac, always considered the strong one, bit his lip trying not to cry, but tears swelled in his eyes and drifted softly down his cheeks, like raindrops streaming down a windowpane.

"I have thought about our lives," Joseph moaned through his tears. "If we only keep looking back at what has been, rather than forward into the future, tears will dominate us. For what we and many of our brethren are suffering, it becomes vital for us to convey our mental and spiritual well-being into the future in order to begin a new life, a life that will be different, far different from the past." He hesitated, running his fingers through his beard. "Who would have known that seeing our parents wave goodbye to us at the rail station was going to be the last time we ever saw them?"

It was a sticky, humid night in July 1945. Joseph was studying Talmud by the light of a small bulb. Isaac was reading the *Shanghai Jewish Chronicle*. Avi lay on his bed with his eyes closed. A low whining sound reached their ears. "It sounds like another air raid," Avi said. He opened his eyes, and they were filled with fear. The wail of the sirens grew louder, and the rumble of aircraft approached. Like a giant dark cloud, a swarm of American bombers filled the night sky.

"No need to worry," Isaac said in a casual manner. "The American planes bomb the outskirts of Shanghai, destroying the factories and Japanese military installations. They know there are about fifty thousand refugees in the ghetto. They will not bomb it."

"What makes you certain they will not bomb the ghetto?" Avi asked. "You act like you know everything because you are analytical and read a lot."

"There is nothing of military value here," Isaac answered. He looked up at the ceiling, as though he could see the planes overhead.

The shriek of the sirens became deafening, and their blaring whine drowned out all conversation. The electric power failed, and the room became as dark as a cave. The city's skyline turned bright red. An explosion in a nearby street rattled the walls in their room, and the building shook. Bombs were falling in the ghetto.

"Are we the targets?" Avi yelled in a panic. "Or are these stray bombs? Death could find us during this bombing!"

"Don't talk that way! We must leave the building and go down to the street." Isaac yelled. "Let's hurry. This is not a usual air raid. Follow me. I know my way through this building even in the dark. Be careful. Take small steps. If you hit something, at least you will not lose your balance."

Panicking students surged into the pitch-darkness. Chaos reigned among them as fear stripped them of their senses. Shouts were heard.

"Where shall we go?"

"How will we get out of this building?"

"It is too dark to see our way down the stairs."

"We escaped the Germans, survived the Japanese, and tonight we will be killed by the Americans."

"Shut up. Let's get out of here."

"Why is this happening?"

"Where is God?"

Joseph stood in the darkness at the top of the stairs with a newspaper shaped into a megaphone in his hands. His voice boomed through the crudely made megaphone.

"Quiet! Quiet! Quiet!" Joseph shouted.

They recognized Joseph's voice. The din lessened.

"Quiet!" Isaac and Avi yelled.

Joseph spoke quickly and calmly at the top of his voice. "Hold someone's hand. No, I mean grip someone's hand or arm. Now begin walking down the stairs one step at a time. Those in front, make certain that all of the steps are still in place. Do not hold the banister, it may be weak or loose. And go as fast as you can. Now go."

The ghetto was miles from the recent incendiary targets, and these bombs were either dropped in error or were jettisoned by bombers returning to their base. Bombs fell throughout the ghetto. Flashes of white light illuminated a building and a street for a second, and then red flames brightened the darkness. More bombs fell, and the flashes of light appeared in one street after another. Flames engulfed the night as bomb after bomb shattered the ghetto.

Burning buildings acted like torches giving off light from their burning shells.

The students evacuated the building. Sirens wailed. Bombs fell on Shanghai like a hailstorm in winter. The roar of the bombers sounded like claps of thunder. More planes arrived. More bombs fell. Shanghai was burning. The stench of burning wood stifled the night air. Flames illuminated the sky as fires spread through the city. The whine of a bomb whistled close to the students.

"Get down! Everyone down!" Isaac yelled.

The bomb struck the building next door, and the sound of the explosion ripped through their ears. Flames shot from the crumbling building. Night appeared like sunrise. Their building trembled. Burning timber and debris flew through the street. What remained of the building was consumed by fire. People screamed from within the ruins, crying in pain, begging for help. Shouts were heard.

"Help me. Help me. I can't move."

"I'm in here. Please save me. Someone save me."

Avi panicked and screamed, "We are the targets! Tonight we will die for certain."

"I was wrong about our safety," Isaac groaned, his absence of fear fading. "Just stay calm and pray we survive."

Hearing Isaac's voice and seeing how well Joseph organized the evacuation, Avi appeared to calm down and said, "Refugees used to watch the American bombers fly over Shanghai on their missions and cheer for them. Now the Americans are bombing Shanghai."

"Be quiet," Joseph said in an annoyed voice. "Concentrate on helping those trapped in the building."

Seldom did Joseph allow himself to become angry, but the bombing and the suffering undid his usual calm disposition.

The whistling of another bomb followed by a thunderous explosion destroyed three houses on the next street. The piercing whistling warned those within hearing range how close the bomb was to striking its target. Knowing its proximity did not lessen the fear. The explosions devastated the wooden buildings and left the remains in flames. Rubble was everywhere.

Joseph, Avi, and Isaac stayed close together as they moved deftly from street to street searching for survivors. Isaac removed his top shirt, tore it in two, and wrapped each piece around his hands to minimize the risk of burning them. Joseph and Avi copied him. Suddenly, Isaac saw an arm struggling against the pile of wood on top of it. Reaching into the burning rubble, Isaac removed a wooden post and grabbed hold of the arm. Pulling gently, he lifted an unrecognizable person from the destruction. Covered with burns, the voice of the survivor spoke several words in Mandarin before collapsing. Isaac looked around, seeing the chaos, and yelled, "Someone please help! Someone please help!" His shouts seemed like whispers as they were drowned out by the sounds of people screaming and bomber engines roaring overhead. They moved on down the burning street.

A hacking cough overwhelmed Avi as he covered his mouth with both hands. Isaac rushed to him and tore off a piece of his hand covering and placed it like a bandana covering Avi's nose and mouth. Isaac and Joseph did the same to themselves to prevent smoke inhalation. From within the shell of a bombed-out, burning building, the shriek of a child broke through the commotion. Without warning, Avi ran past Isaac, who tried to stop him, and into the blaze. A Chinese woman and her child crouched terrified in the corner of what remained of their home. Extending his hand toward them, Avi signaled with his fingers for them to follow him. The woman's eyes were blank. She was in shock. The child remained motionless.

Isaac peered in and shouted, "Get out, Avi, the rest of the building is going to collapse!" Avi pleaded with them in Yiddish to come with him. Maybe, he thought, the softness of his voice would persuade them. Hearing a flaming beam creak above him, he looked up and saw it beginning to topple. He raced for the street as it fell into the house. Avi sat on the debris-strewn street, with his knees bent, and placed his head on top of them. Isaac and Joseph just stared at him. Reaching into his pocket, Avi pulled out a keychain with a stained brown key dangling from it. He stared at it intently, clutching it tightly in the palm of his hand, and next ran his fingers around it. The fear dissipated from his eyes, replaced by a calm that Isaac and Joseph had never seen before.

Hesitatingly, Joseph delicately asked, "Avi, are you okay? Is there anything we can do for you?"

Avi's reply was tears, tears that swelled in his eyes and cascaded down his cheeks as he clutched the keychain. "There are tears in things," stammered Avi.

Isaac look at Joseph in bewilderment, not understanding what Avi was talking about. Joseph shrugged and turned up his hands to Isaac to show he did not know what was happening either.

"There are tears in things," Avi repeated, opening his hand and looking at the keychain as though in a daze.

Joseph moved toward Avi, placing his arm around his shoulder. Not understanding the meaning of what Avi said, Joseph consoled him. "You were brave in trying to save those people in the building. Please do not blame yourself. With God's help, you survived its collapse." Joseph paused as Avi sat without acknowledging anything Joseph was saying. "But what do you mean by 'there are tears in things?' What is the meaning of your keychain?"

Avi remained silent, staring into space, unaware of the chaos around him. Fires raged, panicked people ran through the streets, Japanese soldiers fled, and bombs fell like autumn leaves from a tree.

In a monotone, Avi recited without looking at Isaac or Joseph, "There was a poem named *The Aeneid*, written by Virgil. It told the story of Aeneas, a young Trojan prince, one of the few survivors of the destruction of Troy. His city destroyed, all of his family and friends murdered, Aeneas traveled the world seeking a place to settle and begin again. Stopping in Carthage, he saw a mural on the wall depicting the Trojan War, the war that destroyed everything he held sacred. To Aeneas, the picture on the wall was a picture of his life, and he began to lament and to cry. At this moment, he uttered the famous line, 'There are tears in things.'"

Joseph listened, and his mouth dropped open, and in a rare moment, Joseph was at a loss for words. Avi turned and looked at Joseph and at Isaac. He showed no sign of recognition of who they were. He continued like he was in a trance, "My father gave me this keychain when I was bar mitzvah, and the key is to our front door. I, like Aeneas, will never see my friends or family again, never see my home again, and now must seek a place to settle and begin anew. We are living in the time of Noah. In that *parashat*, the portion of the Torah, in the story of the flood, God planned to dissolve his creation. God's act of dissolution took the form of a deluge. After the destruction, God commenced again with creation among the few survivors and reestablished mankind on earth."

Acknowledging his friends, Avi added, "That is me. That is you. My past life has been destroyed. I ran into the burning building to save those people. It did not matter what happened to me. What else was I to live for if not to help others? Running into that building showed me that there was still purpose to my life. Life has to mean more than just studying, more than just remembering. I will study and learn. I will remember. Joseph, do you have any keepsake from your family? What about you Isaac?"

"No," Joseph replied, "I cannot think of anything with me. I did not plan on life coming to this."

"I wear this wristwatch that my parents gave me," Isaac answered, holding out his left arm.

"Strange, is it not?" Avi added. "Joseph, you speak about memories often, how we will remember events in our lives and they will become future memories. I agree, but, Joseph, you hold dearly to your memories without any keepsakes. We may not hold our memories as clearly as you, yet we possess keepsakes from our past."

Joseph's memory floated back in time. He saw himself sitting on his mother's lap. She wore a white apron and beamed at him, a broad smile across her young smooth face. He was young, four years old. This was one of his earliest memories. As he sat on her lap, she would bounce him up and down on her knee and sing, "*Yedga, yedga, yedga, yedga, hup, hup, hup, nocko, nicka, nocko, nicka, clup, clup, clup.*" Joseph loved that. This memory was a keepsake to him.

After the bombing ceased,* the Japanese guards did not return. A blaring siren sounded the all clear signal. Joseph, Avi, and Isaac walked toward Seward Road, passing where once buildings and shops stood. Fire and smoke spiraled upward into the sky. Passing a partially destroyed burning building, they saw a line of Chinese passing buckets filled with water from one to the next one on line until the men at the front of the line threw the water on the fire. The fire seemed too strong for their efforts to contain it.

Crossing the road to avoid another burning building, they saw burned bodies smoldering in the lot where the building once stood. The stench of burning wood and burning flesh smothered the air. Joseph tightened the cloth around his face. Avi gagged at the sight. Isaac turned his head away from the scene and covered his mouth with his hand. Chinese and Jewish refugees staggered through the streets in shock, walking as though in a daze, an empty look in their eyes. Many were bleeding from shrapnel cuts. Passing a house that had been bombed, Joseph saw the head and arms of a dead man protruding from the rubble. A half-burned Chinese doll, a charred rickshaw wheel, a child's crushed tricycle, and a scorched rat lay in the street. Bomb craters decimated the streets. Reaching Seward Road, they saw that the large concrete building used by the

---

* On July 17, 1945, thirty-one Jewish refugees died in the bombing, and hundreds were injured.

Japanese was destroyed. The building had been a military communications center with its many rooftop antennas. The area surrounding the building was wiped out from the bombing. Walking through the streets of Hongkew, they came upon the large prison across the road from the Ward Road Heim.

"I have an idea," said Joseph. "The building we live in may collapse since it was close to the bombed area. It may be safer for living and for future air raids if we can find a place to stay in the prison."

They entered a concrete building, one of several in the prison compound. The compound was one block wide and six blocks long. The cell doors were open, the prisoners gone, and refugees already occupied some of the cells. Joseph, Isaac, and Avi decided to join them and found an empty cell that became their home until the end of the war. The prison had become a sanctuary.

One day in early August, Isaac was reading the *Shanghai Jewish Chronicle*. Suddenly he jumped from his bunk waving the paper in the air.

"The war will be over soon if it is not already. It says here that the United States of America dropped an atomic bomb on the Japanese city of Hiroshima."

"That is wonderful news," replied Avi. "Now if only the Americans could stop the monsoon rains from flooding Shanghai, life would be better for us. Yesterday, as I walked in the city, the waves in the Huangpu River overflowed their banks again and flooded the streets. My pants, shoes, and socks were drenched. The floods are the same as the ones Shanghai has every rainy season, except this time there were no dead bodies floating in the water, just mud, garbage, and dead rats."

"I said the war may be over," repeated Isaac, "and you are concerned with the flooding. I am concerned that I want to leave this city now and never think about it again, although I know, as Joseph will tell us, that these years in Shanghai will be part of our future memory."

CHAPTER 14

Shanghai, 1945–1946

On September 2, 1945, the residents of the ghetto and of the rest of Shanghai celebrated Japan's unconditional surrender to the United States. World War II had ended. Before American jeeps appeared on the streets of Shanghai, the Japanese soldiers occupying Shanghai vanished. Chinese soldiers, led by Chiang Kai-shek, the leader of the Nationalist Party, followed the American forces into the city. Yet the joy and festivity was short-lived as the darkness of totalitarian Communism blanketed Eastern Europe and spread like a wildfire into Asia.

In December 1945, Joseph, Isaac, and Avi, celebrated the festival of Chanukah by lighting candles in a menorah, a candelabrum with nine branches.

"Tonight, by lighting these candles," declared Isaac, "Jews celebrate the Maccabees' victory against the Syrian Greeks two thousand years ago. Tonight is the fifth night of the eight nights of Chanukah, and tonight is the darkest night of the year. From this date on, the days become longer, each day with more light. Imagine if the Maccabees were defeated. It would be a different world. There would be no Jews, no Jesus, or no Mohammed."

"No German slaughter of the Jews either," added Avi.

They watched the lights flicker and fade. Tomorrow another candle would be illuminated along with their hope for the future.

"The waiting drags on," Joseph exclaimed. "Now a new enemy threatens China and the foreigners living in the country."

"What are you talking about?" interrupted Avi.

"Remember after the defeat of the Japanese," Joseph continued, "many Chinese thought Americans to be their saviors. A few weeks after the war ended, the Chinese celebrated the parade of American troops through the streets of Shanghai. They jammed the parade streets, waving banners. Children gave flowers to the passing conquerors. The Chinese considered Americans the best warriors in the world, but that was the new beginning for the next battle. And once again, we are caught in the destruction and suffering of another war."*

---

* The adherents of Lenin and Mao Tse-tung, however, blamed colonial imperialism and exploitation for the suffering of the Chinese and made preparations to take over the country through violent revolution and civil war. The Communists believed white people represented these evils and must be killed. They did not distinguish between Americans and other white people. While the shadow of Japanese occupation was being lifted, the Communists of Shanghai began their thousand-mile march to Manchuria to rendezvous with the Communist armies just north of the Yellow River. The communist army totaled almost nine hundred thousand soldiers and in the spring launched a major military offensive against the forces of Chiang Kai-shek and the armies of the Guomindang. It is ironic that during World War II, the Japanese forced the Nationalist government to move inland from Nanking to Chungking, thereby cutting it off from its support in the coastal cities, especially Shanghai.

With the arrival of the spring rain in 1946, the Chinese watched as bamboo shoots grew out of their husks to make new sprouts in the hundreds. Green leaves emerged on trees, flowers bloomed in the parks of Shanghai, and the bleak, freezing winter vanished as spring blossomed. Joseph and Avi enjoyed morning walks especially after a hard rain at night cooled the morning air. Each morning, before they walked, they would peer into the streets, and if they saw no Chinese soldiers, they scurried into the crowded, winding streets. It seemed no one paid attention to them, but they could not be certain because the Chinese tended to avert their eyes from strangers. One day, as they left the ghetto, having moved back in after the war ended, Avi's pants were dirty and wrinkled, his small beard unkempt, his hair uncombed, and his eyeglasses tilted at a peculiar angle on his nose. He still resembled the teenage boy who had arrived in Shanghai six years earlier. Avi noticed the difference between his appearance and that of Joseph.

"Joseph, you seem to look well even after all we have been through. I know you have told me before, 'If you feel good about yourself and are not depressed about life, you will take good care of yourself.' I try, but it doesn't work for me." Avi shook his head in distress. "I still count the years, the months, and the days since I heard the news about my family being murdered. Will it ever go away?"

"Avi, my dear friend, as you know, it is all in God's hands. We make the best decisions based on our knowledge and experience, and we believe that we know what the results will be. Sometimes we are right, but other times, things happen that we could never have imagined. That is what happened to us."

"I suppose," Avi replied, "if I could keep my spirits up like you do, I would feel better and look well."

"I try to be aware of what the hardships of the war did to the people here." Reflecting on his parents, he paused then continued softly. "Each of us will carry the memory of where we came from and who we were, and the hope of what we may become in the future."

"I will try to follow your example," Avi answered.

"Look, we have food, a place to sleep, a place to learn, so why should we complain?"

Avi shrugged his shoulders, nodded, and continued walking.

Crossing Tongshan Road, they walked past the Ching Chong School. Students moved about the grounds like a busy anthill. Walking in the direction of the Huangpu River, they weaved through crowded streets, dodging bicycles and workers carrying heavy loads on poles extended over the shoulders. Bumping and shoving was normal, and no one bothered to say "Excuse me." It was too crowded to matter.

On certain streets, they covered their noses with their hands because the stench of wet garbage and raw sewerage stifled their breathing. Before the war, the fragrant aroma of woodsmoke, onions, sesame oil, spices, and wine coming from the restaurants filled the air. Now a foul, polluted stench made them choke.

"Joseph, will we ever get out of China?" asked Avi as he switched from speaking Yiddish to English.

"Please, Avi, enough lessons. My mind is tired. No English for a while. Let us speak in Yiddish. It is less of a burden on my brain."

"Okay, but I know the answer. I learned how President Roosevelt refused to allow Jews into America during the war, and Jews from Poland were especially discriminated against. Jews whose parents were from Poland remain the lowest on the list for obtaining a visa. Perhaps President Truman will feel differently about us and allow our immigration into the United States."

"I have spoken to Mr. Hirschman," Joseph replied. "He said that it was not the time to expect visas because of the chaos in China and the turmoil at the embassies. Our applications were submitted again after having been completed with our latest information. Mr. Hirschman hand delivered them and received a receipt in return."

Crossing Seward Road was an adventure. They saw scrawny men pulling rickshaws overloaded with material, material used to construct houses and office buildings. Other men and women carried poles across their shoulders. On the end of each pole were large bundles of supplies. Those carrying heavy loads scurried along the street with short, quick steps, clothes wrapped around their foreheads to stop the sweat from dripping into their eyes. Walking carefully and weaving their way through the crowds, Joseph and Avi avoided being struck by the bundles. Joseph thought of the contrast between a street in Chemelnick with a few dozen people on it and a street in Shanghai inundated with a thousand people. The thought of Chemelnick overwhelmed him, and he said, "I wish I knew if my parents were alive or dead."

He stopped speaking because he did not want to express what was on every Jew's mind in the Hongkou Ghetto. His thoughts flashed back to the newspaper stories of the millions of Jews murdered in concentration camps. Was it true? The number seemed like an exaggeration. He did not like to think about it, yet it preoccupied his thoughts. Could it be, he asked himself, that all those who stayed behind were slaughtered?

They crossed Broadway East as they continued south toward the river. As the morning became warmer, a haze from the mixture of smoke and sunshine hung in the sky. Avi walked with his eyes straight ahead. Joseph moved through the crowds, his eyes roaming in every direction. He wanted to see everything, to remember it all, because Joseph knew that once he left Shanghai, he would never return. Joseph believed strongly in Divine Providence yet still possessed a sense of control over his future. They passed disabled beggars, men missing a limb lost in the war or blinded by disease or war injury. Peddlers jostled through the streets, most selling old, salvageable household items, others selling cotton-padded tunics and pants. Chinese women stood in doorways waiting to escort American soldiers. Yet in spite of all the people and activity filling the streets of Shanghai, offering the specter of a thriving economy, reality dictated a city plagued with abject poverty.

"What will happen to the Ohel Moishe Synagogue in the ghetto once all the Jews are gone?" asked Avi. "Who will watch it? Who will use it? Who will take care of it?"

"You ask too many questions," Joseph replied. "I do not know. Maybe some Jews will stay here."

"Why would they? A civil war is coming, and I see a future without the Synagogue in Shanghai."

The Huangpu River ran through Shanghai. Besides the oil slicks and garbage in the water, the Huangpu was muddy, causing its color to be a thick dark brown. At the river, Joseph and Avi found two empty crates to sit on. Across the river was Pudong, an area of open fields and wharves. Sitting quietly, they watched a US Navy minesweeper return from patrolling the river in its search for mines planted by the Japanese. At the number one buoy, an American cruiser, the USS *Columbus*, rested at anchor. At the number two buoy, the USS *Rocky Mount* turned with the current as it, too, rested at anchor. An old freighter moved silently up river toward the docks. Originally painted green, the green had faded, and parts of it were covered with splotches of rust or white paint to hide the rust stains. A Chinese flag hung limply from its pole at the stern. Beneath the flag, the name of the ship was painted in white letters, in Chinese characters. Under the name was painted a red dragon, curled and half standing, as if ready to strike. The ship was low in the water because of its heavy cargo, soon to be unloaded in Shanghai. After a brief time in port, the ship would collect another cargo from Shanghai to transport to another part of the world. Joseph and Avi watched as the freighter passed in front of them.

"I wonder if that freighter could cross the ocean to America," Avi suggested.

"That is funny. I am surprised that old ship is fortunate to make it from one Chinese port to another," answered Joseph.

"What kind of ship do you think we will sail to America on?"

"I don't know," said Joseph, "perhaps on an old ocean liner that was in dry dock during the war. I suppose we will have tiny cabins or even be in steerage. It certainly will be better than these old freighters we have seen moving in the Huangpu."

They sat quietly staring out at the river, neither one speaking. After twenty minutes, Joseph said, "One day in the future, what will we remember of our years living in Shanghai?"

Avi stared at the wakes of the ships churning through the river.

"Let's head back," said Joseph. "We do not want anyone to worry that we have been out too long."

Quietly, they walked back to the ghetto on a narrow, unpaved street to avoid most of the crowds. Passing apartments, stores, and hotels, they saw the destruction the war wreaked upon Shanghai. Buildings were gutted and plundered by the Japanese. Doors, doorknobs, electrical appliances, plumbing fixtures, and piping were stolen. A scarcity of materials caused the rebuilding to proceed slowly.

After they returned to the Mirer Yeshiva, Joseph was unable to concentrate on his studies. Placing his elbows on the desk and bending them upward toward his face, he rested his head on his hands and covered his eyes. His mind drifted back to the Huangpu River, and he began to daydream. He thought of the ships moving up and down river. *Do any of the sailors on the US Navy ships come from New York? There must be some from New York. New York is a large city. From which cities did the freighters come? Where do they go after leaving Shanghai? Did any of my letters reach my parents? Did they write to me? How could they, they did not know how to reach me. Are they alive? Did they survive the war? Yes, of course they survived. No, they didn't, they are dead. Will I ever know the truth? I should have stayed no matter the conse-*

quences. They wanted me to stay but were too courageous and proud to ask. One life of mine ended in 1940, and another life began in Shanghai, a life without family. Now I am in an uncertain period, waiting, waiting, waiting for another new life to begin. I have friends and I have God, and I will make do with that.

The loud voice of Sol Hirschman pierced his reverie and rose above the din of the students studying. Wearing a rumpled suit, a wrinkled white shirt, and a dark-blue tie, Hirschman's face was pale white with worry lines etched in his forehead and at the corner of his eyes. His usual calmness was gone, and his left eye twitched from nervousness. The students were shocked at his appearance. Skipping his casual greetings, he stammered as he announced in a piercing voice, "I was promised that tomorrow, we will know if our visa applications are approved. An official at the US Embassy promised me that."

The students listened intently as Hirschman took a deep breath to calm his nerves. "Please excuse me. You know that I am not normally like this. If the visa applications are accepted, I will be told when they will be issued."

Applause erupted, and a great din filled the room. Hirschman raised his hand, and the cheers abated and a hush filled the room.

"The embassy official said, 'It looks good.'"

"When would we go?" asked a student.

"Who knows?" replied Hirschman. "Let us pray we obtain the visas and then worry about when we go. The visas will be good for six months. We may wait a few months, but we will definitely be leaving once we receive them. To keep your minds at ease, I suggest that you plan for another four or five months in Shanghai."

That evening at dinner, visas were the main topic of conversation. Joseph caught snippets of what was said.

"Did the embassy tell Hirschman the truth?"

"Was the promise made to give the Americans time to stall again and stop us from bothering them?"

"Even if we are granted visas, maybe there will be no ship to take us for six months and the visas will expire."

"The Americans know that if we remain here long enough, the Communists will kill us when they take control."

After dinner, Joseph, Avi, and Isaac went to their room. Looking at Joseph, Isaac said, "You were quiet tonight."

"Are you feeling okay?" asked Avi.

"I am fine. Just thinking about all that is happening," replied Joseph. Joseph lifted one of the chairs, carried it to the tall cupboard, and set it down. He mounted the chair and reached the top of the cupboard, where he lifted a small, dilapidated suitcase. Setting it down next to his side, he stepped off the chair.

Avi and Isaac looked at each other with furrowed eyebrows. Isaac said to Joseph, "What are you doing?"

Joseph placed the suitcase on his bed and opened it. "I am packing for our trip to America."

"Joseph, you heard what Hirschman said about the visas. It may be six months. It may never be. Why are you packing?" asked Avi.

"My friends," answered Joseph with a Cheshire cat smile, "we are leaving soon, very soon, possibly within the next few days. I want to be ready."

Avi walked to Joseph, took him by the arms, and shook him. "Stop dreaming. We cannot be ready to leave within a week or two, much less than in a few days."

"Before, they told us 'No,'" said Joseph. "Now we are told 'Maybe.' There is no reason to say 'Maybe' unless 'Yes' was to follow. The United States is a wonderful country."

"What does that have to do with us obtaining the visas?" asked Isaac.

"Isaac," replied Joseph, "Thomas Jefferson wrote the Declaration of Independence when he was thirty-two years old. Before he wrote it, he read the first five books of the Talmud. Jefferson was a brilliant scholar."

"So?" said Avi.

"When a country's ideals are clear, and the government follows them, it is obvious to me that Hirschman was told 'Yes' but not officially. The official part will happen soon. You both will be surprised and I will be ready. Tomorrow, I will begin saying my goodbyes to people I will never see again."

"From your mouth to God's ears," said Isaac.

"I wish I could believe you and be as optimistic as you are," said Avi.

"I suppose people are not that optimistic," said Isaac, "because they are afraid of being disappointed. But after all, what is disappointment? It is only a hurt to your ego or pride. Maybe I will learn from you how to become an optimist."

Joseph laughed, his laugh mixed with a big smile and a chuckle. "Well then," he said, "your first lesson in being an optimist is to start packing for America."

The next day, Joseph said goodbye to friends. Surprised looks greeted his good wishes for a safe journey and a healthy and happy future. Joseph knew that his group would depart together and other groups would travel earlier or later to different destinations. Joseph entered the cramped Jewish cemetery adjacent to the yeshiva. It had existed before the war, but during the war many Jews had been buried in it. Grave sites were crowded together, leaving just a few inches between each one. Watching where he placed each step, Joseph walked carefully in search of the grave markers of friends he once knew. Sadly, he reflected, *There are things in life one cannot recover, like a friend or family member after the person dies.*

Leaving the cemetery, he walked along Dixwell Road, drifting through the streets of Shanghai. Oblivious to the crowds and street noise, he passed the former Japanese school, now being repaired and converted into a Chinese school. Workers moved along like pack mules, carrying supplies to buildings. He stopped at the northern settlement boundary without crossing it, still conditioned from the war not to leave the International Settlement. Knowing this would be the last time he would see Shanghai, he wondered how many people ever sense the feeling of the last time. How differently people would behave if they knew this was the last time, the last time they would live at home, the last time they would hug their parents, the last time they would kiss their children, and the last time they would have the chance to tell those they love just how much they loved them. He thought, *In life, there are too many last times.*

Two days later, life had returned to its normal routine. Joseph was studying in his room when Avi and Isaac burst in like a bolt of lightning racing across the skies.

"What is all this commotion about?" asked Joseph.

Avi and Isaac were speaking at the top of their voices at the same time. Joseph cupped his hands over his ears. "Stop screaming. I do not know what you are saying. Tell me one at a time."

"We have them!" shouted Isaac. "We have the visas. They were issued today. You were right. Congratulations."

Joseph looked from one to the other with a look of disbelief. "It is true? This is not a joke."

"It is true, absolutely true. Mr. Hirschman has them in his possession. He will tell us the details at dinner," said Isaac.

Joseph quickly said a prayer to God thanking Him for his mercy and kindness.

That evening, the dining hall was quiet, as the usual loud conversations and noise were subdued. As they ate their dinners, the students kept glancing to the main door waiting for Mr. Hirschman to appear. Each time someone entered the dining hall, all heads turned toward the door. During dessert, the door opened, and Mr. Hirschman entered carrying a scraggly-looking leather case that was nicked and scuffed and its dark-brown color faded to a whitish-brown hue. Silence greeted his arrival as he undid the straps on the case, removing a pile of papers fastened together by a thin string. Walking from the table to the middle of the hall, he held up the papers. "I have in my hands the visas for our freedom."

Shouts of joy bellowed forth from the students, followed by singing. Joseph sat silently, staring intently like an owl with his eyes wide open, watching the spectacle.

"What is it, Joseph? Why are you not celebrating?" Isaac asked.

"Sometimes," Joseph replied, "when you pray for something for a long time and it finally happens, there is an emotional letdown. I have no energy left to celebrate."

When the singing subsided, Hirschman held up his hand for quiet, and silence engulfed the room. Hirschman looked haggard and exhausted. Black charcoal-colored rings hung under his eyes. He glanced slowly at the faces staring back at him. Speaking deliberately, he addressed the students. "Some of you have been here for six years. That is a long time. All of us have been hurt in some way, whether by disease here in Shanghai or from the news of personal tragedy back home. We can never pretend we have not been touched by adversity, but we can refuse to be held by it. I hope that along with the tragic memories of the war, you will take with you good memories of friendships you have made here. After all, it is through Divine Providence we are placed in circumstances we may never have anticipated. Only then do we make our choices. You will choose whether to maintain friendships or to store them in your future memories." Clearing his throat, he continued, "You will not be leaving together, and you will not be going to the same places, but you will be going to America." The students pounded the tables showing their approval. "The *aleph* group will leave the day after tomorrow and must be ready at six in the morning. We expect the trucks taking you to the harbor will be on time and they will not wait. The *bet* and *gimmel* groups will be here a while longer because no definite date for a ship has been made, maybe within the next month or two."

He paused, looking down, and covered his mouth with his fist. When he continued, a note of sadness crept through his voice. "We suffered through the war and we survived. Rather I should say, we prevailed. You studied and learned Torah and Talmud, yet I pray that the years here taught you more. Adversity is one of God's ways to test man. You have struggled and suffered and learned to live without basic necessities. You have lived without comfort, without food, without proper sanitation, and without family. Remember these days, do not hide from them. After all, we are the fortunate ones when we remember how the Germans killed our friends and families. We are alive. We can see, we can hear, we can pray, and we can remember." He paused, and his eyes filled with tears. "And we must remember for our children and grandchildren who have yet to be born. They, like all people, must know what happened during these terrible times. In the future, when you are older, you will remember all of this. And the memory of who we were and the hope of what we become shall guide us the rest of our lives. I pray that you all have a safe journey, and with God's blessing, we meet again someday in America."

CHAPTER 15

Shanghai to America, 1946

Joseph, Avi, and Isaac waited for the truck as the sunrise cast sparkling rays of light through the clouds flooding Shanghai with daylight. It was five forty-five in the morning, and without having many hours of sleep, they were not tired. By five past six, the group was assembled and waiting.

"If the truck is late," asked Avi, "will we miss the boat?"

"Do not worry," said Joseph, "we are too many for the ship to go without us. They will lose plenty of money if they do not take us. I just hope that the ship is a good one."

Fifteen minutes later, an old army truck stopped outside the yeshiva. Splattered with mud and with a torn canvas top, this truck was their transportation to the docks. Each student helped the next one climb up into the rear of the truck.

Carrying a box tied with rope and a suitcase, Joseph sat on a wooden bench facing another bench. The seats were rough and splintered, and there were not enough of them forcing four students to stand. Ownership tags dangled from strings hanging on the suitcases that were shoved to the front of the truck and stacked behind the divider in back of the driver. Before the rear gate was lifted and fastened in place, the students staying behind handed bags filled with chocolates, candies, and cookies to the students in the truck. The *aleph* group had not expected this wonderful departure. Joseph held a brown bag in his left hand and waved goodbye with his right. The students shouted goodbyes as the truck cautiously departed. Joseph cried as he waved, knowing he would not see them again. He wondered how his memory of the past would affect his future.

At this early hour, the streets were already crowded. Chinese pushed through the streets carrying their wares. Merchants were busy setting crates filled with goods in front of their shops. People hovered around the crates choosing things to buy. The smell of food cooking blended with the smell of garbage in the streets. Moving slowly, the truck maneuvered its way through the crowds, finally arriving at the docks. Wooden crates and large corrugated boxes were being unloaded from trucks and carried by laborers aboard the cargo ships docked in the harbor. Walking along the docks, the students searched for the ship that would transport them to America. The US Navy had marked each pier in English for the convenience of the Navy. The students searched for Pier Number 9. The workers peeked quick glances at the students, never having seen a group like this, with long hair and beards, dressed in black, except for their shirts and socks, which were white. The workers smiled at this sight.

Joseph walked at the front of the group absorbing the beehive-like activity on the docks. When he saw the ship that was to take them to America, he smiled, shaking his head sideways in disbelief.

"What are you smiling at?" asked Avi.

"Wake up, Avi. Look at the ship."

"I see the ship. What about it? It looks like all of the other ships we have seen at the docks."

"Avi, this is the green ship," said Joseph.

"I can see that. I still do not know what is funny."

"Remember a few days ago, we sat at the Huangpu watching the boats. One of the decrepit ones was green and had a dragon at its stern. This is the same ship, the one I said could not make it to America."

"Oh no, not that ship," said Avi.

"Oh, yes, we sail on this ship today. Let us make the best of it because I believe this will be another adventure that we will add to our future memories."

"We have endured enough adventures for a lifetime," said Avi. "I have enough memories. It would be better if we could enjoy a life of peace and calm."

"During my six years in Shanghai," Joseph replied, "I studied, I prayed, I suffered, and I am alive. Unfortunately, tragedy and sadness occurred, and I learned to accept the permanence of the tragedies. My choice was to either live in the past or to begin a new life. It is all in one's attitude that dictates the choices one makes. I chose to begin a new life. That does not mean that I do not miss my family. I miss them very much and think about them every day. Many people quit on life because it is easier to quit than to continue. There is a famous quote from Rabbi Moshe Luzzatto, 'All that befalls us in this world, the good as well as the bad are tests.' I want to pass my test."

His friends looked at him, somber expressions on their faces, and did not reply.

The students climbed a rickety, wobbling ladder to board the ship, named the *Rising Dragon*. The ship was scheduled to depart at ten that morning. In Shanghai, ships did not depart on time, usually being hours and often days late. Once aboard, a seaman wearing a dark-blue shirt and trousers and a white cap motioned them to follow him. The deck was cluttered with crates waiting to be stored below. Ropes swung from the hoists, and others lay on the deck. A boathook stood in a corner to be used to push the boat away from the dock. To pass the next pyramid of crates, it was necessary to move around it away from the railing. In doing so, a metal protrusion hung low over the area. Joseph warned everyone to duck their heads to pass safely below it.

Joseph, Avi, Isaac, and a fourth student named Yossi shared one of the small cabins below deck. Yossi's dark-brown beard and black thick-rimmed glasses dominated his face. His beard was fuller than those of his peers, and the combination of the glasses and the beard allowed only his short, straight nose to be noticed on his face. His black hat was worn with the brim turned down in front.

The cabin paint was peeling, and rust stains spotted the walls. Boat nails with a convex head, and a chisel point protruded from the upper and lower corner of the doors. Space was scarce, and the cabin consisted of two upper and two lower bunk beds and a tiny closet. With the four of them in the cabin, there was not enough room to move about without banging into someone. Only when they lay on their beds was there enough room for four in the cabin. The sinks and toilets were located in a common bathroom down a narrow passageway off the hall. Cobwebs hung in the corners, and finger- and handprints had turned the once white door black.

"How long will we have to be squeezed into this cabin?" asked Yossi.

"Only God knows." replied Avi.

Later that afternoon, the *Rising Dragon* steamed from Shanghai harbor laden with passengers and cargo. Her course was east, southeast to pass through the East China Sea, the Ryukyu Islands near Okinawa, and to the Pacific Ocean. Joseph and the students gathered on deck, finding spots to stand among the crates, ropes, nets, and pulleys. They saw a man in a straw cape and bamboo hat holding a long rod by the river. White egrets flew back and forth searching for fish. Shanghai began to fade into the horizon.

"Leaving Shanghai marks the end of a phase of our life," said Joseph, "and the beginning of a new one. I pray that God grants us a better life in America than we had in Shanghai."

The first evening at sea was a Friday. Before dinner, the students conducted services for welcoming the Sabbath and made *Kiddush*, the blessing for wine, followed by *Hamotzi*, the benediction for bread. Food had been prepared and stored in the ship's refrigerators to assure that there would be kosher food for the students' meals. After dinner, they all sat and recited the grace after meals.

The *Rising Dragon* churned through the sea, having left behind the lights of Shanghai. That night, Joseph stared at the sea and saw darkness without light other than the illumination of the stars that filled the skies. The fresh salt air felt good to breathe after years of inhaling the humid, polluted air of Shanghai.

The next day, the weather was sunny with white clouds scattered against a pale blue sky. The *Rising Dragon* passed through the Ryukyu Islands, south of Japan, and plodded eastward over the Japan Trench into the open sea of the Pacific Ocean. Cool breezes and a calm ocean prevailed during the early days at sea. Yet many students became seasick. Studying was difficult because of the sounds of the ship's engines, the crew moving cargo into the storage holds, and their shouting as they worked. The swells of the sea caused the *Rising Dragon* to rock from side to side and to pitch from bow to stern. After seven days at sea, the students had become lethargic.

Early one morning, an ocean-like expanse of dark clouds filled the sky and lingered into daytime as a light mist mixed with drizzle obscured the sun. Shortly, a cold rain began to fall, and the intensity of the wind increased. Flashes of lightning displayed an instant of bright light followed by the rumble of thunder sounding like artillery fire. Crew members battened down the hatches and secured items that could move during the storm. The *rat-a-tat-tat* pounding of the rain on the deck sounded like a machine gun. Whitecap waves embraced the sea, breaking against the hull, causing the *Rising Dragon* to pitch violently from bow to stern.

Joseph awoke and felt a rush of nausea. He took several deep breaths and waited for it to pass. The growling storm awakened them. They dressed quickly and tried to go to the upper deck. A crewman, shouting in Chinese, and motioning in pantomime, made it clear that it was dangerous on deck and they must stay below. Students gathered in the narrow hallway and, gripping the handrails, moved to the mess hall. The pans, utensils, metal dishes, and pots had been sealed in cupboards fastened with heavy ropes. As waves battered the ship, the banging of pots and pans caused a crescendo of loud clanking noise.

Then the lights went out, and pitch-blackness gripped the students. The shriek of the howling wind ripped through the vessel and mixed violently with the clatter from the banging pots and pans. Students sat on the benches at the tables, others sat on the tables. Every so often, a student fumbled his way out of the mess hall to find the toilet and throw up. The fury of the storm intensified as waves slammed over the bow of the ship, seawater flooding the deck. Water seeped into all the cracks, and leaks sprouted in the mess hall. Puddles, like miniature ponds, formed on the floors. Avoiding becoming wet was impossible, and the sea won the battle against staying dry. Another sound, more ominous than the crashing of the waves, threatened the vessel. The walls, floors, and ceiling of the mess hall sounded like a tree crashing to the forest floor. The *Rising Dragon* was on the verge of breaking up. Seawater poured through the openings in the hallways and through the cracks in the doors. Surging waves continued smashing against the ship and breaking over the deck. Small puddles expanded into small lakes, deep enough to cover the shoes and ankles of the students.

Unable to see in the dark, a rush of water poured through an opening in the corner of the ceiling. Ice-cold seawater sprayed down and chilled their bodies. The storm intensified. Twenty-foot waves tossed the ship like a cork on the sea. Cargo broke loose from its ties on deck and slid through railings tumbling into the ocean. The engines, working to their limit, lost the battle as they spluttered, coughed, and finally stopped. The *Rising Dragon* was at the mercy of the storm, all control having been wrested from her.

In total darkness, their clothing drenched and the water above their ankles, the students believed that their death was imminent. A solemn silence filled the mess hall. In the midst of this chaos, Joseph's voice rose from the darkness, "We do not surrender hope. For without hope, there remains only despair and the surrendering of oneself. You must never allow that to happen." Joseph began to sing softly as tears fell. "*O-say shalom bim-ro-mav, hu ya-a-say shalom a lay-nu v-al cawl Yisroel v-im-ru, v-im-ru, amen.*" He sang it again, in a stronger voice, the words meaning, "He who makes peace in his heavens, may he make peace for us and for all Israel, and say amen."

Avi, Isaac, and Yossi joined the singing, and soon everyone in the mess hall was singing. The soft melody, part of a prayer, bounced off the walls of the vessel and drowned the sounds of the storm. Students banged their hands on the benches and tables, keeping rhythm with the melody. The more intense the sounds of the storm, the louder the students sang. "*Ya-a-say shalom, ya-a-say shalom…*" Everyone was singing. "*Shalom a lay-nu v-al cawl Yisroel. Ya-a-say shalom, ya-a-say shalom, shalom a lay-nu v-al cawl Yisroel.*"

For two hours, huddled in the wet, cold, dark, they sang songs in Yiddish and Hebrew. They sang every song they had ever learned. They became oblivious to the storm. And then during the morning sunrise, as the sliver of the moon faded in the sky, the storm subsided. The wind eased, the ocean calmed, and the monstrous waves disappeared, replaced by small swells of three to six feet. Small white caps covered the sea, but the violent pitching stopped. The engines started, power was restored, and the lights went on.

Bedraggled and soaked, the students went on deck. The fresh air and the cool breezes invigorated them. Crewmen worked cleaning the deck of water and debris. Near a broken railing, several crewmen gathered around a small crate lodged between a larger one and the railing. Shouts erupted, and the rest of the crew ran to the place. Beneath one of the crates, a sailor was buried. During the storm, he was crushed as the lashings broke loose and the crate fell. The crate was lifted from his body. The captain yelled something, and two men came forward with a thin board shaped like a stretcher. The broken body was placed on it, covered with a blanket, and brought to the railing. The captain spoke a few words, the board was tilted toward the sea, and the body slid into the ocean, an eternal burial ground of sailors. The students watched this quick burial, and the crew returned to work as though nothing unusual had happened. The next day was overcast, and a westerly wind blew across the deck as a memorial service was held. After the solemnity of the service, Avi reflected to Joseph, Isaac, and Yossi, "From the time I left Lodz, I have been pursued by death, my family and friends killed in Poland, friends killed escaping from the Nazis, and fellow students and Chinese dying because of the Japanese in Shanghai."

"In life, there is sadness and tragedy mixed with happiness," Isaac replied. "Happiness has its limits as does sadness. Dwell on the sadness and you become pessimistic and depressed. You should try to live with a positive attitude over life directing your free will towards good deeds and leaving the unknown to God. And the attitude you choose is what you bring to others around you. It is what you will leave them. For you never know what it is you say or do that will have a lasting effect on another person."

The *Rising Dragon* continued east-southeast following the Tropic of Cancer, toward Hawaii. Since the storm, the weather was clear, and the seas calmer. The students used the isolation of being at sea to study. Joseph carried a book during the day and studied from it for hours at a time. As the ship passed some of Hawaii's 122 islands before reaching Honolulu, the students viewed their first glimpse of a United States possession.* They saw coral and volcanic islands, a few of them inhabited. Coming from a crowded and tumultuous life in Europe and Shanghai, they felt it strange that people could live their lives in a tranquil setting, on a secluded island, away from the crowded and stressful civilization.

After a day of cruising past the islands, the ship passed Pearl Harbor. Sharing a pair of binoculars, the students saw the protruding deck of the sunken USS *Arizona* as it lay at its mooring, destroyed by the Japanese on December 7, 1941. The *Rising Dragon* entered Honolulu, the main seaport of the Pacific Ocean. The students gathered at the railings watching as the ship tied up. In the background, they saw the magnificent Koolau Range of mountains. Few realized they were only two thousand one hundred miles from California. The captain, a Chinese man in a crum-

---

* Hawaii had once been an independent kingdom and in 1898 requested annexation to the United States.

bled green uniform, spoke to the passengers through an interpreter. He explained that this stop was necessary to take on fuel, make repairs, and unload and load goods. The students could not leave the ship because their visas were for entry into New York.

For many days, in between their studies, the students observed the activity in the port and enjoyed the warmth of the sunshine and the solid feeling underfoot as they walked on deck. One of the ship's sailors brought a wreath of flowers to the students and said it was called a lei, a special name for such flower arrangements in Hawaii.

Early one morning, the crew untied the ship from its moorings, and the *Rising Dragon* departed, sailing southeast on its last segment of the journey toward the Panama Canal, through the Caribbean, and to New York. The students stood at the railings as Hawaii became a dot on the horizon and disappeared. Isaac looked healthier than he had in many years. Where his beard did not cover his face, it was suntanned. The tension from the years in Shanghai had dissipated from his eyes. Wistfully he said, "I wonder what it would be like living in Hawaii, where life is calm and the weather is warm and sunny."

"Keep dreaming, my friend," said Joseph with a smile. Joseph was smiling more, having accepted his new reality that a new life had begun and that his former life was a memory. He knew that he was a different person and that there was no going back to that other person and to that other place. "That will not happen. Once we arrive in Brooklyn, we will be content there and seldom want to go anyplace else."

"How much longer until we reach New York?" asked Avi.

"Twelve more days," replied Joseph.

"That's good. I can't wait." Avi had changed his perspective on life. His attitude was, "Give me the insight into today, and you may have the antique and future worlds."

"Although we have not been at sea for forty days as Noah was in his ark, I pray that we will become as righteous as Noah in his generation."

The afternoon sun, directly overhead, cast circular shadows at their feet. Seagulls followed the ship, flying above it and off its port and starboard sides. Diving toward the stern, the white and gray birds retrieved garbage dumped overboard by the crew. Other than the birds splashing after a meal, the surface of the sea glistened from the sunbeams striking it. Joseph turned from the railing and faced Avi and Isaac, his eyes shimmering like the sea. "I have been thinking about this voyage, and I believe that through God's mercy, we have survived. Consider that during our days aboard this ship, we endured a terrible storm, a storm where one life was lost and seawater had reached above our ankles in the mess hall. We thought the ship would sink."

"In today's world," Isaac said, "there are people who are adrift for most of their lives. Their ark is, like Noah's, a symbol of their behavior. They remain isolated and suffering in what they consider an unfriendly world, an uncivilized world."

"What instigated the savage killing by the Germans and the Japanese against civilization?" asked Avi.

Squinting from the sunlight, Joseph replied, "A complex answer is needed for a simple question. I suppose it began in their homes, when people still knew the difference between right and wrong. Then gradually, through propaganda from the leaders, the people lost their shame and immoral behavior became normal. They believed they were superior and smarter than everyone else and yet envied what others possessed. After the first innocent victims were put in jail or murdered, it became easy to kill and justify what the masses had been conditioned to believe. I know there are other interpretations, and for generations there will be discussions about the causes and the horrors of World War Two."

"Joseph, wasn't appeasement a contributing factor?" asked Isaac. "What did France and England do when the Nazis reoccupied the Rhineland in March 1936? Nothing. Had they acted decisively against them in 1936, there may not have been a world war."

"True, very true," interrupted Avi. "Appeasement is the easy way, the comfortable way. No one has to act at all. Simply allow the tyrant whatever he wants, and he knows how to take advantage of this human frailty."

"Enough," Joseph said. "Let's enjoy the remaining days at sea."

From Honolulu, five days at sea passed. The ship moved closer to land, although it was not visible from the deck. Early one morning as night shed its blackness and bright rays of dawn illuminated the horizon and the sea, Panama came into view. The *Rising Dragon* steamed toward the Panama Canal.* The passengers slumbered in their small cabins, crowded into their bunk beds, unaware

---

* Panama became free in 1821 from Spain. In 1903, Panama signed a treaty with the United States allowing them to control a 10-mile-wide Panama Canal Zone for a down payment of $10 million, plus $250,000 a year. After clearing Panama of mosquitoes, the Americans completed the canal, which the French had begun in 1879 but abandoned in 1889. The canal, built in 1914, cuts across the Isthmus of Panama between the cities of Balboa and Colon and links the Pacific and Atlantic Oceans. Thirty-six miles separates the two oceans.

that of the ship's position. Cutting its speed until it was barely moving, it waited its turn to traverse the fifty-one-mile-long canal.

Red streaks mixed into the white clouds, tinted with bands of pink sunlight, brightened the morning sky. A sharp blast of the ship's whistle woke everyone. Dressing quickly, Isaac nudged Avi and Joseph telling them that the ship was at the canal. On deck, they watched in awe as the *Rising Dragon* moved through the six pairs of locks. These locks could raise ships of up to sixty-seven thousand tons to a maximum height of eighty-five feet above sea level. On this day, forty-two ships would pass along the canal, and the *Rising Dragon* would take eight hours to get through. Like a vision in a dream, where one awakens to describe an incomprehensible site, they witnessed one of the world's unique structures. The pictures Joseph had seen of the canal did not compare to the actual sight before him.

The following days passed leisurely under the warmth of the tropic sun. Cruising through a soothing Caribbean Sea, the *Rising Dragon* churned along the eastern seaboard, arriving at New York. As the ship passed through the Narrows, passengers squeezed themselves in at the railing and watched as the largest city in the United States loomed closer. At last, the Statue of Liberty came into view, and shouts of joy erupted like a volcano.

"There it is."
"We have made it."
"I cannot believe this."
"We are free."
"Thank God."

Before veering up the Hudson River, the passengers saw the three bridges along the East River connecting Manhattan with the Borough of Brooklyn.

Joseph stood still like he was frozen, oblivious to the passengers struggling to obtain a better view of France's gift to the United States. He reflected that after nearly seven years, he had attained his goal. *Only God knew,* he thought, *that I would reach America alone, without my mother and father, without my loving grandparents, and without any family. Who do I share this joyous moment of freedom with? All that remains of my family are memories. I am overwhelmed by mixed emotions, of joy at arriving here safely, and of sadness by missing my family. By some miracle, did they survive?* The faces of his parents seared through his memory. *How they would have relished this moment had they been here.* As his tears fell, he made no attempt to dry them. The memories flooded through him—the calmness of the Sabbath; his mother's endearing smile; the wrinkles on his father's forehead and along the sides of his eyes; the proud smile his father gave him whenever they studied together; the taste of his grandmother's cookies; his ailing grandfather giving him a coin to buy a treat; an entire wall filled with books; dinners with aunts, uncles, cousins, and friends who came to their home for the holidays; the delicious beets his mother cooked; and the belief that this would continue forever. A voice in his head spoke and said, "Nothing is forever. Spend the time given to you on this earth wisely." The tears fell harder. Joseph's life in Shanghai was a life in transition. Now in New York, it was time for another transition, another test, another life. He remembered that there are tears in things.

CHAPTER 16

Brooklyn, New York, 1946–1947

The *Rising Dragon* followed its escort tug through the Hudson River. The students gawked at the Empire State Building,* the tallest building in the world. It was beyond their imagination seeing the spectacle of the skyscrapers standing close together like an army of towers reaching to the heavens. North of the Statue of Liberty was Ellis Island, the processing center for newly arrived immigrants. This was the America's main port of entry beginning in 1892. After the *Rising Dragon* tied up at a berth, an immigration inspector, attired in a dark-navy-blue uniform and a matching cap, boarded the vessel. Ordering the crew to disembark first, he told the passengers to wait for his signal to follow them. Shortly, the passengers set foot in America for the first time. Many kneeled and kissed the ground. Others prayed. Carrying everything they owned in battered suitcases or boxes tied with rope, they heard the command of

---

* The Empire State Building, completed in 1931, stands 102 stories high, with its top 1,250 feet above the ground. It is built of limestone and granite and trimmed with sparkling stainless steel.

an official demanding, "Have your papers ready. A small boat will transfer you to Ellis Island for immigration processing. Move it along." A strange silence set upon them. On board the ship, as it approached New York harbor, animated conversation, like jumbled music, flowed through the air. They feared authority, and hearing this command, they remembered how officials in uniform treated them in the old country. Once inside the immigration building on Ellis Island, fear caved in to chaos. Long lines waited to pass through immigration and then customs. Joseph thought of the tumult as music to his ears. "America, America," he hummed to himself. "I am in America." Yet mixed with his elation, part of him was filled with sadness, a sadness he never felt before.

Was it my letters that were not answered? Sometimes we do not know the psychological burdens we bear.

Hundreds of immigrants crammed the registry, pushing their way along the lines. Fans hung from high ceilings, spinning slowly in an attempt to move the air in the stifling, overcrowded building. Long wooden benches filled sections of the large hall. They waited for hours to enter a country where they believed the streets were paved with gold. The commotion and the noise were deafening. Most of the immigrants, either Europeans or Asians, carried suitcases, boxes, and bundles and tied smaller ones around their backs. Older children gripped the hands of their younger siblings. Mothers tightly held babies in their arms. The pandemonium of children crying, people shouting answers to the immigration agents, and a sense of confusion caused a din like the constant shrill of the tugboat's horn. The immigration agents and customs inspectors seemed oblivious to their surroundings and worked with an appearance of frustration on their faces, as though this was their first day at work.

A stout, middle-aged man wove and squeezed his way through the crowds in the customs building searching for someone. Oblivious to the noise around him, he stopped in the middle of the hall, took a deep breath, and exhaled in frustration. Straightening his old felt hat, he smoothed his beard and walked slowly as he was bumped by the mass of people surrounding his passage. Sweat dripped from his brow, and his crumbled white collar, already brown from too many days of steady wear, was soaked with perspiration. His brown suit fit snugly, and threads were separating from the cloth. He moved like a hunter waiting to pounce on his prey. He lost track of time. Finding a flight of stairs, he climbed halfway up and cast his dark-brown eyes through his glasses at the clamor below. Across the hall, in the farthest corner away from him, he spotted the students from Shanghai. He hustled and bumped his way through the crowd and went to meet them. A big smile crossed his face as he spoke in Yiddish to the students.

"Welcome to New York. Welcome to America. I am Zalman Canavitch, an emissary from the Rebbe, the chief Rabbi, in Brooklyn. I will help you clear through immigration and customs and get to the bus we have arranged for you. Have you been waiting long? I am sorry if I am a late, but you know how it is."

The students bombarded him with questions, none of which he answered, because he did not hear one clearly through the chorus of shouts.

"Please follow me closely. Make sure you have all of your things. If you forget anything, it will be lost and gone forever."

Zalman Canavitch, followed by the students, pushed, shoved, and maneuvered through the crowd, looking back to see if the group was close behind him. Arriving at the desk of an inspector, Canavitch leaned over toward him. Placing his hand over his mouth, he whispered to the inspector and passed him a small white envelope. A clutter of forms and applications covered the inspector's desk. Canavitch returned to the students waiting on line. The inspector finished the processing of several immigrants and then announced through a hand megaphone that Zalman Canavitch come to his desk. Canavitch walked from the line and handed the applications and entry visas to the inspector. The inspector studied each one for a moment, signed and stamped them, and returned the stack of approved papers to Canavitch.

An hour later, they boarded the bus. In a voice of astonishment, Joseph said, "Imagine, we are in New York and traveling in a bus. Who could ever believe such a thing would happen to us? Look at how clean and organized this city is compared with Shanghai. We have arrived in a civilized country."

"Isn't it unusual there are this many buildings in New York?" Avi questioned. "I could not imagine this amount in the entire world. It is beautiful to see them here. I will always remember my first day in America."

"See," Joseph replied, "when something unimagined or beyond belief or unexpected happens to you, it is a time in your life you know you will remember. By announcing

FUTURE MEMORIES

today, your first day in America, as a day to remember, you claim a future memory. And best of all, we shall share this memory. After all we have endured in Shanghai, sharing good memories is a blessing. For life without memory is nothing."

The Lubavitcher rabbi handed an envelope to Joseph containing a letter and a smaller sealed envelope. Having been told the letter was delivered many years before, it felt like a lead weight in his hand. Joseph thanked the rabbi and left his study. Joseph was shocked that this letter waited his arrival. The stamps on the envelope were from Poland, and the handwriting was scrawled but legible. Joseph shuddered with fear and trembled. He studied the stamps and the handwriting.

"It cannot be," he repeated to himself. Looking closely at the postmark, he saw a blurred black ink imprint and saw the outline of the faded numerals 42. "This is my mother's handwriting, and it is postmarked in 1942."

A cold sweat broke out on his forehead and neck. Turning the envelope over, he saw smudged fingerprints and dirt marks on the back. On the upper left side, the return address was written in small script. Joseph recognized immediately the return address. It was his home in Chemelnick. He located a seat in the entrance foyer and sat down. He fumbled with the envelope, and it fell to the floor. Bending to pick it up, he dropped it again. He wiped his forehead with the sleeve of his jacket. With the envelope firmly in his grip, he unfolded the letter. The letter was dated June 1942 and addressed to the Lubavitcher rabbi.

Dear Rabbi,

I pray this letter finds you in good health. I write to you for two reasons. First, our son, Joseph Shalosky, left home to escape the Nazis and fled to Shanghai. I pray one day he arrives in Brooklyn. He read your telegrams about leaving Poland. You had the wisdom to recognize the impending danger that swallowed Europe. Joseph is our only child, and we did not want him to go. At first, I was angry with you because I love my Joseph very much. He and my beloved husband make my life worth living. Now I am beside myself for having felt that way towards you. Please forgive me. Second, we miss Joseph and pray that we are reunited after the war. If he is in Brooklyn, or one day arrives in Brooklyn, please see that he is looked after and taken good care of, and give him the letter I put in this envelope.

With my humblest greetings,
Sophie Shalosky

Joseph pressed the unopened envelope to his chest. He remembered his mother, her hand brushing back hair in her face, the sound of her voice, and the strong planes of her cheeks. He wanted these memories to stay with him forever. He wondered whether they would fade in time. He told himself that he would not let them fade away. Remembering his father, tears filled his eyes.

FUTURE MEMORIES

Opening the letter, he noticed that his mother's handwriting was weak and unsteady. He read the letter dated June 1942.

> *Dear Joseph,*
>
> *We pray this letter reaches you and that God has blessed you with good health to read it. You know what is happening to Jews in Europe. The situation is desperate, and crying seems to be all I do. I cried when your father was forced to shovel snow in winter. He nearly froze to death. I cried for those who refused to shovel or did not work fast enough and were shot. I cried for our rabbi, his wife, and their children who were shot in the village square. The Germans placed their bodies in the synagogue and burned the synagogue. With God's help, we saved one of the Torahs. I cried as the Germans came with their dogs and hunted for Jewish children. They put them on trucks and carted them off, never to be seen or heard from again. I cried because I wanted you to stay with us. How foolish it now seems. We believed that the Nazis will pass soon and that all would return to normal. I believed the saying that "when tyrants or kings stand on the backs of Jews, they will not reign for long." It has been too long that the Germans reign. Staying with us would have doomed you to the same end that we may now face. I cried for the*

life we once had and will never have again. I cried to God to save us. Always remember who you are and where you came from. I miss you and love you dearly.

The handwriting changed, and Joseph, through his tears, recognized the bold strokes of his father's hand. With anguish tearing at his heart, he continued reading.

If we do not survive, you, my dear son, will be all that remains of our family. God has protected you and blessed you for survival. I know the pain and suffering you will feel in your heart. Both pain and suffering are opportunities to challenge the way we look at life.

Joseph's heart sank, and he sobbed. His hands trembled as he read each word.

But you will remain our reason for having lived. Remember us through your children and grandchildren. I believe that in spite of what has happened to the Jews in Europe, God has a plan, and his plans are for the good. Perhaps one day, you will understand the reason for our suffering today. In the book of Psalms, it says, "Those who sow in tears will reap with songs of joy." May your life be filled with songs of joy.

FUTURE MEMORIES

Take good care of yourself. We miss you and love you.

Momma and Poppa

CHAPTER 17

Montevideo, Uruguay, 1947

Joseph studied Talmud during the twelve-hour flight from Miami to Montevideo. Pausing in his studies, his thoughts traced back over parts of his life. It seemed that he had lived two lives during his first twenty-six years, one growing up with his family in Chemelnick, and the second leaving Poland and living in Shanghai and arriving in Brooklyn. Now at age twenty-seven, a third life was about to begin in Uruguay. Whatever happened, he believed, was decreed through Divine Providence, by the hand of God, and not by luck, fate, or coincidence. Man has freedom of choice but not control of the results. He knew that suffering seeks explanation, that people overwhelmed by tragedy ask why. Sometimes there were obvious answers. At other times there were not. For life is like a story, a story being painted brushstroke by brushstroke on a large canvas. As the final brushstrokes are added, one sees the finished picture, if one lives long enough to comprehend what the finished canvas looks like. Yet all that happens in one's life, whether happiness or tragedy, is part of that large canvas.

He remembered the story about the concept of justice. In it, Moses asks God for an example of justice. God tells Moses to take a step up the spiritual ladder toward his light. God continues, "A man and his son are walking along the road. From the forest, a bandit attacks them and kills the father. Reaching for the father's pouch filled with the gold, the bandit sees a stranger on horseback watching his actions. In fear, the bandit flees and leaves the gold behind. The stranger approaches the son, sees the dead father, takes the gold pouch, and rides away. That is the end of the story."

Moses replies to God, "I do not understand the story. Where is the justice?"

God tells Moses to take another step up the ladder, to come closer to his light. God says, "I will tell you another story. A man on horseback stops at a stream to drink and to water his horse. A man sleeps nearby in the shade of a tree. A short distance away, a shepherd watches his flock. As the man drinks, his pouch filled with gold falls from his pocket. Unaware of this loss, the man mounts his horse and rides off. Discovering the loss, he returns to the stream and searches for the pouch. He cannot find it. Seeing the sleeping man, he wakes him demanding the return of his pouch. The awakened man denies knowing anything about it. The rider slays him and searches him for his gold. Not finding the gold, he mounts his horse and rides away. That is the end of the story."

"I still do not understand the story. Where is the justice?"

God replies, "The two stories are connected. In the second story, the horseman who lost his gold pouch was the one who stole the gold pouch from the dead father. The sleeping man killed by the horseman was the bandit who killed the father. As for the pouch filled with gold, it was found by the shepherd boy who was the son of the man killed. That is justice. That is the end of the story, an ending you could not imagine from hearing the first story."

The Douglas DC-6 circled Montevideo, the capital city of Uruguay. Having flown over the River Plate, only sixty-two miles across the estuary from Argentina, the aircraft began its approach toward the runway. Joseph looked out the window at the old Spanish city below. What he could not see and did not know was that Montevideo, because of the successive hordes of immigrants from Spain and Italy, possessed a mostly European culture. Prior to and after World War II, they chose this city because of its Mediterranean climate, its variety of palm trees, the shady parks, its nineteenth-century buildings, and a look that seemed to date the city to a time in the past. The approach was low enough for Joseph to see the beautiful roses in the El Prado Park. The bumpy landing jolted the passengers as the aircraft bounced along a rut filled runway before stopping. A set of stairs was rolled to the door, allowing the passengers to disembark. The glare from the sun blinded Joseph for a moment as he walked down the steps. It was July 11, 1947, and a sharp, cold wind sent a chill through his body. Joseph forgot that at the thirty-fifth parallel in the southern hemisphere, it was winter in July.

Waiting among a handful of people stood Solomon Shalosky wearing a dark blue double-breasted suit, white shirt, red-striped tie, black shoes, and a dark-gray hat. He was clean-shaven. Standing beside him were his wife,

Chaya, and their two daughters, Rebecca and Dvorah. He waved to Joseph, and Joseph walked toward them. Joseph greeted them with a smile as if he was basking in the sunshine. Rebecca, the eldest daughter, at age twenty-two, was the reason Joseph made the journey to Montevideo. She was petite, and her height matched Joseph's. Her smooth face with round cheeks and glowing hazel-colored eyes greeted him. Joseph was surprised by her gaze, a gaze of intense scrutiny. Her dark-brown hair fell straight below her shoulders, adorned by two bright-pink ribbons. A necklace with a Star of David on it hung down on to her navy-blue dress. Handing him a bouquet of flowers, Rebecca betrayed a trace of girlish self-consciousness. They were first cousins meeting for the first time.

Joseph placed his dilapidated suitcase in the car's trunk. Carrying a box tied with rope, he placed it on his lap as he squeezed into the rear seat. In Shanghai, Joseph learned that boxes were good for storage and for transporting things. His box contained gifts for the family wrapped in large sheets of tissue paper. Driving to their home, Solomon asked about Joseph's life in Brooklyn and how he survived the war in Shanghai. Joseph offered brief answers, omitting most details.

Joseph inquired of Solomon as to why he moved his family from Poland to Uruguay, and Solomon related this story. "It was 1928, and we were living in Warsaw. Our daughter Rebecca was almost three. and her sister, Dvorah, was a few months old. I received notice from the Polish government that I was to be drafted into the army. Being drafted meant a term of service for twenty-four years. The Polish government did this to destroy Jewish families.

Immediately I went to the United States Embassy to apply for visas to emigrate from Poland to America. I was told that the quota for Polish Jews was filled and no more visas would be issued. It seems strange that this all happened almost twenty years ago."

Joseph listened to the story from his uncle, his father's brother, and reflected on how Divine Providence brought them to this country to survive and how his parents and family had chosen to stay in Poland. He thought of his trips every Friday in Brooklyn to HIAS (the Hebrew Immigration Aid Society) and the Red Cross to inquire if there was any news about the survival of his parents. The answer was the same, "Nothing new at this time."

"A friend of mine," continued Solomon, "told me that he had a visa for a foreign country and that he and his family were leaving Poland. I asked him to what country, and he said he did not know, but that it did not matter as long as they left Poland. I thought it amusing that he did not know, but I knew that he was desperate to leave. He walked with me to that embassy, and a tiny plaque on its outside front wall identified it as the Embassy of Uruguay. I applied for visas, and to my astonishment, they were issued. I raced home and looked in an atlas for Uruguay and learned that it was in South America, not far from Buenos Aires, Argentina." Solomon took his eyes off the road to glance at Joseph. "Joseph," he said in a soft, sad voice, "I begged my brother, your father, to leave with us. I pleaded with him and your mother that life in Uruguay would be better than life in Poland. Your father answered that I was a pessimist and saw only a dire future, and other than the draft, Poland had been endurable for Jews for centuries, so why would he want to leave?"

He drove in silence and after several minutes said, "I miss my parents, my brothers, sisters, all of them. Not a day passes when I do not think of them. And here you are, my dear nephew, the survivor of Chemelnick, and the survivor of our family. I pray that your visit here results in the continuation and blossoming of the Shalosky name throughout the generations."

Arriving at their home, Solomon carried Joseph's bag and box inside. The house was constructed of concrete blocks and stucco, colored in a shade of burned red orange. Arches over the doorways and windows contrasted with the black wrought iron gates surrounding the house. The entrance hallway ceilings rose ten feet high, causing a majestic appearance. Bright red tiles adorned the files. The large rear windows offered a splendid view of the garden and the forest.

Joseph reflected on the purpose of this trip. From Brooklyn, he had been corresponding with his uncle and, with the rabbi's encouragement, began writing to Rebecca. Joseph knew that if they liked each other, they would be married. In his religious world, a man and woman were introduced to each other, and if they were compatible, they married. If they did not like each other after one or two meetings in a public place, there would be no marriage. Each would seek another mate.

"Welcome to Uruguay, cousin Joseph," said Rebecca in Yiddish. She was also fluent in Spanish and English. They were in a large sitting room. The walls were painted a pastel red and were lined with bookcases. Several chairs and a small sofa covered in bright floral prints surrounded a large mahogany desk covered with neatly placed stacks of papers held in place with strings. Brightly decorated area rugs covered the orange-red tile floor. Uncomfortable being with him, she blinked her eyes rapidly several times, took two deep breaths, fidgeted with her hands, and concealed them behind her back. "I have been told much about you, mostly about your life in Chemelnick. On the ride from the airport, I listened to your story about your life in Shanghai." As she became more confident, she added, "You were brave to travel to Shanghai on your own. I mean, to leave your family at such a young age must have been difficult."

Joseph forced a smile. Having spent his life studying in all male yeshivas, speaking to a woman was unusual and difficult. He sat with his right elbow on the arm of the sofa and his left hand rested on his knee. "I was in conflict over what to do. Now, Shanghai and Poland are memories, a history of my life. It is strange how memory works. After I left home, everything seemed to be happening like in a whirlwind. I did not think about what events or people would become memories. I suppose that living in Shanghai built short-term memories, and now many of them developed into long-term ones. I pray that in the future, I will be able to recall all that has happened." He started thinking about his parents and slumped down into the sofa. Rebecca studied her cousin and replaced the word *cousin* with the word *man* and perceived a man in conflict. Intuitively, she recognized that Joseph was a good person, one who still agonized about his parents and his family. She wondered whether people who lose loved ones through tragedy ever overcome their losses.

In a whisper, he added, "I think of them every day." Looking directly at Rebecca, "Maybe they survived. I check with HIAS and the Red Cross often." Sitting up, he continued, "What is difficult for me is that I must make decisions on my own, without any guidance from my parents. The rabbi advises me, but I must still decide on my own. After leaving home and eventually learning that there was no going back, I was forced to begin a new life. So here I am in Montevideo, meeting you, maybe my bride-to-be, and without any knowledge or experience to determine if I will make the right decision. With God's guidance, I will make the right decision."

Without being able to explain it, Rebecca felt herself becoming bound to Joseph, and this encounter drew her closer to him. Rebecca deftly changed the subject. "You will adjust to your new life. After all you have experienced, it takes time. Wounds take time to heal." She paused and smiled at him. "I would like to hear more about your life in Brooklyn. I would like to know what life would be like living there."

"I teach in a yeshiva for teenage students." Joseph relaxed as he spoke of his life in Brooklyn. "I live on a street named Eastern Parkway. The students are sixteen through eighteen years old and are at their highest level of learning. As I teach, they learn, and I do too. Acquiring knowledge is never ending. I enjoy teaching. It fills my day from early morning to late in the afternoon. Besides the actual teaching, I must prepare the lessons and be ready for the never-ending questions the students ask. I do not know all of the answers, and that is when I am forced to learn more. Being a teacher is exciting."

"Are you nervous being here with me?" Rebecca asked, her hands clasped in her lap, her palms becoming sweaty.

"Well, yes," he stammered. "The rabbi insisted that I meet you and that we marry. This is very difficult for me. I am stumbling with my words and thoughts and ask your kindness in bearing with me."

"I understand." She unfolded her hands and smoothed her skirt. "Joseph, if it is meant to be, we shall marry. Meanwhile, tell me about the rabbi in Brooklyn."

Feeling comfortable, Joseph continued as though Rebecca was a student in his class. "The rabbi and his wife, Chaya, escaped from Poland and sailed on the last ship allowed to leave Portugal during the war. I arrived in Brooklyn only last year. During my first Rosh Hashanah, the Jewish New Year, in Brooklyn, there were not ten men present to have a *minyan* for prayer. That situation will improve. As for the rabbi himself, he prays for love and kindness to possess the world for the good of every person. He work twenty hours a day and never takes a vacation. I do not know how he functions on hardly any sleep."

"Go on," she encouraged. "I want to hear more."

"I have been studying and teaching at a yeshiva. Oh, excuse me, I told you that already. I am sorry. The rabbi wants to help the Holocaust survivors and all Jews in America establish a cultural and social renewal. It is our way of fighting back against what the Germans did to us. The goal is a spiritual initiative, to search for every Jew with love, just as Jews were once hunted down in hate. I learned from him that remembering the past is a source of strength." Joseph fought to hold back the tears.

"What is it? Are you all right?" she worried.

"I was remembering my past, and the memories filled me with mixed emotions. The joyous times I had with my parents, and the sadness of knowing it will never be that way again. I suppose we imagine the happy times in life will continue, and then one day they vanish, and a new life replaces the old one. I dare not compare them because each life is different. Before I left to come here, the rabbi spoke to me. He said that I may use my mother's name for future generations. After I heard that, it was a confirmation of what I dreaded. Finally, I had to accept the reality that my parents were killed in the Holocaust. Memories are all that remain."

"I understand your losses. My parents felt the tragedy of the war although we were thousands of miles removed from Europe. They did not want to know the number of Jews murdered by the Nazis. If they knew, it would add to their grief. Having left Warsaw when I was three, I have no strong attachment to the city or the country. My attachment was to the relatives who stayed behind. My parents wrote to some of them and learned about other family through their letters. They did not know they would never see them or receive a letter from them again. My parents changed after learning of the killings. My father reveres Mordechai Anielewicz. He was the leader of the Warsaw Ghetto revolt and a hero in my father's eyes." Rebecca bit her bottom lip and shut her eyes, and tears flowed from the corners of her eyes. "Everyone was murdered, except you. You are the lone survivor."

They stared at each other in a shared moment of empathy for what each had suffered.

"For your parents, it was too many last times," added Joseph.

"What do you mean?"

"I have learned that there are too many last times in life and we do not know when it will be the last visit or the last letter or the last time you will hear their voice. I suppose that lesson is part of me because I try to do the best I can and enjoy every day as it happens."

"I feel the same way but could not express it as you do. What I know about you is that for six or seven years, you wandered through the world before arriving in Brooklyn. The tragedy that befell our family in Poland is unspeakable. How could we not suffer pain and emptiness? In Brooklyn, the rabbi and his friends became your new family. I understand why he wants you to marry. In that way, you will become independent and begin your own family and start a new life. Then you will be able to convey your memories to your children and, God willing, to your grandchildren. We live and we die, like flowers blooming in the spring and turning colors and dying in the autumn. You must tell your story, because in the future after we pass, people will forget. Who will remain to tell the story, to relate the truth of those terrible years in Europe? Without you telling your story, then the tragedy of the Holocaust will become as distant as when the Romans killed Jews in Jerusalem two thousand years ago. It will all become history without memory. Without memory, there can be no passion."

"You are wise, Rebecca," Joseph answered. "It will be necessary to be true people, true to one another and true to everyone we know."

Joseph admired her sensitivity and assertiveness. He understood that this decision would change his life forever.

"Yes, Joseph, and we will remember our roots from Poland. To remember everybody who was killed. My mother lost four brothers." Tears streamed down her face. She dabbed at them with a handkerchief. "I am sorry to be crying, but how can I think of them without tears? One of my mother's brothers was a grandfather, and he, his wife, his children, and his grandchildren were murdered. No survivors. Not one." She hesitated and added, "They remain with us spiritually for their souls are with us for all time, and remembering them is a blessing."

Joseph looked at Rebecca listening to her every word. Thoughts fumbled through his head. *Is this the woman for me to marry? She is gentle and kind. The rabbi said she is the one to marry.* He remembered the telegrams from Brooklyn before the war. *I listened when the rabbi said to flee Poland. I must listen again. If only Momma and Poppa were here to guide me. I forgot that the words "if only" are not allowed to overcome the words "what is." We must accept what is because we cannot change the past. As to the future, it is in God's hands.*

"Yes, it is good to remember. One of the great joys of life," she added, "is to share memories with someone you love. For life must be cold for those with no warm memories."

"Words that emanate from the heart," Joseph whispered, "must enter into another's heart. Your words do that to me."

Four months later, they were married. It was November 14, 1947.

CHAPTER 18

Los Angeles, 1991

Time is life and time hurries by. Joseph and Rebecca asked themselves what most people ask, "Where did all those years go?" They had five sons, each one a rabbi, and three daughters. The children lived in Los Angeles, Montreal, Brooklyn, Lexington, Massachusetts, Chicago, Israel, and Boca Raton, Florida.

It was 1991 in Los Angeles. Joseph and Rebecca planned an eight-week visit with two of their eight children who lived there. On this hot summer day, the sun's rays blazed through a blanket of smog that hung over the city, making the air quality unbearable. The pollution index soared toward the two-hundred mark. Ozone danger warnings were issued by the city. Children, the elderly, and people with breathing difficulties were advised to stay indoors. Mainly the elderly paid attention to the warnings.

The majestic coastline along Santa Monica Bay vanished like a ghost into the smoggy white haze. Residents, used to bragging about the good weather in southern California, forgot to mention these polluted air days and what it did to their respiratory systems. In Westwood, at nearby Gayley Avenue, there was no escape from the foul air.

"Joseph," a voice called from the kitchen, "you cannot go out today. Find something to do until this smog lifts."

Mumbling, he replied, "Okay, I'll find something."

Joseph was dressed in black except for the long-sleeved white shirt he wore without a tie, buttoned at the neck. His trousers, jacket, shoes, and hat were black. Instead of changing styles every few years, as was the popular fashion of American society, the Lubavitcher sect of Hasidism mimicked the fashion of the wealthy Russians of the eighteenth century. Weather changes did not affect what they wore. Deciding what to do this smoggy morning, Joseph saw a heavyset student enter the main hall. His brown curly hair was covered with a baseball cap that read Dodgers on the front. Dark-rimmed sunglasses dangled from a chain around his neck. Dressed similar to most of the students, he wore faded blue jeans, dirty sneakers, and a T-shirt with a logo saying UCLA #1. He placed his pack on the floor and walked to a cabinet and removed a hammer and some nails. Joseph watched and greeted the student with a hearty "Shalom."

"Hi" came back the greeting. "How are you? Looking for something to do? How about giving us a hand? The house was just painted after the fire, and we need to hang all of this stuff," as he gestured toward a stack of photos and plaques. He studied Joseph's clear eyes, slightly wrinkled forehead, the beard, and the broad smile, and said, "I'm Mark. I hang around here a lot."

Joseph stared at Mark like he knew him. Remembering Mordechai and his bright round face, squinty eyes, and his overweight body, Joseph was drawn back fifty years, for that is what memories do. Joseph replied, "Excuse me, I just thought, oh, never mind, it couldn't be." *Of course it couldn't be. It was such a long time ago.* "You just reminded me of someone." *Too many times a person reminds me of someone, and then memories of that time and place reappear. It deepens my nostalgia and highlights my memories.* "I'm sorry. What did you ask me?"

Mark smiled at this befuddled man. "You know how to use a hammer, don't you?"

"Excuse me again," Joseph answered. "I am Rabbi Joseph Shalosky. What fire are you speaking of?" His mind was wandering back to the beginning of their conversation.

"The fire, you know, the big one here."

"No, I don't know about any fire here. Fires in Poland, I heard about, but not here. I live in Brooklyn. Tell me about the fire."

"I am not sure of the date, but about nine or ten months ago, this house burned to the ground. Not a clue who started it."

"What do you mean 'not a clue who started it'?" Joseph asked.

"There was a rumor that it was arson, and the fire department's investigation concluded that it was probably arson because all other possibilities were ruled out. Yet no clues were found and no one ever learned who did it. There are many people around here filled with hate."

Joseph hung his head, his chin touching his chest, and placed his hands over his slumped forehead and muttered to himself as was his habit, "Many people filled with hate. What a shame. What a pity. Will it never end?" He prayed silently. Joseph's longing to study Torah that morning gave way to a desire to help finish the house. "What can I do to help?" he asked. "I know about building and fixing things. I do it all the time at home and in the yeshiva."

Thirty minutes later, Joseph was hanging paintings, plaques, and pictures. Other students had joined in the work, none noticing that Joseph's left index finger and thumb were taped because of the few hits with the hammer that missed the nail. He raised a photograph filled with rabbis. It was taken in the 1890s in Lvov, Poland. He studied it, staring intently at the men, their bearded faces, their black coats, each rabbi looking the same as the one next to him. *How much they resemble my father. How much I resemble them.* Joseph saw the photograph of these men, filled with energy and vigor, yet knew they died long ago. *Did they realize when the photograph was snapped that the clock of their lives was running? Now they were dead, only memories. After several generations, there will be no one to visit their gravesite. What would future generations say about the photos taken today, photos that will be old ones tomorrow? There is always much to accomplish and insufficient time to do it. And how many people waste their precious allotment?*

In the realm of memories, Joseph closed his eyes tightly and heard the voice from his spirit asking, *Why did I leave my parents? They stayed behind and I left, and they knew we would never see each other again. I know it is part of God's plan, but that thought is part of the emptiness in my missing them, something I do not speak about.*

As he stood on the chair, holding the hammer in his right hand and a nail in his left, tears swelled in his eyes. He swallowed hard and bit his bottom lip not to cry. His inner voice of memory repeated thoughts that he carried ever since he left Poland five decades ago. *I wrote them letters from everywhere, and I do not know if they received any of them. I wanted them to know that I was sorry for leaving, and if I had the chance again, I would have stayed. I loved them very much. I would have stayed to take care of them and to suffer whatever happened. They wanted me to stay and were too proud to ask. Sometimes, it is better not to remember.*

A student's voice brought him back to the present and away from his memories.

"You okay?"

"Fine, just fine and dandy," he replied. Joseph banged the nail into the wall with four small taps of the hammer and hung the photograph. "I was daydreaming, that's all. Just daydreaming. By the way, how long is this smog supposed to last?"

The student smiled, shrugged his shoulders, and turned his hands out, palms up, telling Joseph, without speaking, that he did not know. Work continued all morning. Rolls of carpet were carried in and laid in the living area and bedrooms. Boxes of new tile were emptied and installed in the kitchen, bathrooms, and dining area. Blinds were hung on the windows. The activities in remodeling the house were like entering a beehive, filled with motion and buzzing. All the carpet and tile had been donated by local businesses. With the volunteer labor of the students, the cost to the synagogue was mainly for food and drinks. The rabbis had learned that food was the chief ingredient in bringing out the faithful. No matter the event, food made the turnouts greater. It was even successful with the volunteers.

After lunch, Joseph went upstairs to his bedroom, read several chapters in the Book of Psalms, and took a twenty-minute nap. During the afternoon, the volunteers washed the windows inside and out, and the kitchen and bathrooms were scrubbed clean with soap and ammonia. Everyone had to walk on the brown paper paths that led around the newly installed floor tiles, allowing the tiles time to set.

Late in the afternoon, the students drifted away, back to their dormitory rooms or apartments. The pollution alert remained in effect. Joseph found four more framed photographs and decided to hang them. Since most of the wall space that could be reached by standing on the floor or on a chair was filled, he needed a ladder. He found one in the hallway leading to the storage room, and with the hammer, a picture hook, and a photograph in one hand, he climbed the ladder. Hammering with small taps, he nailed a hook into the wall and hung a photo. He studied each photo after it was hung.

Standing on the ladder, he looked for space to hang the last photo. A knock on the entrance door startled him. *Someone will get it.* Stepping down from the ladder, he moved it to a spot where there was an empty space. He climbed the ladder, hammer, hook, and photo in hand.

"Excuse me," said the woman standing at the foot of the ladder. Concentrating on what he was doing, he had not heard her enter the room or come up behind him. "Excuse me," she repeated in a frail voice barely above a whisper.

Peering down from the ladder, he saw an old woman, bent over, looking like she was one hundred years old. Wrinkles and lines covered her brow, and sunken cheeks exaggerated her emaciated face. Thin black rings sagged below her hazel-colored eyes, eyes sunk deep into her head, and a sense of weariness enveloped her. Wisps of thin gray hair protruded from beneath the brown scarf she wore. Her mouth was thin and disfigured, like it was slightly dislocated. Beneath the veneer of this worn, aged face, Joseph recognized the life of anguish that this woman had suffered. Gazing at her eyes, he remembered that the entrance to one's soul is through the eyes.

"Sorry," Joseph said, "I did not see you come in." He smiled, but she did not react. She stared back at him with a look of sadness, like she had just returned from a funeral.

"I was lost in thought about hanging these beautiful photographs," added Joseph. "When I look at them, I think of my home and my parents in Poland. I miss them very much." *Why did I say that to a stranger?* Descending from the ladder, he asked, "Why are you here? Is there any way that I can help you?"

"Yes, yes, I pray that you can help me. As you see, I am an old woman. I cannot go on much longer. Since my family was killed, I have no one, nothing. I have no feeling in me. I am drained of emotion. It was destroyed along with everything I ever loved."

"Without feeling," Joseph replied, "life is empty. I am sure that you have not lived an empty life."

With her eyes half closed, her sad stare gazed into his eyes. Neither one spoke. She looked around the room, unsure of her surroundings. Many times in many places she had felt this strangeness. Joseph was uncertain how to react. He went to the kitchen and brought her a glass of water and bread and jam. She thanked him.

"I know you are a good person," she said. "Everything we do affects somebody. We should use this influence to do good things as you have just done. The positive acts that are done create positive energy for all those around."

She sipped the water and settled back on the sofa. "Certain things I no longer remember, but my memory recalls the details of how my family and I suffered. I was born in Poland and came to America a few years after the war. While I was in Poland, I made a promise to a dear friend that I must keep. Until now, I have failed, and my time on this earth is limited. How can I face God when I have failed in this important matter?"

Her body sagged into the sofa. With her long brown dress hanging limply, she looked like a cushion on it. Sighing deeply, she held her purse tightly.

"Tell me about it," Joseph asked. "It is written that important matters must not go unattended."

"I am looking for a boy, no, I mean a man. He was a boy when this happened a long time ago. I am so confused. Please forgive me. I must find him. I have a compelling obligation, and it has been painful for such a long time. Why did God choose me as his messenger? Me. After all I suffered through. In the Bible, Job suffered. I suffer like him. All of the rest who know how much I suffered were killed."

She grabbed each of her arms with the opposite arm and rocked from side to side. From deep within, she uttered a sound, a sound of grieving, a sound of suffering, and a sound like the pain of an animal crying with its leg caught in a trap. Not knowing how to react, he sat motionless. "I have searched everywhere," she continued. "I looked in America, in Canada, in South America, in Israel, and in Europe. I have inquired at Jewish organizations. I visited synagogues, prominent Jewish businesses, and Jewish schools. I suppose I chose the wrong places to look." The old woman put her face in her hands and cried, "It's no use, no use. How long can anyone endure the suffering? Sometimes, I believe it is easier to quit, which is how most people behave when they fail or are disappointed. Maybe then the suffering goes away."

"Sometimes the suffering lasts longer than one's lifetime," Joseph replied. He gazed at the wall where he had just hung the photographs. *Everyone in the photographs was dead. Some lived a good life, a secure one. Others suffered like the slaves in Egypt or the Jews in ghettos.*

"In New York, I learned he lived in Brooklyn. I phoned the number for days and there was no answer. Maybe it was the wrong number or he moved. I decided to come with my daughter to visit her in-laws in Los Angeles. Today, I was supposed to visit the Jewish Museum, but the air pollution kept me indoors. Finally, after the air became better, I decided to go for a walk, and I found this Chabad house."

"What is the name of the man you are searching for?"

"Joseph Shalosky."

Stunned, Joseph's eyes widened in astonishment and went dry. He stared at this frail woman trying to remember her from a distant past. All he saw was an old woman of five feet six inches in height, who weighed ninety or ninety-five pounds. Joseph searched his memory of every woman he could remember from his youth in Chemelnick. Since childhood memories are strongly embedded in memory, he recalled all his neighbors and his parents' friends. Struggling to identify her, he focused on the old woman's face, but no memory came forth. He knew that every memory cannot be recalled, yet he was confident that she was stored in his memory. *Why am I not able to remember her? This makes no sense. Not everything that happens is understood logically. After all, there are no man-made explanations for everything that happens.*

"I am Joseph Shalosky," he replied in a soft, wavering voice that was barely audible. "I am Joseph Shalosky," he repeated, making sure that she had heard him.

"Excuse me, I cannot hear you. Please speak louder. It is hard for me to hear."

"I am Joseph Shalosky from Chemelnick, the one you are searching for. But who are you, and why are you looking for me?"

"I am Tuvia Blancowitz. No, excuse me, that is incorrect. That was my married name. My husband and three children were all murdered by the Nazis. Only one daughter and I survived. Now I call myself by my maiden name, Tuvia Kovner, my name before my life was destroyed."

Tuvia's voice was gentle, and as she spoke, her eyes alternated between being closed and being wide open, like an owl staring directly into Joseph's eyes. Listening to her, Joseph felt like he was suffocating. His mind tried to remember the face, the face as it looked in the 1930s, as it once had appeared to him. *Could suffering and anguish change a person's appearance beyond recognition? Of course it could. I must remember.* In frustration, he stood and paced and sat again. Beads of sweat formed on his forehead, and a few drops trickled through his eyebrows into his eyes. He removed his glasses and wiped away the sweat with a tissue. After putting his glasses on, he stared again at Tuvia. Suddenly, superimposed on Tuvia's face, he could not believe the image he saw, like a photograph set on another photograph: it was Tuvia's face in 1938 on the body of Tuvia in 1991. From deep within his memory, her face had been recalled.

"It's all part of God's plan. Truly this is Divine Providence," she wept.

Tuvia leaned forward in her seat and looked into the disbelieving eyes that looked back at her. "Is this true? Perhaps I am dreaming." Tuvia's eyes came to life, and from the depths of her soul, she laughed, only a small laugh but one of the rare laughs she allowed herself. Looking up, she said, "Dear God, when I had given up all hope, and despair became my companion, you helped me find him." She sat up straight, brushed the sides of her head with her hands, and spoke with a voice filled with emotion and choked with tears.

Joseph waited for her to pause in her excitement and asked again, "Why are you searching for me?"

"In Chemelnick, my father was the cobbler," she said. "When you were a child, he used to repair your shoes. Do you remember him?"

"Perhaps vaguely," he replied politely, not wanting to hurt her newly gained energy. "It was a long time ago and I was a little boy. It is hard to remember everything, even the things that you want to remember. Memory plays tricks with the mind. Different people remember the same person or an event in different ways."

"My family lived across the street from your house, about five or six houses up the street. Your dear mother was a friend of mine. We grew up together, went to school together, married, and had families. Don't you remember? Try to remember," she pleaded.

Joseph sat still, numbed by what he was hearing.

"For the Sabbath," she continued, "I baked sugar cookies and gave them to you and the children in the village. Of course I looked very different then. I had dark-brown hair, a lovely complexion, and was one of the tallest women on our street."

Like a bolt of lightning illuminating the darkness of a night sky, Joseph suddenly remembered. For decades he had placed a lid on what he thought of as his bucket of memories, a bucket filled with the memories of his youth. Recalling the sad memories of loss caused him pain, and seldom did he ever speak of the life he had before arriving in America. Now he sought to retrieve certain memories from this bucket. Focusing his mind, he remembered his life in the village of Chemelnick, and he remembered Tuvia Kovner and her husband. He savored the taste of the sugar cookies and thought of his mother's admonition that they were only for the Sabbath because too much sugar was not good for you. *How did she know in the 1930s what medical science would advocate years later?* Memories flooded through him. He remembered himself as a little boy and his father reading the newspaper or studying and calling to him, "Come, my little one, sit here on my lap." As Joseph grew older, he sat alongside his father and listened as his father taught him and spoke about what was happening in Poland and the world. He remembered his father's glistening dark-brown eyes, slight eyebrows, and a smile hidden under a full-grown dark-brown beard. Joseph's memory wandered to his mother and how she looked. He saw her dark, short brown hair tied neatly behind her head, dark-brown penetrating eyes filled with love, heavyset eyebrows, a long narrow face, and the kindest smile he had ever seen. Being the only child in the family, Joseph recalled the special affection received from his mother and father and the gentleness and spirituality that they bestowed on him.

The faces of his friends, uncles, aunts, cousins, and grandparents appeared in his mind. With his eyes shut, he forced himself to remember. He saw each of them clearly. They were laughing, talking, knitting, eating, smiling, cooking, walking, studying, and praying, each one doing a normal activity, each one expressing a different emotion, all done routinely. The routine is taken for granted until it is there no more, until it has become a last time. *Too many last times*, he reflected. The more he exerted his memory, the more memories rose from what he labeled his bucket of memories. Since the photographs of his family were destroyed in the war, all that remained were memories. *I remember Tuvia. I remember her. Does she know if my mother survived? And my father?* He knew the answers, but he had to ask because hope must exist even in the darkest times.

"Please listen," she implored. "Now I must tell you the story, the story I carried with me all these years. I never told anyone, and I waited to tell you. It is, after all, for you and about you."

FUTURE MEMORIES

Joseph knew when to be a good listener and said nothing. She began her story. "When was it? Oh, forgive me, I am not good with dates, but you will understand anyway. It all began after you left, maybe one or two years later. I'm sorry, I don't know exactly." She twisted and fidgeted on the sofa. Her right hand twisted her bare left ring finger like she was moving her wedding band around. The finger bore no wedding band. "Life was hard, very hard in Chemelnick," she continued. "Jews could not work in Gentile businesses. There was little work, no money, barely any food, and people were forced to share their flats and homes with displaced Jews from other towns. Unbearable, it was unbearable."

Her voice was monotone, without emotion, as though she was far away, alone. "You cannot imagine the crowding, the filth, the illness, the hunger, and the death. Worse than death was the degradation of the human spirit. Even if you have seen documentary films about this, you cannot know the horror of it. And the stench, the stench from the people being murdered, and the stench of their dead bodies."

Tuvia Kovner stopped, and her head drooped. The pain of telling this story for the first time drained her emotionally. "One moment please," she begged. "Having survived all of my yesterdays, I must tell you the story. Who knows if there will be a tomorrow?"

When her nerves calmed, she continued as though there was no interruption. "Must I tell you of the screaming from pain and hunger that I heard or about the sadness of the suicides? It was terrible. It was worse than terrible. Are there words to describe what the Germans did to us? I hope not because what they did should never be allowed to happen again. But I suppose it will happen again, but in different ways with new methods and by different people. That wonderful woman, Golda Meir, said, 'Until parents learn to love their children more than they hate their enemies, there will always be war.'"

Joseph's eyes widened and his mouth fell open and a state of shock embodied him. He tried to strike out thoughts about his family suffering like this. Like pages in a book that he did not want to read, he wanted to tear the pages out of his mind. He tried, but the images were too vivid.

"God alone knows how we endured," she said. "My dear Joseph, God gave man free will, and man chooses between good and evil. The Germans chose evil, and the world suffered. Fifty-five million people died in the war, more people killed than in all of the wars before that combined."

Joseph felt queasy. He tried to look out of the two front windows, but the shades were drawn shut. No trees, no sky, no fresh air, and Joseph feared what he was about to hear. *Don't listen. Don't tell me. My life was going along smoothly until she came into this room. Smoothly, that is untrue, and you a man who seeks truth. Just like most people who deny reality, who cannot face the truth, and who would rather live with old beliefs rather than new truths, you must live in reality. It is not easy. But how do you nourish your soul if you live a lie?*

Now it was Joseph who fell back on the chair, body slumped, head down, and energy drained. In contrast, Tuvia was filled with energy as she leaned forward on the sofa and continued.

"We kept saying that this will pass, that this is a temporary nightmare that will go away. How we deluded ourselves. In time of crisis, how easy it is to delude oneself, how difficult it is to be decisive. Well, we succeeded in deluding ourselves. As bad as things were, we still spoke about them being temporary. Temporary, we continued to tell ourselves. Don't confront it, pretend it will go away. After all, it is just temporary. The main argument from the Jews was, 'How can they do this to us, we who are loyal citizens and have lived in Poland for over seven hundred years?' The Jews thought seven hundred years gave them immunity from anti-Semitism. They had not learned one of the lessons from *The Ethics of Our Fathers*. In chapter two, paragraph three, it states, 'Be wary of those in power, for they befriend a person only for their own benefit; they seem to be friends when it is to their advantage, but they do not stand by a man in his hour of need.'

"Jews have lived in America for over two hundred years, and today there are Jews in America who defend those who speak against Jews. These Jews do what they can to shed their Jewish identity and in the extreme turn against their fellow Jews. Anyway, I came to tell you another story.

"Where was I? Oh, yes, I remember. I remember it well. I think of it often. That day possesses me. It was a bleak day when the Germans arrived. I suppose every day is bleak when terrible things happen. Trucks, dogs, armed guards carrying truncheons and rifles. 'Out! Out! Out!' they screamed from the streets. They always screamed like wild animals just caged. Everyone knew what that meant. Quickly, most of us scampered out of the houses, carrying whatever one could, a suitcase, a coat, a child's toy, and clinging to a frightened child."

She slumped back in the chair, her eyes wide open, and stared blankly around the room. Her voice became sharper, and she spoke like she was back in that time describing a day in which she was living.

"Not all of us came out. Some hid. Anywhere they could. In attics, in closets, in basements, in pianos, in beds, in chests, in bureaus, behind walls, under floors, anywhere, anywhere, just to escape death. Some tried to escape over the rooftops. No use. It was no use. It did not help."

Tuvia and Joseph were in the same room physically, but she was living in another time, another place, and suffering through the pain again. His eyes riveted on Tuvia. "Next, the gunfire started. Inside the houses and out on the streets, Jews were being shot. Shot for being too slow, shot for being too old, shot for being too young, shot for being too anything that a German soldier did not like. We were killed simply because we were Jewish. It did not matter if a Jew was religious or if a Jew had assimilated or if a Jew denounced his heritage, the bullets did not discriminate. Jews caught hiding were beaten into unconsciousness and dragged, broken and bleeding into the street. Chaos reigned.

"Oh! The screaming. I close my eyes and still hear it. The screaming of my neighbors, my friends, my family, and the screaming in my soul suffocated me. I could barely breathe. The chaos was loud. *Loud* is not a strong enough word, but I have no other word. Let me describe what I remember. The yelling and shrieking were loud enough at times to drown the sounds of the gunfire and the barking of the shepherd dogs.

"Desperately, parents gripped their children's hands hoping to bring safety and solace to them, dreadful of the impending terror. Unknowingly, the parents were holding their children for the last time. You know how important it is for people to touch the ones they love. Whether it is a kiss or a hug, there is touching between people who care for one another. As parents struggled to prevent the inevitable loss, the Nazis ripped apart these clasping hands of love and protection, and families were shattered forever. And every loss was the loss of not just a child or an adult, but of generations, the children who will never be born, the grandchildren that will never snuggle in the laps of their grandparents, and the destruction of young lives full of hope. Parents bore the unbearable burden of losing their children and grandchildren, wives lost their husbands, and young men and women would perish before they could experience anything of life's promises."

She stopped speaking and looked around the room as though in a trance, not knowing where she was. Joseph stared at her, and neither one spoke. Recognizing where she was again, Tuvia's voice weakened as she brought forth memories stored away like jewels hidden in an old chest. Joseph waited for her to begin the episode about his parents, the story he had waited forty-five years to learn. He leaned forward to catch every word.

"I am certain God never heard this much crying," she continued. "I forgot to mention the blood. It was everywhere. On walls, on floors, on clothing, there was blood. Blood dripped down the street from the dead bodies. Why must I remember? Why can't I just forget? Sometimes remembering may be dreadful.

"There is much to tell you, and as I tell you the story, I keep remembering the details of that day. It is easy speaking to you about this. It is just that for all these years, I have suffered because it was difficult to think of anything else. Strange, is it not, how we forget the past? First you forget the details, like the touch of your mother's hand holding yours, or the aroma of your grandmother's freshly baked cookies, or the strength of your father's arms hugging you, or the kindly smile of your grandfather. Next the memory forgets more general things like the room you grew up in, what the interior of your house looked like, and what the village's streets and shops appeared like. And finally, memory records only that you had a mother and a father and you remember them as your parents and that is all. In a way, that is good. You see, I remember my family in the details. I even hear the sound of their voices. And because I remember, my life without them has been a sad one. Perhaps without that much detailed memory, I could have lived a different life, a happy life."

"Is this the first time you have told this story?"

"Yes." She smiled. "Out loud, that is. I have carried this story in my memory, in my soul, for two generations. Until today, it was never the right moment to tell it. Many people, especially Jews, did not want to hear it."

Tuvia Kovner seemed to travel in time between the present and the past and transformed herself back to Poland in 1942.

"Trucks rumbled into our street," she continued as though there had been no break in the story. "Large trucks with brown canvas covers. The rear flap was let down and the Germans began loading us into the trucks like we were furniture. Anyone who could not climb up on his own was lifted by a soldier and then pushed or thrown in. The inside of the truck was dark and damp. The stench from urine and vomit stifled the air. I always remember the stench. It doesn't leave me. It is in my nostrils always. After we thought we were settled on the narrow wooden benches, more people were lifted in, and soon it became unbearable. There was no room to sit, no room to stand, no room to breathe, no room to cry out. We almost suffocated. Squashed together worse than berries in a box, we could not move an inch. The men were put in separate trucks from the woman and children. Again, the wailing sounded from every truck. Voices pleading to be heard by their loved ones swept up in the terror and fright of the moment. A German soldier yelled out for everyone to be silent. A man's voice cried out for his wife. His answer was a bullet from a German's rifle. Then it was quiet. No other voices cried out."

Joseph tried to remember the faces he knew from Chemelnick, picturing them being loaded on trucks and taken away to be murdered.

"My parents," he interrupted, "what happened to them?"

"Your mother, Sophie, and I were on the same truck." Tuvia cried, tears streaming from her eyes. She stopped speaking, stood, walked to the window, and looked out at the trees. Turning to Joseph, she said, "That day was the last day in our lives that your mother, Sophie, and I ever saw our husbands." Tuvia inhaled deeply and sighed. "Joseph, Joseph," she said in a weak voice. "Time hurries by, and I must finish my talk with you." Smiling, she said, "Young people think there is always plenty of time. Then one day they are not young anymore and realize that time in life is limited. Time is precious, more precious than money. As the rabbi has said, 'Time is life.'" Joseph smiled at Tuvia, a smile of agreement.

"You, Joseph, are part of every grandparent and great-grandparent that came before you. You cannot know which part or from which generation makes you what you are, but what you are is a composite of your inheritance of all past generations. And when you die, the memory of your father and grandfathers live on in your children and grandchildren. They will not know what your father looked like or how he spoke. But always remember this, Joseph, everything you have done in your life, everything you have said, everything you have written, every deed you have done is embedded in generations yet to be born. And through these generations, the essence of your ancestors will live."

Dabbing at his eyes with a tissue, Joseph told her about his life. His description read like a listing in a job wanted advertisement. He told her that he was seventy years old, had eight children, thirty-six grandchildren, had been married for forty-three years, and that he was a principal at a yeshiva high school in Brooklyn.

"Please allow me to finish the story. I must tell you what happened to your mother. You know the end already, yet I am certain you want to hear the details. Listen to me."

"Most days in our lives run together. We remember periods of time as a composite without remembering every day. It is difficult to remember one day from the other because of the similarities of each day. Yet there are days that are vivid in our memories, days of joy and happiness, and days of suffering and sadness."

Her voice dropped to a whisper, and her eyes sunk back deep into her head. Joseph leaned forward to grasp every word.

"In the boxcar, some of us were standing, some of us lying down, some were dead. The train crawled through the countryside slowly. The slower it traveled, the faster we died. The freight train of box cars was traveling to a death camp. The boxcar was dark except for the slim rays of sunlight fighting their way through the cracks in the boards. The stench is what I remember vividly. I cannot describe it, but can you imagine a boxcar stuffed with a mass of people, without sanitation, without running water, and with dead bodies stacked in a corner? No, you cannot imagine. Seeing a transport boxcar used by the Nazis sitting in a museum does not convey what happened during that transport. It was horrible. Seeing my neighbors and friends lying dead and stacked like cords of firewood is beyond human description. I huddled with my three-year-old daughter in a corner of the box car."

Joseph looked down at his shoes and then up at the ceiling. He fidgeted with his hands trying to find a comfortable position for them. In frustration, he placed them under his thighs and sat on them.

As happened before in their conversation, Tuvia Blancowitz drifted back in time, back to Tuvia Kovner in Poland, in 1942.

"We had little left of the food we brought with us. The Germans gave us nothing to eat, and only once in three days did they bring us a pail of water. I prayed to God, asking, 'Is there no escape from this calamity?' Looking through the car, I saw faces that had no hope, eyes that had no feeling, that were glazed and empty, and bodies withered and nearing death. Joseph, as your dear mother lay on the floor, she asked me, 'What will become of us? Will I ever see my husband Jacob again? And Joseph, where is my Joseph? I miss him.'

"The train crept along, almost as though it was planned this way so that most of the Jews would be dead when they arrived at the death camp. The Germans were smart in killing Jews, but not as smart in fighting the war. I often think about how many of their soldiers and trains were used to support the killing camps, soldiers and trains that could have been used fighting against the Russians. I said to your mother, 'Only a miracle can save us.' She answered, 'I will just have to pray harder.'"

Joseph's breathing tightened, and the blood rushed from his face, turning it pale white. With the light-gray rings under his eyes, his face became exaggerated and contorted, appearing like a ghost wearing a false beard. Placing a hand over his forehead, his head drooped.

"We were on the train that was bringing us to the end of our lives, to the end of our identities. The train rolled slowly. Daylight penetrated the cracks in the wood sidings. After listening to your mother's prayers, I walked to the boxcar door and tried to open it. It was not locked. I was surprised and frightened. Perhaps it was done deliberately by the Germans as they waited for someone to attempt to escape and then shoot him. Cautiously I left the door slightly ajar because I did not want a German to spot the unlocked door.

"I looked out the opening and noticed that every time the train came to a curve, it slowed even more than usual. It was barely moving. I whispered to your mother, 'Sophie, your prayer is answered. We can escape. When the train reaches the next curve, let's jump off.' She looked at me and smiled, a smile filled with friendship and love, a smile like yours, Joseph. I will carry Sophie's smile with me until I die.

"She said, 'I am too weak to do such a thing. You go, yes, you go without me. Bring a message to Joseph. Say to him how much his mother and father loved him and will always love him. Tell him that after he left, I was sad for weeks, but after that, happy for years that he was safe. We did not want him to end up like this. And thank him, for the letters. They meant a great deal to us. We read them over and over. We read them to our parents and brothers and sisters and to their children. Joseph's letters and his freedom were our salvation. We wanted to answer the letters, but we had no address. Find him, Tuvia. Tell him this for us. Please find him. He must know that he survived for all of us. His children and his grandchildren will be part of us, and that is all that will remain. And tell him how much we loved him.'

"Your mother removed a tissue from her pocket and pushed it into my hand. 'Here,' she said, 'take this with you. It will help you get to freedom.'

"In the tissue were three small diamonds. I placed them in the belt I wore inside my dress. I bent down and hugged your mother and whispered 'Thank you' into her ear. Her strength was fading, and weakly she smiled back at me. 'You will always be in my future memories,' I said.

"Time on the train crept along as it does when life is sad. Then the train slowed for the next curve. I waited. I pushed open the door and picked up my little Ruchel. Turning to see Sophie for the last time, I blew her a kiss and mouthed the words 'God bless you.' A minute or two later, holding Ruchel against my chest, I jumped from the train. Landing on a slope, I rolled down the embankment. The sound of gunfire erupted, and bullets hit near the area where we lay. I lay still, not moving, and the shooting stopped. I saw the train shrinking in the distance, and we were free. The resistance found us wandering through the forest the next day and hid and protected us for the rest of the war."

"A miracle from God," Joseph said.

"What miracle?"

"Your escape, you reaching America, and you finding me," said Joseph.

"Perhaps it depends on how one views life. For me, since Poland, since World War II, my life has been a tragedy."

Joseph changed the subject by asking, "Do you know what happened to my father?"

"I know a little," she replied. "You remember a neighbor, Mr. Pereles? It does not matter if you do. He had a son, Aaron, about fourteen years old at the time of the Nazi roundup in Chemelnick. Several years ago, I met this boy, now a man, at a dinner in New York. I asked about my husband and sons and about your father. He told me they were all gassed in Treblinka. I asked if he remembered anything specific about anyone from our town. Aaron told me how he had helped the elderly men into the Nazi trucks. One of the men he helped was your father, Jacob. Aaron remembered your father's words as your father climbed into the truck. 'Dear God, thank you for your blessing of not having our son, Joseph, with us on this tragic day. I pray that wherever you have led him, that he is safe with your love and ours.'"

The sorrow in Joseph's tears flooded his eyes as he remembered all the years thinking about his parents and how they died. He recalled the letters he had written them, letters that could not be answered because of his years of hiding. Joseph wept at the thought that he had abandoned them. His shoulders shook and his body trembled, and he sobbed.

"Everyone who was killed," she spoke like in a trance, "was not only the loss of an individual but of generations. There are the children never to be born and the grandchildren never to snuggle in the arms of their grandparents. It was the destruction of young lives full of promise, their mothers and fathers whose lives are forever shattered, wives who lost their husbands, children who lost their parents, and young women who died before they experienced anything of life's promises."

Then there was silence. Several moments later, Tuvia's mind returned to the present, and she told Joseph that she had to leave.

"Where will you go? Will I see you again? I would like you to meet my family," Joseph said.

Reaching into her purse, she removed a pad and then fumbled around in the purse until she found a pencil. She wrote an address on it and handed the paper to Joseph. "This is my daughter's address, where I stay."

Reading the address, he blurted out, "This address is in Brooklyn. You live within a few miles of me. We will definitely see each other again."

"I hope so, Joseph," she replied. "In life, we meet people who we would like to share a friendship with. We exchange addresses and phone numbers and promise to stay in touch, but usually there is no contact again. It is not because we did not mean it at the time. It is only that we are concerned more with preserving the past and all that it means to us rather than looking to the future and what it may bring. The past is comforting and people cling to it. Maybe that is why I am the way I am, because the future I had hoped for was destroyed. My life was burdened with too many last times."

"It will be different this time. I will call and we will meet again. I know it."

"Yes, of course, we will," she answered without enthusiasm.

As Joseph escorted her to the door, she said, "I am sure you know that the first letter of the Torah is *beit* and the last letter of the Torah is *lamed* and those two letters spell *lev*, which means 'heart.' You, dear Joseph, encompass the Torah because you have acquired a good heart.

"Look at the difference between us. We both suffered terribly because of the war. I, like many other survivors, have lived a life of sadness, despair, and hopelessness. You, who lost all of your family, your friends, and had your town destroyed, suffered pain and emptiness. People cannot imagine what it would be like to suffer such losses. Yet you decided to possess a positive attitude towards life. You married, raised children, and enjoy your grandchildren. Most people looking at you would never suspect the losses you have endured."

At the door, Joseph said goodbye to Tuvia and watched as she walked down the street and blended into the crowd. He stepped outside and stood on the stoop. He reflected on her story. A wave of sadness overcame him at the thought of his parents. Yet by having heard the truth from Tuvia, the pain of uncertainty that had burdened him for forty-five years was gone.

Muttering aloud to himself, he said, "I will see her again."

Back in Brooklyn, Joseph telephoned the number Tuvia had written. Her daughter answered and said her mother had not returned from one of her trips yet. He called regularly for two months. One day, in the early afternoon, a man answered Joseph's call. He told Joseph that Tuvia Blancowitz had died one week earlier.

EPILOGUE

"The Life of the Dead Is Found in the Memory of the Living"
—Cicero

In January 1998, Joseph Shalosky died. His family remembered a father and grandfather imbued with goodness and kindness, a man full of vigor, the life of the party, singing, dancing, telling stories, but not stories of his life in Poland or Shanghai. People wondered, "How could someone with those memories possess a positive outlook on life?" Joseph once commented, "Every day, people have a choice about the attitude they will embrace for that day. They cannot change their past or change the fact that people will act in a certain way, but they can change their attitude and their reaction to what happens to them."

During his lifetime, most of Joseph's stories contained mementos of his life with Rebecca. Wearing a grin that overwhelmed his beard, he relished in relating his stories. Their first apartment in Brooklyn forced him to become a handyman, learning to paint walls, install wallpaper, hang mirrors, repair dripping faucets, install a fuse box, and construct bookcases. A joy for Joseph was cooking potatoes and kishke (i.e., the intestines of beef or fowl stuffed with a mixture of flour, fat, onions, and seasonings) and making dinners. Years later, with five children, and three more yet to be born, they bought a house on East Fifty-Second Street at Church Avenue in Brooklyn. On a wall in the house, Joseph hung a small framed sign dedicated to Rebecca that read, "As water mirrors a face, a heart responds to another."

A favored memory was their 1989 trip to Israel. Praying at the Wall in Jerusalem, being stoned in Hebron after having left the tomb of the Patriarchs, and breaking down in tears at Yad Vashem created new memories and revived old ones. He did not tell anyone of his memories that floated back in time, like clouds drifting through a gray autumn sky, to the time of saying goodbye to his parents, taking the train ride, having friends shot and killed along the way, of being saved by Ruth, Samuel, and Michael in Sofia, of the students in the forest who helped him get to Nesebur, the walks past the shops and tenements in Hongkou, the diseases and the deaths in Shanghai, and the joyful day he, Isaac, and Avi left on the *Rising Dragon*.

For how can anyone imagine the unimaginable? he thought. *Memory illuminates the past. You see the house where you grew up, the school you attended, and the shop you bought candy. The vision of memory intensifies. You see your parents as a young couple. You return to your old neighborhood and remember the streets, parks, shade trees, bicycles, and games you played. Your memory rekindles friends from another time, and you wonder whatever became of them. Who has survived? You remember your family and friends, many of whom have passed, and relish their love, hugs, and kisses. It is not for such a long time that we may enjoy the physical warmth of our par-*

ents and grandparents. Imagine it destroyed with no remains but memories.

Praying that his children and grandchildren will preserve their families' memories, Joseph understood not to be afraid of the tragic and not to yearn after happiness, for neither the bitter nor the happiness lasts forever.

ABOUT THE AUTHOR

William F. Tanenbaum was born in Brooklyn, New York. He received his BA from Columbia University, where he majored in art history and studied psychology with an emphasis on memory function. While in college, he developed a passion for travel. William has visited more than fifty countries, studying their history and culture. He has also visited all fifty states. For over forty years, he operated residential mobile home parks in Florida. William currently resides in Boca Raton, Florida.